SKINNER'S LUCK

A roar brought Chavez to his feet. He stepped through the door, fumbling the magazine into his unfamiliar weapon.

The dragon flowed along the ground with a low, scuttling stride—a great, moving boulder with eight-inch teeth. Blood trickled unnoticed from a long scar along its jaws, highlighting that terrible maw in grisly scarlet.

Chavez lost an eternal second groping for the charging handle of his rifle with fingers that suddenly seemed to have lost all their deftness. Then a sliver slammed into the battery, and he brought the weapon to his shoulder and fired, the rifle-scope full of looming grey dragon-flesh . . .

SKINNER by Richard S. McEnroe
author of *The Shattered Stars* and *Flight of Honour*.

D1328878

Also from Orbit by Richard S. McEnroe:

THE SHATTERED STARS
FLIGHT OF HONOUR

RICHARD S. McENROE

Skinner

Futura

An Orbit Book

Copyright © 1985 by Richard McEnroe

First published in the USA by Bantam Books

This edition published in 1986
by Futura Publications, a Division of
Macdonald & Co (Publishers) Ltd
London & Sydney

ISBN 0 7088 8191 2

Printed and bound in Great Britain by
Cox & Wyman Ltd, Reading

Futura Publications
A Division of
Macdonald & Co (Publishers) Ltd
Greater London House
Hampstead Road
London NW1 7QX
A BPCC plc Company

1

Chavez Blackstone knew the stranger was trouble before he ever saw him.

The rasp of the doorbuzzer was a coarse-pitched drill bit grinding into his temples, goading Chavez to hungover wakefulness. He stumbled, shirtless, out of the cramped, cluttered back room that passed for home behind the made-over storefront Blackstone Freighting called an office and squinted blearily at the second-hand timepiece dangling crookedly on the wall behind the dusty counter. There was no way the numerals flickering erratically across its cracked face added up to anything later than too goddamned early.

He turned and stared at the indistinct shape of his caller, silhouetted against the slender white spires of the First Wave residential towers as they rose above the older, cruder buildings of the Stonetown slums. The towers shone like ivory, like filed teeth in the dazzling morning sunlight cast by Hansen's Primary, bright enough to hurt Chavez's drink-sore, bloodshot eyes even through the grime-caked display window. Chavez didn't recognize him. He hadn't expected to. Most of Blackstone Freighting's few paying customers did their business by screen rather than risk the mean Stonetown streets, and Chavez rather doubted that any of his many creditors had suddenly decided to come beating down his door, overdue cash in hand.

They hadn't.

The man standing there when Chevez threw open the door was everything he didn't want to see waking him up at such an ungodly hour. Fat, office-pale and balding, the stranger stared down disapprovingly past the terraced ramparts of his several chins and across the broad lower

slopes of his fashionable gray First Waver's robes. The
effect, to Chavez's expatriate Terran eye, was rather as if
someone had tried to stuff an elephant seal into a Bedouin
jellaba. Chavez slumped against the doorjamb, whippet-
thin in comparison with his visitor, with the whipcord
definition that came of running the streets, a nut-brown
Terran mongrel unimpressed by fossilized First Wave
ethnic purity and native-son status.

The gray robes gave the stranger away. His great-great-
grandfather or whomever might have been one of Wolkenheim's founding fathers, but he still had to work for a
living and his betters surely hadn't let him forget it, any
more than they would let a scruffy latecomer such as
Chavez forget his place. Chavez saw no reason to let them
have all the fun.

"Chavez Blackstone?"

"Who's asking?"

The First Waver's reaction was to produce a holotab from
his pocket and compare its projection with the young man
before him. Chavez could recognize the back of his own
head from where he leaned. Satisfied, the man put away
the tab and produced a folded sheet of fax with a familiar,
official seal. A noterunner, Chavez realized, and himself so
burnt-out that he'd simply walked right up to him.

"This is an official writ, Mr. Blackstone," the runner said,
with the pro-forma voice of utter indifference. "You're
required by law to accept."

"A breakfast treat," Chavez said sourly. "Shit. Who says I
owe them what this time?"

"That's none of my concern. Thumb here, please.

Chavez thumbed the proffered receipt book at the
indicated spot, to get it out of his face. "Hell, if you aren't
worried about it, maybe I shouldn't be either."

"I'm not worried about it," the runner admitted. The
receipt book spooled out Chavez's copy; the runner
stripped it off and handed it over. "But then I wouldn't have
the labor marshals after me, would I?"

"Labor marshals?" Chavez straightened. "Who dropped
them on me?"

But the fat First Wave bastard was already halfway back

to the waiting groundcar. Chavez stepped down out of his doorway after him. "What the hell is this?"

He got no answer as the groundcar door locked down and the runner pulled away from the curb on surging fans. Ground-effect cars were better suited to the cleaner streets around the towers; Chavez ducked back from the eddying swirls of paper and gutter trash thrown back from the car's flaring skirts. Then he was left alone on the street, staring down at the sealed fax in his hand, unable to remember when he had taken it. He unfolded it nervously.

> BUREAU OF COLONIAL CUSTOMS
> AND REVENUE
> OFFICE OF LABOR REGISTRATION
> —HANSEN'S LANDING
> NOTICE OF RECLASSIFICATION
>
> TO: BLACKSTONE, CHAVEZ ALLENDE
> HL61935284/ZTU
> CAUSE: INSUFFICIENT SOLVENCY
> IAW: COLONIAL CODE SECTION 104(F)

. . . where it has been so determined that BLACK-STONE, CHAVEZ ALLENDE has been found deficient in means of personal support, this office is charged to declare him a ward of Council, and establish him in such a position as will best permit him to resume the status of contributing citizen, effective this date. Appeals or submission for processing must be submitted within twenty-four (24) hours of receipt of this notice."

Chavez felt as if the bottom had dropped out of his gut as he sagged back against the frame of the dirty window with its peeling gilt lettering.

"Oh, shit," he said again. But this time he meant it.

"Office of Labor Registration, Adjudication and Appeals, good morning."

There were two phrases that didn't go together, Chavez thought sourly.

"Good morning," Chavez said to the Customs and

Revenue graphic on his screen. "I'd like to speak to someone about a problem with a solvency writ, please."

The graphic vanished, replaced by the face of an Oriental woman, her expression locked into calm by a thick layer of white pancake and blush, her hair piled up in an elaborate bird's nest fixed by long mock jade needles, a Meiji geisha in First Wave grays, transmitted in living, pretentious color. "Secretary Koyama, may I help you, sir?"

The voice was flat and slightly nasal, bored, cool, and formal, hardly likely to tempt any lingering daimyo's ghost to indiscretion.

"Yes," said Chavez, "I'd like to query a reclassification notice, please."

"Your number, sir?" Chavez gave it, and Koyama looked to her desktop terminal.

"Yes, sir, we have that notice on file."

"I know you have it," Chavez answered, as patiently as he could. "What I want to know is why I got it."

"What precisely is the nature of your challenge, sir?"

"The grounds of my challenge are that there should be no writ to challenge. I am not insolvent."

"One moment, sir." Chavez suddenly realized that she had yet to look out at him at all. She shook her head. "I'm sorry, sir, but your taxable earnings statement shows a significant shortfall of the legislated minimum."

Chavez gripped the edge of the counter, the sweat on his palms smearing the dust. "That can't be possible."

"What is your reported monthly income, sir?"

"Fluid," Chavez admitted. "I'm self-employed—"

"Mister Blackstone, we have no record of your showing a reported income in the past four weeks."

"I know that. I told you, I'm self-employed. Look under the earnings report for Blackstone Freighting."

There was a pause as she consulted her files again. "I have no reported income for any 'Blackstone Freighting' in the past four weeks either, sir."

"I know that. Look at the annual gross earnings."

"That figure does not meet the legislated annual minimum, sir."

"What are you talking about? Look at the invoices I have pending. I should be well above the line."

"Oh, that's potential income." Secretary Koyama brightened, the mystery solved. "Potential income is not relevant to a solvency decision, sir."

"Of course it is. They've allowed it before."

"It's not a mandatory element, sir. Potential income may be taken into consideration, where the adjudicating authority deems it appropriate. But in this case the adjudicant declared the potential income an unreliable asset. It's all there in your writ, sir." Now she looked out at him, now that she possessed the documentation to show that she didn't need to involve herself, now that Chavez Blackstone wasn't going to be her problem.

"Well, what the hell do I do about this?" He flinched inside at the pleading note in his voice, at how he must look, unshaven and scared.

"Adjudication and Appeals maintains regular office hours during the normal business day, sir. That's nine to five," she added, as though she thought Chavez might need reminding. "You may come down anytime today for processing on your writ. Please bring your copy and any necessary personal records."

"Thanks a whole hell of a lot," Chavez said.

"Have a nice day, sir." The phone went blank before Chavez could ask her how he was supposed to do that while surrendering himself to Labor Registration's body-brokers. He leaned on the countertop, staring at the empty screen, at the blank glass wall laid across his future. . . .

Chavez squirmed his backside farther into the corner of the *Irish Missed*'s wardroom couch, as though he sought to draw the sheltering mass of the intrasystem freighter closer around himself. The seam of his hip pocket caught on a strip of duct tape covering a rip in the plastic upholstery, reopening the tear. Embarrassed, he tried to smooth it down again under the amused gaze of Maureen O'Shaunessy, the willowy, red-headed young woman who wore the *Missed*'s crewpatch and the electron-and-rocket tab—"the atomic banana"—of a ship's engineer.

The wardroom hatch slid open and Moses Callahan stepped through, stooping to clear the corridor bulkhead, a sandy-haired young giant whose bulk suggested he would be better employed off-loading ships than mastering one. But a captain's gold braid shone on the visor of his battered cap, and the *Irish Missed* was his.

"Has our caller been minding himself then?" he asked.

"He has not," O'Shaunessy answered. "Look what he's done to your couch."

"Ruining my ship already, is it?" Moses demanded playfully. "And myself gone scarcely an hour, no more."

Chavez shrugged apologetically. "Sorry, Cap'n. I just can't take me anywhere anymore."

"You've got the right of that, from what I've heard." The cushion plumped beneath Chavez as Moses dropped his bulk onto the other end of the couch. The hand at the end of the arm he threw across O'Shaunessy's shoulders was oversized even for its owner, like the paw of some enormous puppy whose full, dismaying growth was still before it.

"What *have* you heard?" Chavez asked. "What's the word out there?"

"Nothing you couldn't have found out for yourself."

"If I could risk being seen asking."

"There is that. Once you're on a ticket, those Labor Registration sorts don't really want to hear anything out of you except what time you'll be in to give yourself up. It's a lucky man who has friends he can trust to make inquiries for him."

"So what's the word?"

"Ah. The word, now, is that you've been having me on," Moses said. "If you're really expecting me to believe you don't know how you earned that ticket."

"Swear to God, I don't, Cap'n," Chavez said earnestly. "I went to bed last night a perfectly solvent, sober second-class citizen—well, a solvent second-class citizen anyway—and I woke up this morning in the labor pool. What the hell could have happened in one lousy night?"

"Last night, nothing," Moses said. "But what about the night before?"

"What *about* the night before?"

"Do you remember it, for a start?"

Chavez scowled. "Not as such," he admitted. "A whole two nights ago?"

"Try to think back about three bottles."

"We don't go in for ancient history down in Stonetown. Live for today, that's the motto of us happy poor folk," Chavez declaimed, "for tomorrow may never come and yesterday's paid for."

"True enough," Moses said. "You're paying for it now. All right, if you really don't remember what you did with the evening—"

"I really don't. I wasn't exactly there at the time, if you understand."

Maureen O'Shaunessy looked at Moses. "Say you don't and you're a liar."

"I wasn't about to," Moses protested. Then, to Chavez: "Then do you at least remember who you did whatever you don't remember doing with? A young woman by name of Jonelle Thorson?"

"What about Joni Thorson?" Chavez asked defensively.

"Actually, you should have asked, 'What about Joni Thorson's father?'," Moses said.

"Oh, really?"

"District Councilor Thorson."

"Oh. Really."

"How do you come to know such influential people, Chavez?"

"Well, I ran a delivery up there about six weeks back—"

"In the course of which you made the young lady's acquaintance?"

"In the course of which any number of things got made, one way or another."

"Vulgar man," Maureen O'Shaunessy said.

"Something glandular, I expect," Moses told her.

"Oh, yeah," Chavez grinned. "Absolutely. You'd be surprised how many proper little First Wave daughters like to go slumming once in a while."

"And you might be surprised how many proper First Wave fathers disapprove of the practice."

"Hey, he still hasn't paid for the damned delivery yet,"

Chavez said. "If he doesn't like his little girl going for the rough trade, that's his problem."

"True enough. But PanDistrict Councilors have ways of solving problems that lesser mortals such as ourselves can't call upon."

"Wait a minute," Chavez said. "You mean I caught this ticket 'cause Thorson doesn't want me pulling his kid? She's legal, damn it."

"I doubt if that would matter much to the likes of Councilor Thorson," Moses said. "But I gather that wasn't the whole of the problem."

"Then what is?"

Moses Callahan shook his head, eyeing Chavez ruefully. "You really don't remember, do you?"

"Remember what, for God's sake?"

"Now how could you forget such a party as His Honor, Councilor Thorson, must know how to throw?"

"Uh . . ."

"Because as near as I've been able to piece the thing together, you did attend, presumably at Mistress Thorson's invitation. And you were having yourself a fine old time, as well—also presumably at Mistress Thorson's invitation. Certainly with her ardent cooperation. But not, I'm afraid, with Councilor Thorson's countenance."

"Oh, no," Chavez said. "He found us out, huh?"

"And took no pleasure in the sight, you may be sure."

"I still don't believe he'd have me ticketed for the pool just for that," Chavez said.

"Do you mean to say, then, that if *you* were a proper First Wave parent and you walked out onto your very expensive scenic tower balcony and found your very well and very, *very* expensively bred daughter contributing to the delinquency of a semi-employed latecomer hauler jockey, within spitting distance of the cream of First Wave society, you might not be somewhat peeved yourself?"

"Assuming I possessed party, balcony, or daughter, most likely I would. But I wouldn't ship him off to the pool for it."

"That's because you lack the refined subtlety that is the hallmark of the better classes."

"No. It's because it just isn't that big a deal."

"Of itself alone," Moses said, "I might agree with you.

But then what would you do if the drunken lout responded to your admonitions by lurching to his feet and knocking you on your backside?"

Chavez blanched. "I didn't."

"Of course, His Honor might have been prepared to overlook even that affront, you being an invited guest and plainly under the influence of spirits His Honor had set out himself, and so at least in part he shared the blame for his own upending. But you weren't prepared to leave it at that."

"I wasn't."

"Several of the guests tried to intercede."

"They did."

"The final score was two PanDistrict Councilors and the compradore for one of the bigger offworld conglomerates, along with quite a good selection of statuary, left in various states of disassembly."

"Agh."

"The morning fax had quite a bit of fun with it. They don't usually run the society column so far up in the printout."

"Oh God."

"'A mystery man who may not know much about art or politics, but he knows what he likes.' Unquote."

"Stopstopstop." The words came out muffled by the tabletop and the arms wrapped around Chavez's head.

"There isn't much more to tell, anyway. You've a gift for pillage and rapine, but you stopped short of salting his gardens and driving off his housepets."

Chavez lifted his head up from his arms and glared at Moses Callahan. "I'm glad you're taking this so well."

"I can afford to. I haven't physically assaulted half the government, have I?"

"No, you haven't, have you? Well, hell."

"Indeed."

Chavez sighed and straightened in his seat. "I guess we can take it as a given that there's no way in hell I'm going to beat this writ, not if Thorson's pushing it."

"Doubtless he is. First Wavers don't go around brawling on patios. They've got too many other ways of doing up their enemies."

"So I've learned. But I didn't come all this way out here

just to wind up playing plantation lackey for some First Wave one-blood. What the hell did they ever do to get put in charge of this place, anyway?"

"They got here first," Maureen O'Shaunessy said.

"Good for them. If they were the first to arrive, I'll be the first to leave."

"So you'll be asking after passage, then?"

"To the next starliner insystem, right. I'll pay, of course."

"How kind of you to offer," O'Shaunessy said.

"And what can a legally insolvent citizen expect to pay me with?" Moses asked.

"I'll unload the hauler before I leave. Hell, I can't afford to take it with me, can I?"

"I suppose not. But you'll get enough for it, will you?"

"I'll get enough to get by on."

"Enough to book passage on the *Missed*, and then to book passage on a starliner, and then to live on whenever you get where you're going?" Moses shook his head. "I don't think so, Chavez."

"It'll be enough. It'll have to be. The hauler's all I've got to sell. I've got to do it this way, Cap'n. The only chance I've got to duck this writ is to get out of the Hansen System's jurisdiction. Otherwise I'll be in the pool for as long as it suits Councilor Thorson. And I think he knows how to nurse a grudge."

"It's certain you've given him ample encouragement," Moses admitted. "You know you're asking me to break the law, don't you? Aiding in flight to avoid prosecution, or whatever they call it around here." His bantering manner had evaporated, now that they were moving beyond Chavez's problems to possible troubles of his own.

"Not yet I'm not," Chavez answered. "I've got until five o'clock local to report in for adjudication. Until then, I'm a free man. If you booked my passage before then, you'd have broken no law—and once I'm back on port ground they can't touch me. You know that."

"Extraterritoriality is a noble concept," Moses agreed. "But the Confederate lawboys aren't fond of tramp masters who abuse their hospitality like that."

"I hadn't thought of that," Chavez admitted. His shoulders slumped. "Hell. I've got no business asking you to put your neck on the line, Cap'n."

"It isn't yours to ask for, Mister Blackstone." Moses stared at the young man seated across from him, backed into a corner of the couch, into a bigger corner outside. "All right. Be aboard the *Missed* before five o'clock local and you've got a berth."

"Thank Christ. Thank you, Cap'n. How much are you asking?"

"You'll dead-head it. No charge."

Chavez looked at him warily. "I'm not looking for a handout, Moses."

"And I'm not offering one. I have to go out to meet the starliner anyway, and I have the space to hand. Besides, if I don't declare you on my manifest, no one's going to ask me what I'm about running writ-skippers, are they?"

"No, I guess not. Thanks. I'll be there."

"You know, if you're smart, you'll stay right here aboard now."

"I wish to hell I could. But I've got to sell off the hauler. I need that stake."

"Is there any reason I couldn't buy it?"

"Yeah, a couple. I'd feel like a shit gouging you to get the price I have to get. And if you don't want a record of me on your manifests, you probably don't want to have a transfer of registration on file downtown either, do you?"

"Probably not," Moses agreed. "Well, take care of yourself, then."

"Don't I wish I could." They all stood to let him get up.

"You know, this situation seems familiar, somehow," Moses said.

"It should," Chavez said. "Chavez Blackstone, getting dragged through life by his hormones once again. It's getting to be a habit. His Excellency, the premier, would be proud of me."

"Painful as it sounds," Maureen O'Shaunessy said, "I'd love to hear the story behind that statement."

"Sorry," Chavez said. "I may be a vulgar man, but there are certain stories I refuse to tell in mixed company. Particularly when they make me look like the prize idiot I sometimes think I am. Thanks again, Cap'n. I'll be back."

"You're pretty free with our cabin space," Maureen O'Shaunessy said, once the wardroom hatch had closed behind the departing Chavez. "What's provoking all this charity now?"

"Nostalgia, mostly," Moses said. "Chavez was my first paying customer when I arrived insystem. He took passage down from the *Natchez* with me, and I've been referring hauling work to him when I could ever since."

"You recommend the likes of him?" O'Shaunessy asked. "After such stories and all?"

"Don't you be fooled," Moses said. "He's a good enough worker, when there's work to be done. And that's as much as you can expect from him."

"Why is that?"

"Because he's never going to get anything better," Moses said. "Not here. Not on this world."

"No?"

"No. This isn't his world, you see, and the owners are not disposed to share it with every empty-handed wanderer who falls out of the sky."

"But they'll throw him in the pool, just like that."

Moses shrugged. "You'll learn. It's the usual First Wave situation. The families from the original landings have had theirs for generations, and if anyone else wants to come play in their sandbox, they'll have most of his, too. Wait until you've been insystem a while longer; you'll see."

"What a lovely place to call home."

"Isn't it?" Moses said. "So I trust it won't distress you if I thumb my nose at the hardy colonists a bit?"

"I'll live through it."

"I hoped you might."

"I'm just glad we don't have to play their game."

"I haven't had to yet. . . ."

2

Secretary Koyama didn't like Lakim Tovas. But she couldn't afford to ignore him.

In her mind, Tovas was no proper representative for any reputable firm. He had the slight, dark, furtive manner of any Stonetown latecomer mongrel, an impression only heightened by the fine cut of his suit—Stonetown fashion but the best Xen How nearsilks, equal to any a First Waver could afford—and his impeccable grooming. He was as smooth and polished as an oil slick on puddle water. And he had a way of looking at you, she thought, that could make you feel *used* just by meeting his gaze, and all the while remaining so perfectly polite that you might even begin to think it was something wrong with yourself. But Lakim Tovas worked for Eli Santer, and if one of the most powerful men in the Hansen System wanted one of the latecomers' own kind to do his body-snatching, that took the matter entirely out of Secretary Koyama's hands.

"How many are we signing for today?" he asked.

"We have ninety-one writs pending assignment—"

"Let me have them."

"And one default."

"Just one." Tovas smiled archly as he accepted the dataplac. "Perhaps we scummy latecomers are finally learning our manners. Has Enforcement been notified?"

"The notification is pending, Mr. Tovas."

"I think you can cancel it. Let me have his file too, please."

"That's highly irregular, Mr. Tovas."

"Dear woman, every week you tell me that."

"Enforcement won't accept responsibility once you've signed for the writ."

"And every week, don't I agree to sign the release?" Without his asking, she slid the short form over the desktop to him. "Thank you."

Tovas signed the release with qualms. He rather doubted that the men and women whose lives he was taking possession of would have appreciated any regret on his part, even had he felt it. And of course he didn't, because Lakim Tovas wasn't signing for people.

Lakim Tovas bought failure. The names on the dataplac Secretary Koyama handed him were the names of latecomers like himself, different only in one respect. They had never learned the rules of the game they were trying to play.

Latecomers were intruders in the Hansen System, an imposition. Tovas had learned that in his own first days on Wolkenheim, when he had been a penniless, optimistic Terran immigrant himself.

Latecomers hadn't *earned* the Hansen System, not in the eyes of the First Wave natives. They were barging in, looking to get fat off the sweat of generations of First Wave toil, a mass of swarthy, swarming humanity bearing with them echoes of the blackest First Wave legends of an Earth their ancestors had fled, retreating before just such a flood of hungry half-breeds. First Wave fairy tales of old Earth told of a Europe staggering under the ethnic detritus of half-a-dozen empires, a Mother Russia soiled by an outpouring of Islamic fundamentalist barbarity, an America where the fair-skinned language of the textbooks and boardrooms was no longer spoken on the streets. But there was no way the First Wave cream of the Hansen System crop was going to let that happen again.

The latecomers knew nothing of that when they shuttled down from the starliners, of course. And in Tovas' case, as in so many others, it would have made no difference. The Hansen System was as far as he could take ship, lured outward by the deceptive, dated immigration information on file at Marrakesh Emigration Station. Looking back, Tovas had often wondered if that information had been wrong out of laxity or by policy. The First Wavers might hate Terran mongrels, but they loved cheap labor with all the passion of their *pukka sahib* ancestors.

It was a passion Tovas had no desire to satisfy, even as he realized that its satisfaction was unavoidable. He had looked on with bemusement as the latecomers around him went about the business of trying to build lives of their own in the Stonetown slums, not realizing or not admitting that those lives could never be their own while the labor pool went forever hungry for new bodies. Tovas scorned their naïve hopes of avoiding the pool, of proving themselves solvent, worthwhile citizens, when solvency was an intangible chimera, shifting with every contraction of the labor pool, and a latecomer's worth was determined before he ever set foot off the starliner.

But it was a passion Tovas could use to assure his own survival.

Fast as the labor pool machinery was, as thorough as their files were, there was no way Labor Registration could ever know of an insolvency case before the streets did. They kept records of poverty; the latecomers lived with it. And that firsthand knowledge was something a latecomer could sell.

Labor Registration had its informers, of course. But Tovas never sold to them. There was no future in selling a commodity to a market that already had all it could use from a hundred other sources. Tovas went straight to the First Wave families that did most of the buying. He bet that they would rather secure the pick of the labor pool for themselves, rather than squabble over the undifferentiated mass of workers Labor Registration put on the block each day. He was right, particularly in the case of one buyer:

Eli Santer.

The Santers were an oddity, even in the Hansen System—one of the few First Wave families whose base of power rested off Wolkenheim. The Santers were the last remnant of the failed Trollshulm colony, settled at the same time as Wolkenheim and Trollshulm's binary sister, verdant Hansenwald. The other families were long gone, dead or fled in the face of a savage world that resisted all efforts at terraforming, whose befouled, arid earth poisoned off the nurturing plants and organisms men sought to seed there, and locked away even the moisture men sought to sustain themselves.

Now there was nothing there but the Santers and the savage, enormous beasts they preyed on. But their offworld insularity made it awkward to do business in an economy that was ninety percent social contact and old-boy network. If Tovas could provide a link with that economy, Eli Santer would use him.

It started with the usual thing—informing, letting Santer take out writs of insolvency and claim the indentured latecomers without having to compete with the other First Wave families for colony-assigned workers. Then Tovas discovered that he could use First Wavers as readily as he used his latecomer neighbors, and association with Eli Santer made him respectable enough to be dealt with.

Now, ten years later, after shuffling penniless and confused off the battered lighter, there were few First Wavers and no one in Santer Holdings who wielded the power Lakim Tovas could wield in the Hansen System, short of Eli Santer himself. And that was a restriction Tovas was less and less willing to accept these days. . . .

"Now you realize Mr. Santer will be held accountable if the writ continues in default, of course," Secretary Koyama was saying.

"Of course," Tovas smiled, the smile of a ferret discovering a populated rabbit warren. "But they never do, do they?"

Chavez slouched impatiently against the high flank of the eight-wheeled hauler as the dealer slammed shut the engine-deck hood and climbed back down.

The Stonetown dealer shook his head dubiously, running his hand over his balding scalp. "Well, I don't know," he said. "You've sure as hell made this old girl work for her supper. How many times have you turned the odometer over?"

"Just the one time since I've owned it."

"Yeah, since you've owned it. But it sure looks like it's been around a time or two maybe before that."

"I couldn't say. Look, you're not going to push my price

down on me." He slapped the side of the hauler. "This is a Mitsui Leyland, damn it. You can't wear them out."

"Somebody's sure tried. I don't know," he mused aloud. "I'd have to pull the tranny and refurbish it front-to-back—"

"You'd have to do that anyway."

"—and that number-three fuel cell's cooking on nothing but trace metals and memory. God only knows what kind of life's left in the suspension. Hell, I wouldn't be taking too much of a chance at nine thousand."

"Take a chance. Twelve."

"No way in hell I could go over ten."

"Give me a break."

"That's not what I'm here for."

"All right. Five thousand—in Confederate standards, not colony marks."

"Listen to him. I say I can't go over ten thousand marks, he asks for five thousand standards. Do you know what the going exchange rate is?"

"That's ten thousand, two hundred and forty-three marks, point three. Tell me that's going to break you."

"I'm eating right into my margin," the dealer complained. "But all right. Gimme your plate."

"Uh-uh. I need a hard draft, made out to bearer."

The dealer eyed him with new suspicion. "We got some kind of title problem here?"

"The title on the hauler's good," Chavez told him. "It's my ass I'm not so sure I own."

"Goddamn." The dealer looked up at the towers of Hansen's Landing above them, cutting off the sunlight like toppling monoliths. "You ducking a writ?"

"I've ducked it, if you give me that draft."

"I'd love to know how you figure to do it. You never know when it might come in handy."

"I'll drop you a tourfax, once I pull it off."

The dealer shrugged and chuckled. "What the hell. They never did me any favors. Come on."

The dealer slotted his card into the phone in his cluttered cubicle, keyed in a sum, and pressed his thumb to the screen. There was a second's nervous wait, and then a cashfax tickered out of the copy gate. "I wish I'd known you were skipping before I made my offer. I bet I could have knocked you down to four."

"I know you could have. That's why I forgot to mention it."

"I can't say as I blame you. I never did anyone any favors either. Lemme have the registration. Thanks. Good luck."

"I think I've had it already."

"Maybe." The dealer looked at the gaudy timepiece on his desk, a snarling, plastic dragon with a clock in its belly. Chavez imagined he'd growl too if someone stuck a clock in his gut. "It's four-thirty. You'd better get moving if you're going to keep it."

He'd just started across the street as the limousine floated to a stop at the port gate.

Chavez stepped back quickly into the shade of a doorway. The Port Security Police weren't terribly impressed with the two civil marshals, but they sharpened up smartly as the third man, smallish and well-dressed, emerged from the vehicle. Chavez recognized him at once. Tovas. The most notorious body snatcher in the colony was a more familiar face in Stonetown than some popcart stars.

Tovas was showing a holocube to the gate guards. He might not be after him, Chavez told himself. He probably wasn't. There were dozens, probably hundreds of insufficient solvency writs issued every day.

But the thought that he might be scared Chavez silly.

Tovas turned back to the limousine, leaving the marshals waiting by the gate. As the hover turned toward him, Chavez stepped back through the doorway he'd been sheltering in.

It turned out to be the entrance to a trashy gift shop, the kind that clustered around the gates of starports throughout the Confederacy, specializing in overpriced junk for ship's crews on liberty.

Chavez picked up the first article that came to hand—a small, transparent globe. He shook it and a hail of meteors streaked past a gleaming starliner at the heart of the sphere. He bought it and stepped back into the street, letting the package wave in plain sight of the marshals as he moved away from the gates. They were looking for writ-skippers trying to get into the port, not consumers walking away from it.

He rounded the second corner he came to and turned right, paralleling the course of the port fence. Several blocks down, he turned right and approached the barrier again.

There was no sign of the perimeter patrol. Chavez looked closer, harder and finally saw the flashing blue lights of the PSP sled winking between a warehouse and a grounded lighter far across the field.

He scrambled quickly over the horizontal bars of the fence and started across the wide, empty stretch of permaplast reserved for the intrasystem freighters.

He got perhaps halfway.

Suddenly a rectangle of shadow engulfed him. He spun and looked up as the down-draft of a closed-fan sled, hovering silhouetted against the glare of Hansen's Primary, plucked at his clothes and hair. Another sled was settling to the ground. From the powerful winch and tackle mounted on its prow, it looked to be a cargo handler off a grounded freighter. The markings on its side identified it: it was from *Abilene*. A Santer ship.

Three spacers had dismounted from the grounded sled, the blunt potato-masher shapes of heavy bass stunners in their hands. Chavez started to back away from them, trying to circle and get the port fence behind him once again. The junk ornament was heavy in his hand; he clutched at it hopelessly.

The nearest crewman spoke.

"All right, friend, just take it easy now. This is business, right?"

"If you say so."

"Sure it is. So why not just come along and get it over with?" He grinned. "What else is there to do?"

"You could let me go, but I'm not counting on that."

"That's not what Mr. Tovas pays us for."

"No—" Chavez snapped the ornament into the face of the nearest crewman, turned and bolted for the fence—

—the sequence never progressed that far. As the ornament left his hand there was triple impact deep in his chest,

the sound of a thunderclap heard from the inside. The
world was shaken into a featureless blur as the bass
stunners picked him up bodily and slammed him into the
ground.

Then the darkness came.

The purple horizon silhouetted the towers of Hansen's
Landing, orderly columns of fireflies stacked up toward the
twilight sky. Moses Callahan stood in the open passenger
hatch of the *Irish Missed*, staring glumly out over the
deserted field.

"He isn't coming, Moses," Maureen O'Shaunessy said,
entering the lock behind him, toweling the grime of a day's
work from her hands.

"Isn't or can't," Moses agreed unhappily.

"You made the offer," she said, trying to console him.
"There isn't anything else you can do, is there?"

"No, I suppose not."

"After all, now, you can't be picking up every stray that
walks past your door."

Moses looked back at her, and forced himself to smile.
"*Nighean aig Éirrin Og*," he named her. "Daughter of New
Ireland." "I couldn't leave a fellow citizen to the exploit-
ative employ of those slave drivers, now could I?" He swept
a hand across the outer lock to indicate the lesser ships
docked around the *Missed*.

She grimaced at the dirty towel in her hands. "Do you
mean there's worse than yourself, then?"

"Oh, vastly worse," he assured her wryly. "Why do you
know then that some of those unethical swine might even
make demands of you that go right beyond the bounds of a
sober professional relationship?"

"No," she said, her astonishment as mocking as his
indignation.

"Yes. Why some of them might even feel entitled to take
liberties."

"Good heavens. How can that be?"

He grinned honestly this time. "Very nice, I expect. But
memory fails me, I must confess."

She slid her arms around his neck, kissing him lightly.
"Then it will stand for some refreshing, won't it?"

"I expect it might." He slipped an arm around her waist,
and turned back to the lighter field. Still . . . nothing
moved.

"Come inside, Moses. It's out of your hands now."

"You're right, damn it. I just hope it's still in his."

Chavez had no idea how long he'd been aboard the ship.

The cabin was devoid of portholes, screens or any fixtures
at all but the three berths and the small, exposed head
bolted into one bulkhead. There was nothing at all to
identify his surroundings; he only guessed that he was
aboard *Abilene*. His mind shied away from that thought
though, and the fate it implied for him.

He had been unconscious when they brought him
aboard, unconscious when they presumably lifted out—
don't think of that, don't think about where he was going—
and he had been alone in the cabin when he awoke. He had
not seen anyone since then, although three times since he
awoke an access panel in the door had opened and a
packaged ship's ration and plastle of water had been tossed
in. But he had been unable to judge the duration of his
confinement from that: The time between meals had
varied, and he suspected that he was being fed only when
one of *Abilene*'s crew remembered to get around to it. It
might have been once a day, or perhaps even less frequent-
ly. It didn't matter. There was nothing he could do about it,
in any case. . . .

"Hey, it's the admiral!"

"Very funny, Klepper," Moses grumbled.

Hans Josef Klepper waved Moses over to the small knot
of captains waiting outside Mariner's Hall for the day's
bidding to commence. The starliner *Walkabout* had begun
broadcasting its arrival notice three days ago, when it
dropped below lightspeed on the borders of the Hansen
System. Now the intrasystem freighter captains were
gathered at Mariner's Hall in the Confederacy's Mission

House, the interface between colonial and interstellar affairs, to bid on the various cargoes the FTL ships of the Confederacy bore between the stars.

It was an anachronistic system: In theory there was no reason why the starliners could not have brought their wares directly into planetary orbit for purchase by the merchants of the colony themselves. But involving the captains was a simple means of keeping shipping available insystem for local use between starliner calls, a vital consideration in a multiworld colony such as the Hansen System. The captains stayed where they could make a profit; thus keeping the shipping tonnage available at a reasonable level for each colony's wealth, and it allowed the masters of starliners—Confederate officers rather than private shipowners—to remain objectively distant from internal colonial affairs, much to the approval of the local powers.

Moses joined the waiting captains, not entirely unaware of their envy. The *Irish Missed* was a split-drive fusion/ magnetics brig, a newer and swifter ship than their older magnetic-drive freighters. It might have been a point of hostility between them, but Moses Callahan's ambitions had been largely sated by his taking command of his new ship four years before, and he had no desire to bite off a larger share of the market than he could chew, even if he could have beaten their united competition. And he had the memory of his own first voyage to keep him humble, a pocket-scraping passage aboard a starliner out from Confederate center, where the *Missed* herself was undersized and obsolescent.

"What's the latest gossip, Hans?" Moses asked.

"We might have a price war on our hands," the older captain told him. "Protherall, off *Flute*."

"What's he about then?"

"You heard about his last survey, didn't you?"

"I can't say as I have."

"He's got troubles. *Flute* needs some heavy structural work; the surveyors turned up a lot of fatigue-shearing, I heard even down into her backbone."

"Ah, that's bad now."

"It isn't the worst of it. The colony's looking to replace *Vigilant*, you know."

"That I'd heard about."

Klepper nodded. "Yah. Well, the word is, they're looking at *Flute*."

"Protherall isn't selling, surely."

"He might not have the choice. When the underwriters heard about the fatigue-shearing, they were all set to push his premiums up. Then the colony heard about it, and from what I hear, they're leaning on the underwriters to really hike it."

"Will they go for it?"

Klepper grimaced. "They're all reputable First Wave businessmen, Moses, and taxpayers all. Even with a fifty or sixty percent structural upgrading called for, it's probably cheaper to, ahem, buy *Flute* and convert her than it would be to commission a new revenue cutter from the keel up."

"I'm sure it would be." Moses looked sidewise at the captain under discussion—a gray, sagging man standing apart from the group, lost in his own worries. "Poor bastard. So you think he's going to hype the bidding?"

"He's going to try. I almost wish we could let him, if it would make any difference. But if the colony's after *Flute* they'll get her—or they might come looking for one of us, instead."

"So we lock him out, and he can't make his premiums, and they pull his coverage, ground him, and impound *Flute* against his debts."

"No. We don't lock anybody out, youngster. We bid against him just the way we'd bid against each other. He takes his chances, just like the rest of us. That's how it is. He knows that."

An aging man, grim lines of worry graven into the edges of his mouth, eyes bleak. "Yes, he does, doesn't he?"

A three-note chime sounded, and the captains moved forward as the doors to Mariner's Hall swung back. They moved into the Hall, a surprisingly small space for the function it served, through the holographic columns inscribed with the names and numbers of spacers looking for new berths, names most of the captains knew by sight. The broad holoboard of the auctioneer's stand hovered above them all, glowing green with the carrier signal from *Walkabout*.

An attendant moved among them, handing out packets of fax listing the cargoes the starliner offered for their consideration. Moses found himself watching Protherall as the man paged through the packet, searching for the one magic cargo that would save him.

A young woman, blond and severely tailored in the functional uniform of Mission House, stepped up to the stand.

"Good afternoon, ladies and gentlemen. I am Second Assistant Administration Clerk Holstadt, and I will be conducting the bidding today on behalf of Captain Whitlam of *Walkabout*." She looked up to some unseen technician. "This auction is now in session; close the doors, please."

The double doors to the Hall clunked softly shut behind them all, leaving the room lit only by the muted light-bars overhead and the reflected light from the holograms.

The board above Holstadt came to life as the first listings flashed into view. "Now, lot number one, a selection of . . ."

Moses tuned out the descriptions, and the first bids from the back of the room. These first cargoes were small stuff, that the freighter captains usually left to the lighter-masters. Otherwise it was possible to clutter up your hold space and tie up your working cash in several smaller lots and wind up with surplus space inadequate to the really substantial cargoes, and insufficient free funds to bid on them.

"Lot number seventeen, a software package and templates for a new series of ghost-path multiprocessors from Miyama Technics of Amaterasu. A similar package went for one hundred thousand standards in the Arcadian Worlds, today's floor is one hundred and fifteen thousand. Do I hear an opening bid at that level?"

"*Irish Missed* bids one-fifteen," Moses said. That was the sort of cargo you could count on a two- or three-fold return on, properly marketed. But Klepper thought so too, unfortunately, and drove Moses up to two hundred and twenty-five thousand before the younger captain conceded.

"No new shoes this year then, Hans?"

"Just let me sell those off and I'll be able to pay somebody to carry me!"

Holstadt gave the chuckling time to die of its own accord.

The bidding continued, Moses beating out the pack on a substantial cargo of imported wines (of good ancestry and report) and specs and demonstration model on a forty-ton industrial loader. Moses was relieved that the last could drive itself home under its own power; delivering it would have been a bitch.

Yet through all the bidding, Protherall remained silent, his eyes fixed on the last page of the faxpack. Moses retired from the bidding briefly, flipping ahead in his own sheets, curious as to what so obsessed the desperate captain.

There were only three items on that page. None of them would have done much to raise Moses' hopes. Another software package, popcarts that would never be within Protherall's price range, a sample and specifications of a new and improved synthetic protective fabric—it couldn't be that, he thought. Not in the Hansen System, not while Eli Santer was in business with dragonhides to sell.

The time came to find out. Moses passed on the software package, and retired from the popcarts at one hundred and sixty thousand.

And Protherall never bid. Dear God, Moses thought, he's lost touch completely.

"Lot number fifty-six, a synthetic protective fabric and full formula and specifications, as summarized on your sheets. . . ." The room filled with a buzz of dismissive conversation; the captains knew their market.

"*Flute* bids one hundred thousand standards," Protherall called out into the sudden silence.

"We have a bid of one hundred thousand standards," Holstadt announced. "Do I hear one hundred ten? One hundred ten—"

"One-ten," Klepper called back.

"*Bremerhaven* bids one-ten, can I get one-twenty, one-twenty ladies and gentlemen—"

Moses looked at Klepper. The expression on the captain's face was closed, unreadable. Not so Protherall's. He had grasped at a reed on the edge of the abyss, and now someone was plucking it out by the roots. What was Klepper doing?

"*Irish Missed* bids one-twenty." Now it was Klepper's turn for suprise and puzzlement. He looked at Moses as if at a stranger.

"One-twenty, I have one-twenty, can I get one-twenty-five?"

"One-twenty-five," Protherall snapped.

"One-twenty-five, I have one-twenty-five, who'll go to one-thirty?"

"One-thirty," Moses called, almost aghast at himself. What did he think he was doing, competing with a man who had no hope of outbidding him? And for a cargo he didn't want. Protherall had to be bidding against the untouchable funds earmarked for the operation of his ship—

"One-thirty-five!" Protherall blurted it out the way a murderer might have screamed out his confession in a popcart melodrama. It was plain to everyone that he was at the limit of his resources—

"*Irish Missed* yields." Just as it was plain to Protherall that he was being handed a victory he could never have won on his own. He looked at Moses as though the young captain had caught him in the middle of some unnameable obscenity.

"Lot number fifty-six, to *Flute* for one hundred and thirty-five thousand standards." The board flashed blank again. "That concludes the day's bidding, ladies and gentlemen. Bidding will resume again tomorrow at ten hundred hours local. Those parties interested in submitting bids for the colony-administered intrasystem runs may do so at thirteen hundred hours this afternoon. Thank you."

The sunlight was warm on Moses' face as he emerged into the gardened court of Mission House once again. Klepper fell into step beside him.

"Going back to the port? We'll split a cab."

"Not as yet, thanks," Moses said. "I think I'll wait around and put in a bid for one of the insystem runs."

"Thirteen hundred hours this afternoon," Klepper pointed out wryly.

"Or one o'clock P.M. this afternoon, right." Moses chuckled. "Don't make fun of the civil servants, Hans. They give us money."

"Some of us, anyway."

"True enough. What the hell was Protherall playing at? For that matter, what the hell were *you* playing at, Hans?"

Klepper's face grew sober. "He's going to ruin himself with that fabric," he said. "I wouldn't have touched it with someone else's ten-foot pole. But I couldn't let him just take it. It would have been bad manners. I had to leave him the illusion at least that he could still make a deal for himself. I didn't expect you to jump in though."

"I don't think it worked."

"That's because you have a lousy poker face. He *knew* you were doing him a favor. He was ashamed."

"I wish I'd known I was doing him a favor."

"Good God." Klepper looked at him. "You don't mean you wanted that junk?"

"Hell, no. I know what the local poisons are. I'm quite happy to stay as far away from Eli Santer as two planets will let me, thank you."

3

Even twenty feet above the ground, the blown sand swirled in his eyes.

The world was *brown*. Light brown sand blown every which way, gusting across the permaplast roadway and the landing dock, silting up against the sides of the geodesic domes clustered as if for warmth three hundred meters away, flowing in great golden dunes toward the darker brown of the stony mountains on the horizon, half-hidden in the dirty-brown haze of sand suspended aloft in the constant wind. And not the warm, vital brown of chocolate or autumn leaves or even good honest dung but a brown that suggested the more unpleasant sorts of mushrooms, aged and decaying paper, or dusty, mummified remains.

The only spots of color in the whole grim vista were the dirty white domes and the glaring scarlet of his gamy shirt. Even the hulking paneled warehouse beyond the domes was some shade of undeclarative dun.

Chavez's keepers fell into place behind him, and they walked down the long ramp to the ground below. He wondered why they kept the bass stunners to hand now. Where the hell did they think he was going to run?

As they drew closer, details of the gathered domes began to reveal themselves. They were larger than they looked, in the deceptive way such featureless structures had, and they were separated by a stretch of permaplast road along which were parked several six-wheeled haulers, smaller cousins of his own Leyland. Several closed-fan sleds were parked by a dome that might have been a barracks by the long rows of windows set in its sides.

His escort brought him into the anteroom of a smaller

dome than the others, where he waited while one of them
went on in. He came out again quickly. "He'll see him
now." He grinned mirthlessly at Chavez.

"Welcome to Trollshulm. Enjoy your visit."

"We'll understand one another before you leave here."

Eli Santer looked down at Chavez from his raised desk, a
desk that matched the rest of the room's opulent furnish-
ings. It might have been a prime First Wave tower suite,
but for the honeycomb walls of the geodesic, stark and
functional, surrounding it all. Chavez stared at Santer,
interested. He'd never met a man who owned his own
planet before.

Eli Santer was a tall, rawboned man with close-cropped,
silvery hair that had been blond once, and teeth that
flashed startlingly white in his seamed, leathery face. He
spoke in a deep, measured voice, with an unworked-at
undertone that suggested he was capable of pulling off
somebody's arms if it suited him. He had pale eyes,
impossible to read, and the kind of demeanor that one
either quailed before or bridled at. And if Chavez had been
any good at quailing, he wouldn't have been standing there.

"Now, you've read your writ," Santer said, "and you
know why you're here. Hansen's System is a growing
colony, and we haven't got any room for people who don't
pull their own weight. So that's what you're going to do,
friend. You're going to give me all the work you're capable
of."

"And what's in this arrangement for me?"

"Money. You work, you get paid. You work hard enough,
hell, maybe you can even buy your way out of here."

"That may not be easy." Chavez pulled his empty wallet
from his pocket and tossed it onto Santer's desk. "I seem to
have trouble hanging onto my money lately."

Santer picked up the wallet and studied it indifferently.
"Oh, yes, your money. Four thousand, nine hundred and
ninety-seven standards, point four, to be exact." He tossed
the wallet back. "We're holding it in escrow, as an advance
against your initial outfitting and supplies. That leaves you
with a balance of"—he consulted the readout on his desk—

"eleven hundred and thirty-four marks, almost exactly. I'd hold onto it, if I was you. You'll probably need it."

"That was a little premature of you, wasn't it?"

"This isn't a charitable institution, my friend."

"I didn't think it was."

"I'm so glad. Now, until you get your feet under you, we're going to pair you with an experienced skinner, Rafer Stone. You watch him, you learn from him, and maybe you'll be making quota before the year's out."

"What's my quota?"

"Five hides a month, local time, in good condition. Anything else?"

"No. So I guess I shouldn't be wasting my time standing here."

"Uh-uh. You shouldn't be wasting *my* time. You better get used to thinking that way."

"I'll make an effort." Chavez turned to leave. Santer spoke again.

"You know, Blackstone, you really aren't very smart. It wasn't smart to run back at the port. It wasn't smart to get Councilor Thorson mad at you. It wouldn't be smart to get me mad at you. You work for me now. It would be smart to remember that."

"I'll be as smart as I can. I promise."

"You're not being very smart right now. Do you know what's happening here? I buy up twenty or thirty writs a week, did you know that?"

"I knew it."

"And you're the only one I had brought here. That's because you're not very smart, so I had to bring you someplace where I wouldn't have to keep looking for you. You see? If you'd been smart, you'd have figured out some way I could make my money off you back in Hansen's Landing, just like all the others. But I'll make my money off you anyway, easy or hard. And the smarter you are, the easier it'll be. On you."

Chavez left.

"Five thousand Confederate standards don't go as far as they used to," Chavez said sourly.

The dark, attractive Hindustani girl with the disconcerting green eyes of some Anglo-in-the-woodpile ancestor grinned and hefted the jacket of his field leathers.

"Whatever are you talking about?" she demanded. "Where else are you going to get all this"—she indicated the rest of the pile, underwear, toilet kit, field gear, boots and the long knife all dragonskinners carried—"*and* a complete set of dragonhide originals for a lousy five thousand?"

"Yeah, but they're irregulars," he said, opening the jacket to display the thick scar that marred the iridescence of its back. "They should be marked down."

The girl managed to look offended without meaning it. "Five thousand *is* marked down," she assured him archly. "You don't think we sell the good stuff to the help, do you?"

"The help?"

"You and me, friend."

"Somehow, I never considered myself as 'help.'"

"Well, I suppose you could consider yourself a slave or a convict, but that puts things in such a depressing perspective, doesn't it?" The small red dot of her *bindi* caste-mark worked slightly with her quick changes of expression. "Besides, this isn't such a bad place if you go about it properly."

"Mm-hmm. And what's 'properly'? You have any special tricks for getting along with the management that you think I should know about?"

She looked him up and down. "None that you could use, I'm afraid. He can be mean, but he's sexually quite conventional, from what I've seen."

"Ah. Really."

"Really. It beats mucking around with the bloody lizards, doesn't it?"

"I'm not arguing. But, uh, speaking of mucking about with the lizards, don't I get a gun or something to do my mucking about with?"

"Well, as long as you've paid for one—"

"I did?"

"—I don't see why not." She disappeared back into the shelves that filled the bulk of the geodesic, and returned carrying a rifle, still wrapped in its original government-issue plastic. "This is a Kalashnikov-Kern two-by-fifty assault rifle. It comes with stock one-to-three power variable optical sights. It takes the standard military two-by-fifty sliver and fires it at a muzzle velocity of eighteen hundred meters per second. It has three-sliver burst and full automatic capability, and a burst dispersal area of thirty centimeters at three hundred meters, fired from a fixed rest, whatever that means. It's all rather academic anyway, because a two-by-fifty sliver won't pierce dragonhide at that range."

"Then why the hell do you use them?"

She propped her arms on the countertop and looked up at him. Her green eyes were bright and startlingly direct beneath her shining, close-cropped black hair. "Do you want to try to kill a dragon without one?"

"No, no, no," Chavez said quickly. "But why use this model if it's no good?"

"The company got a good price on them when the Wolkenheim militia went over to a new model with a more powerful accelerator. Besides, they'll do the job if they're used properly. That's part of the free lecture."

"I actually get something for free here?"

"Enjoy it; it will probably be the last free thing you get on this planet. Sit down, sit down." Chavez looked around and took the single chair on his side of the counter. The girl sat on her counter, swinging her legs over to face him. They were very good legs, Chavez noted. Her loose blouse of gold synthetic contrasted warmly with the gray shelving and featureless white panels of the dome.

"Free lecture," she began, "as dutifully memorized for newcomers by indentured citizen Shasti Keane, chief and only quartermaster clerk of Santer Holdings, Trollshulman Branch, Limited.

"Dragons are the primary predator in the Trollshulman ecology. They feed mostly on the rooting animals out in the flats and the young of other dragons—"

"What do the rooting animals eat in this dustbowl?"

"Sand."

"Sand?"

"They filter the sand of the flats through their digestive tracts and extract microscopic flora and trace minerals they need. Rather like earthworms with legs. And please don't interrupt, it makes me lose my place and than I have to start all over again."

"Oh, you wouldn't do that to a nice fellow like me—"

She picked up the rifle. "This is a Kalashnikov-Kern—"

"All right, all right, I'm sorry."

"We'll overlook it this time. Dragons average some eight meters in length, some two meters tall at the shoulder, and some seven or eight tons in weight. Unless provoked, they're rather lethargic."

"What provokes them?"

She looked at him, somewhat annoyed. "People shooting at them."

Chavez's resentment of Councilor Thorson plumbed new depths.

"There are three main problems in dragonskinning. First, it is a very resource-intensive industry. The skin accounts for only a minute fraction of a dragon's weight, and no one has ever found a profitable use for the rest of the animal—"

"Don't they serve dragonburgers in the local bistros?"

"There isn't much market for death by silicate poisoning. You do have this problem with spontaneous vocal emissions, don't you?"

"I seem to do. You'd think I'd learn."

"Bit late for that now. At any rate, this means you have to kill a lot of dragons very quickly to keep up your quota. Five hides a month may not seem like many now, but you'll soon find out differently. The second main problem is that a damaged hide brings a lower price. And the third main problem is, of course, that a two-by-fifty sliver won't do much damage to a dragonskin, whether it's attached to the dragon or not. The most viable technique anyone's stumbled across seems to be getting their attention with a short burst in the face and then trying for a brain shot through the open mouth as it charges."

"What if it charges with its mouth closed?"

"It still has to open it to eat you."

"Oh. How did I get into this?"

"Eli says you're not very smart."

"I know, we discussed that."

"You *discussed* something with Eli Santer?"

"Well . . ." Chavez shrugged. Then he looked at her sharply. "*Eli* said?"

She nodded. Chavez snorted with amusement and shook his head. "I've got a knack. I really have."

"A knack for what?"

He grinned ruefully. "I was going to ask you what you did when you weren't giving lectures to newcomers."

She smiled back, a muted expression undercut by private awareness. "Pretty much whatever Eli Santer wants me to, really."

"Oh."

"Well it bloody well beats—"

"—mucking around with the bloody lizards, I know," Chavez chorused. "I'm sorry; I wasn't making judgments."

"That's all right. I do all the time," Shasti said.

"Yeah." Chavez began loading his kit into the duffel provided. "What about ammunition?"

"They give you that when they drop you at your camp. For some reason, they don't want heavily armed employees wandering around the depot."

"I can't imagine why not."

The camp was deserted when the supply sled deposited Chavez before the single prestoplast geodesic hut squatting in the lee of a steep granite outcropping. The pilot of the sled handed him a single box magazine for the Kalashnikov-Kern, one hundred slivers, thirty-three bursts and a single. The sled-loader watched him the whole time, a charged bass stunner ready in his hand, mute testimonial to the quality of Trollshulman labor relations. Chavez turned away, hunching his shoulders as the rising sled blew stinging sand against his back, then shouldered his duffel and trudged up to the door of the hut.

It was deserted. The shaft of bright sunlight that preceded him through the doorway crooked across a rumpled cot and up the wall of the geodesic. Closing the door behind him, Chavez looked around in the relative gloom of the softer light admitted through the translucent walls of the hut. A second cot sat separated from the first by

a cheap stand that held a single lamp and a handful of popcarts. Chavez laid out the cot's bare, half-folded mattress
and dropped his duffel and rifle on it. A combination
microwave cooker/vapor still hung on the wall, outside
which the hut's small monopole generator hummed softly. A
single-side-band radio sat on a shelf by the door, better
communications than a campfire and a wet blanket, but not
by much. Cartons of prepackaged field rations, probably
from the same surplus source as his rifle, were stacked
beside the cooker, most of them already open and well-
rummaged through.

Standing lockers stood on the far side of each cot. Chavez
pulled open the one closest to his cot, expecting to find it
empty.

The shelves were packed with underwear and toilet
articles and several worn, faded sheets. A single scarlet
tunic hung from the clothes rack, frayed at the cuffs and
collar. A handful of tourfax prints sat under a half-used tube
of depilatory. Suppressing a pang of guilt at the intrusion,
Chavez picked up the cards.

They were typical tourfax images, all of them alien to that
arid world. Beachscapes and forest scenes, Westsea and
Fricjk's Wilderness: places on Wolkenheim that Chavez had
known only as names on maps or backgrounds on the free-
channel pops. And there were other scenes: majestic
starliners in golden half-silhouette against distant suns, the
scarlet-roofed pagodas of Peng's Paradise, even an exotic
landscape of UrbAnglia on distant Terra, taken on a rare
clear day.

The messages written in bright green ink on their
reverse faces evoked a world every bit as alien and
incomplete as the universe evoked by the posed, static
snapshots that bore them. The oldest ones all began
"Darling," "Dearest," "Beloved Stefan"; they spoke of
remembered, shared intimacies; they recalled fragments of
stories and occasions that meant nothing to anyone who had
not lived through them; they invoked plans for a future that
made "Stefan's" consignment to Trollshulman servitude a
temporary check in a promised life of fulfillment and
togetherness. "Love, Anya," they ended, "Yours forever,
Anya."

But as the tourfaxes grew more recent, their promises faded, cooling as the two lives they excerpted drifted apart. The intimacies of the earlier missives shoaled, fax by fax, into progressively more rote recitals of day-to-day events; the declarations of passion in salutations and closings cooled to "Dear Stefan" and "Best Wishes"; the dates above the text grew further and further apart.

The last tourfax was dated a year and a half before.

Chavez sat down on the foot of his cot and considered his situation. It didn't bear much consideration. Through the good offices of the paternally cuckolded Councilor Thorson, Chavez Blackstone was stuck on Trollshulm for the duration or until he achieved somebody else's idea of financial solvency by hunting the equivalent of a carnivorous elephant with an army-surplus carnival-gallery popgun, and there wasn't a damned thing he could do except try to live through it.

Having bare survival as the best he could hope for was not very encouraging.

Then the *sound* brought him to his feet, reflexively clutching up his empty rifle. The noise resembled nothing so much as a duet between a submarine klaxon and an aged basset hound suffering the death of a thousand cuts.

The thin prestoplast walls of the hut suddenly seemed terribly confining. Chavez stepped through the door, fumbling the magazine into his unfamiliar weapon.

Rafer Stone came running into the campsite, disheveled and unarmed. The ululating bugle of the dying basset hound was his unceasing, hoarse-throated wail of terror.

The dragon's roar was the counterpointing klaxon. The creature flowed along the ground with a low, scuttling stride, a great, moving boulder with eight-inch teeth. Blood trickled unnoticed from a long scar along its jaw, highlighting that terrible maw in grisly scarlet.

Chavez lost an eternal second fumbling for the charging handle of his rifle with fingers that suddenly seemed to have all the deftness of uncooked sausages. Then a sliver slammed into battery and he brought the weapon to his shoulder and fired, the rifle scope full of looming gray dragon flesh.

His first shot with the unfamiliar weapon went wide,

kicking up sand beyond the charging behemoth. His second caught it in the nearside claw.

The dragon's bellow went up an octave and it fell, rolled, and came up facing Chavez. He snapped a burst into the wide stretch of bone between its deep-set eyes. The dragon shook its head and roared its defiance, revealing the twin half-moons of teeth set three deep and a throat down which Chavez could have slid with no chewing at all. Then it charged, wobbling as it tried to keep its weight off its injured foot.

It was ten meters from Chavez when he fired again and the other foreclaw went out from under the beast. It slammed headfirst into the ground. Chavez thumbed his weapon to automatic. The dragon lurched upright, impossibly tall before him, on its hind legs. That great mouth opened and dragon sound filled the world as Chavez brought the rifle up and fired, not aiming, just pointing the weapon into that gaping vivisectorium and pulling the trigger.

The massive head slammed back into the ground six feet in front of him. The dragon gave a single, violent shudder and died.

Rafer Stone came forward out of the rocks, gasping, a long-faced and gangly man, one of El Greco's elongated saints in dragonhide leathers. "Jesus God, thanks, friend—"

"Where's your rifle?"

"Out there somewhere, with my trac."

"What happened?"

"What the hell do you think happened? I missed."

"Shit." Chavez popped the magazine from his rifle and started slipping the remaining slivers into his palm, counting. There were just three left; he had no memory of firing so prodigally. He started to reload the magazine but the slivers slipped from his fingers into the sand at his feet. He hadn't realized his hands were shaking like that.

Chavez sighed, pocketing the spent magazine and shifting his rifle from the crook of his arm and slinging it over his shoulder.

"You're supposed to teach me how to hunt dragons. . . ."

4

Money was falling out of the rafters all around Ian Protherall, but he couldn't touch a mark of it.

The translucent columns of the holoblocs reached all the way up to the vaulted ceiling of the Warrens, seeming to support the roof itself the way the cascading streams of transactions pouring down within them buttressed the economy of the Hansen System. Bustling runners and floormen jostled past Protherall from all directions to shout out prices and offers or confirm credit or huddle in noisy agitation around terminals tied to unseen offices deeper in the Warrens.

So much money, Protherall thought, such an incredible mass of goods and services, each with a price to be asked and a profit to be made. His own wheelings and dealings, the entire annual business of *Flute*, would not have covered a space on one of those columns the length of his forearm. And the business he hoped to conduct today would have been only one brief line of even that insignificant record—if it wasn't the one thing standing between Ian Protherall and bankruptcy. That made it more important than all the facts and figures tumbling through the air around him put together. That made the small bundle under his arm a weightier, more precious, burden than a bar of gold.

But it didn't change the fact that he had no idea where he was. The mob surging around him had turned him from his path time and again, and the walls with their numbered doorways were lost to sight behind the translucent hologram pillars.

"Captain Protherall?" A thin-faced young man with lank black hair that spilled untidily into his eyes asked politely—

if it was possible to infuse courtesy into a query shouted over the mercantile bellowings all around them. Protherall had not seen him coming.

"Yes," he shouted back. "Can you direct me to the TerraCo offices? They're off door thirty-seven."

"That's why they sent me, sir." The young man grinned, without quite erasing an expression that hinted something dreadful was certainly happening somewhere that he desperately needed to know about but wouldn't until it was far too late. "Nobody ever finds anything in here on their first trip. Follow me, please."

The young man slipped through the crowds on the trading floor like an eel between stalks of seaweed. Protherall shoved and bumped his way in clumsy pursuit, unable to find his way safely through the swarming entrepreneurs. Appropriate, he thought sourly. His guide halted from time to time; only that allowed Protherall to keep the young man in sight.

Then he was through the crowds, and the young man was waiting for him by door thirty-seven, which parted to let them pass into the silence of a carpeted, softly lit hallway. The sudden quiet was almost a palpable thing in Protherall's abused ears.

"A bit overwhelming, isn't it, at first, that lot out there," his guide said.

"Was that meant to be a suggestion or a question?" Protherall asked.

"Oh, well, more an observation rather, sir." The young man seemed to think he had committed some sort of gaffe. Protherall saw no reason to disabuse him of the notion.

"Then I share your observation, my friend. Lead on."

The young man padded softly along the corridor ahead of Protherall, to a door of heavy Kassen's teak. A small ebony plaque with the gilt globe-and-moon crest of TerraCo embossed was the only decoration.

The door opened silently to admit his guide. Protherall started through behind him, only to be brought up short in his tracks by a discreet, melodious chime.

The young man turned back to Protherall with a wounded expression. The young woman seated behind the lucite receptionist's desk looked up at him with composed, clear eyes. But the calm of her expression was of a different nature entirely from that of the blond, square-faced man who stepped quickly from the door Protherall would have sworn was an ornamental panel, to face him with muscular arms loosely folded across the front of his gray, severely cut suit.

"Oh, dear," the young man said, as if embarrassed for him. "You're not carrying any sort of, well, transmitting devices, are you, Captain?"

"Just my pager." Protherall reached into his dress tunic; the blond man's shoulders seemed to get even wider. Protherall suddenly noticed that the man's jacket was unbuttoned—one of those bulges probably wasn't a muscle. He brought the pager out with exaggerated care and offered it to his guide, who handed it to the receptionist. She laid it aside and keyed up a holobloc on her desk, looking from the readout within it to Protherall. She canceled the bloc and looked up to the blond watchdog.

"It's all right, Klaus. Thank you." The silent Klaus stepped back through the concealed door, as silently as he had appeared.

"Thank you," Protherall said. "And now I believe Mr. Rodinov is expecting me?"

"Of course, Captain. Go right in."

Ivan Petrovitch Rodinov rose smoothly from his chair as Protherall was admitted to the executive's presence. He had not gone out of his way to dress up for Ian Protherall— he had no need to impress the captain—but his First Wave suit still made Protherall's well-worn Academy dress grays seem even shabbier than their age called for.

"Captain Protherall, how good to see you." Rodinov extended a firm handshake, whose uncalloused strength suggested it came from sensible exercise rather than the sort of demanding labor the Rodinovs had doubtless been paying to have done for them since Great-uncle Sasha first set up the family business.

"Thank you," Protherall said. "Sorry about all the bells and whistles."

"A regrettably necessary precaution. Unfortunately, the Warrens were not named for their architectural complexity. Some of my esteemed competitors are sadly enamored of some rather byzantine business practices. I trust that will not be the case between us."

"I'm just a simple merchant captain, sir. I buy and I sell; I leave the exotic approaches to others."

"How refreshing. And in which capacity do you approach me today?"

"Well, sir, I'm sure you know that *Walkabout's* just completed her scheduled call—"

"Certainly. That's hardly a secret."

"No, it isn't. And it isn't much of a secret either, that she brought in a major capital infusion from TerraCo-Geneva."

"You can take a serious risk, Captain, paying attention to unsupported rumors like that."

"But in this case they're informed unsupported rumors, Mr. Rodinov. And if they're correct, it's of benefit to both of us."

"Go on."

"TerraCo wants to expand its share of the outer-Confederate market. Simple economic survival demands that."

"Obviously."

"As compradore of TerraCo, you have an advantage over locally based entrepreneurs, in that your operating capital isn't directly affected by the success or failure of local ventures. TerraCo isn't likely to be bankrupted by any given setback in one system, or even a group of systems."

"That's a rather gross oversimplification, Captain. TerraCo expects a return on its outsystem investments."

"Yes, but they still can't afford to retreat from marginal or losing areas. That would mean losing out on the potential market in not just the affected area, but on expansion into every market beyond that. They have to have some kind of executive proximity to the sales-place. So you've got that much security."

"So *TerraCo* has that much security, Captain," Rodinov corrected him drily. "Unless TerraCo's compradore can guarantee that security, he has none at all. That's sometimes a rather uncomfortable position."

"I'm quite familiar with the feeling. And I believe I have a proposition here that no responsible compradore could turn down."

"Why not?"

"Because it's not only commercially viable in its own right, but it offers TerraCo an opportunity to break an outsystem stranglehold on a significant market."

"That would indeed be interesting. And what proposition is that?"

"This," Ian Protherall said. He unsealed the bindings on his package and passed it across the desk.

"I'm prepared to offer TerraCo Eli Santer's hide. You should excuse the pun."

"I'll take it under advisement," Rodinov said. He had pulled the swatch of coarsely woven fabric out and was examining it curiously. "Just what am I looking at here, Captain?"

"A new synthetic protective fabric, Mr. Rodinov, developed for general export by Zion Ring Exports out of Masada Torus, Sol. The key to the dragonhide market and thereby a crack in the basic foundation of Santer Holdings."

Rodinov looked disappointed. "Is that the whole of it? From your first query I was led to expect much more. There have been other attempts to move into Santer's market, Captain. So far no one has been able to provide a product even vaguely competitive with dragonhide—and Eli Santer is willing to go to great lengths to maintain his primacy."

"I know. Santer Holdings can scrap with the best of the insystem firms. But no outsystem compradore has ever challenged him. And no one has ever had this synthetic."

"I see. You have specifications to support your claim."

"I do."

"I would have to see them, of course."

"I can do better than that, sir. The fabric sample is yours, as is a quarter's exclusive option on all rights—for ninety-three thousand Confederate standards. That's as an advance against a full payment, of course."

"An interesting figure, one I believe I've heard before—yes, it just happens to be your updated premium on the *Flute*, doesn't it?"

"You made a comment before about byzantine business practices."

"Yes, they're deplorable—when they're being used on

me. I'm actually quite well informed as to your situation, Captain."

"Very astute of you. Then you'll appreciate why I'm disinclined to dicker. Too little money is no more use to me than no money at all."

"That could tend to harden one's resolve, yes. Did you have an actual final figure in mind, or is that still pending on what the yard decides to charge you for the structural upgrading the surveyors called for?"

"They haven't decided on a price yet; that means I haven't."

"I see. Of course, I'd have to set some sort of definite upper ceiling, in any event."

"I wouldn't be too hasty with that," Protherall said.

"And why not?"

"Because you're buying more than just the fabric here, and you're buying more than just a chip out of Santer Holdings's market in the Hansen System. Santer exports dragonhide to at least three other systems farther out, not counting wherever they might be transshipping to. Offer them a competitive product and you could crash Santer's market at least that far out and more. Wouldn't that be a neat little prize to hand Geneva?"

"To be sure. I suppose in that case this is not a decision that needs to be made immediately."

"No. But whether you want to take an option or not is."

"I would have to see your specifications on the fabric before I could authorize any commitment."

"Why don't we do this, then: I'll make a gift of that sample there. It's yours. Test it to destruction, compare your figures with dragonhide, and then take into account how much more economically the Zion Ring synthetic can be factory-produced than dragonhide can be grown and processed."

"That seems fair enough. Would a week be soon enough for an answer?"

"I've got a week." Protherall rose. "Just one thing, a free tip: To separate that fragment from the roll I had to use a three-megawatt steel-cutting laser on a hundredth-millimeter collimation. It isn't cheesecloth. Good day to you, sir."

"I look forward to speaking with you again, Captain."

Protherall's nervous young guide was still waiting for him in the receptionist's lobby. Protherall retrieved his pager from the young woman and turned to face the guide.

"Yes, well then, sir, how did your discussion go?"

"Well enough, I think. Thank you."

"Oh, good, fine. Then I suppose I should show you back out—"

"That won't be necessary," Protherall said, "I think I can find my way clear from here."

Ivan Petrovitch Rodinov leaned back in his seat as one door closed behind Ian Protherall and a second opened.

"Well, what do you think?" he asked.

"You have to give the good captain credit," Lakim Tovas said, taking the chair Protherall had vacated seconds before. "He does not think small. Or perhaps it is simply his desperation that gives him courage."

"That makes him rash, you mean. If I was in as uncertain a position as his, I would not want to cross one of the major economic powers of the Hansen system."

"You flatter us."

"I'm a realist, Mr. Tovas."

"And you are a man doing business with money not your own. No offense, my friend, but that makes you cautious. You may always assure your station by taking care to at least minimize your defeats. Captain Protherall has to win all, or he is ruined, and so he acts decisively. That is to be admired."

"Do you think Eli Santer will agree?"

"Oddly enough, I believe he would. He will break Ian Protherall, but I think he would admire the audacity of his challenge."

"I see. And do you think he would admire the audacity of your coming to me?"

Tovas contrived to look puzzled. "There is hardly any audacity involved, Mr. Rodinov. Eli Santer trusts me to look after his interests on Wolkenheim. When I learned of Captain Protherall's acquisition I was naturally obliged to express the concern of Santer Holdings."

"Of course. And now perhaps you'll tell me just how great that concern is."

"In what sense?"

"What is Santer Holdings offering TerraCo to refuse Captain Protherall's offer?"

"I do not follow you. What profit would there be for Santer Holdings in that?"

Ivan Petrovitch Rodinov grinned knowingly. "Ah, I see it now. Very good, Mr. Tovas. What consideration may I expect then from Santer Holdings to purchase the option offered? With the understanding that development will prove unfeasible, and quite publicly so?"

Lakim Tovas shrugged. "I cannot see the point in your taking so much trouble for no reason."

"Then I find myself puzzled, sir. You did say you came here to express the concern of Santer Holdings."

"Yes."

"Perhaps I've missed something here. I thought your purpose in coming here was to forestall a potential competitor."

"Santer Holdings has had competition before, Mr. Rodinov. We've survived well enough."

"Then the Zion Ring synthetic doesn't worry you?"

"Worry me? No, not at all. It does interest me intensely, however. I look forward to the results of your tests."

"Now, really, Mr. Tovas. Assuming the test results are as good as Captain Protherall is staking his future on their being, why should TerraCo advertise that fact to our main competitor before we're prepared to exploit it?"

"Because foreknowledge of the properties of the synthetic would do Santer Holdings no good, sir. We can hardly instruct the dragons to begin growing their skins differently, can we? And because," he added, "it would not be a case of advertising that fact to a competitor."

"I don't see what you're leading up to. If the synthetic is viable, TerraCo becomes not just Eli Santer's competition, but his nemesis. The dragonhide export is the key to the whole of Santer Holdings."

"You're not the only person to realize that, Mr. Rodinov."

"Meaning yourself? You work for Santer. The hides are the key to your fortune, too."

"That is a situation that does not please me."

"It pleases Eli Santer."

"I am not Eli Santer. I am hardly a member in good standing of the First Wave community, sir. I have never pretended to be. I have neither the benefit nor the burden of your undoubtedly rich heritage and sense of history. When Eli Santer looks at a dragonhide he sees the essence of everything that let the Santers win Trollshulm and claim it for their own. He sees all the blood, sweat, and tears of a dozen generations of ancestors."

"And Lakim Tovas? What does he see?"

Tovas shrugged. "I am not blessed with such poetic vision. When I look at a dragonhide, I see a serious lack of diversification. I see a product whose availability is limited and cannot be expanded to meet any growth in demand beyond that limit, and which is therefore doomed to be supplanted, whatever its merits, by products more readily available. Seeing all that, I must also see a threat to the future of my employer."

"And yourself."

"My fortunes are those of the Santers. I am quite thoroughly aware of what my status here would be without Eli Santer's patronage. So I collect his indentured labor for him, and run his errands—and sometimes I make the decisions he will not face."

"Why tell me this?"

"Because for all our social disparity, I believe we share a common understanding. The Hansen System and those who own it are too small to compete with the real economic powers such as TerraCo. That is why you elected to become a compradore—First Wave family though you are—and that is why I chose to approach you. TerraCo can survive without Santer Holdings. But it can survive better with us. And we cannot survive at all, ultimately, without you."

"Very perceptive. You display considerable foresight, Mr. Tovas."

"Of course. That's where the profit is."

Ivan Petrovitch Rodinov relaxed, careful not to let his relief show. He understood what was happening now, and that put him back in control.

Tovas' offer itself hadn't thrown him. That was the sort of opportunity TerraCo thrived on, the chance that let them establish themselves in system after system. As a compradore of TerraCo, Rodinov understood that.

But Tovas had been the enigma, the latecomer who broke the rules and thrived by it, enjoying the patronage of Eli Santer and dealing with First Wavers as though he treated with equals. As a First Waver, Rodinov could never really comprehend that. It ran counter to everything he knew about the way things worked in his world. He expected that such confusion was responsible for a large part of Lakim Tovas's success.

But now Rodinov knew how to deal with him, because for all his confessed awareness of his own lack of status, Lakim Tovas was overreaching himself. He had thrived so long in the shadow of Eli Santer's respectability that he still counted on it to give him substance, even as he offered to betray it. He had grown too confident, too self-assured in his past victories. He had come to assume they were the result of his own skills, rather than the resources he was given to attain them.

Lakim Tovas had reverted to type. Stripped of Santer's aura, he was a climbing little latecomer who somehow thought Rodinov would treat with him as he would with a peer.

And as long as he knew that, Ivan Petrovitch Rodinov was in control.

5

Chavez learned, slowly.

They were working fifteen kilometers from camp, two sweat-drenched, sunburnt kilometers from the trac parked in the lee of a dune. The long walk was necessary; dragons had long since learned to avoid the noisy machines.

The dragon-sign they had been tracking from a fresh kill seemed to bend out of sight behind a small dune before them. Chavez slung his weapon over his shoulder and started up over it to pick up the trail. His leathers had yet to break in properly and they chafed at the back of his knees as he climbed.

"Hey, wait—" Rafer began uncertainly.

There was a sudden geyser of dust and the dune stood up. Sand rained away in all directions and Chavez went sliding with it down a broad expanse of dragonback.

A head the size of a horse's chest swung around toward him. Chavez flipped desperately aside, rolling out of his rifle sling and bringing the weapon up before him as a clawed hind foot gouged into the sand where he'd lain.

The dragon came whirling around with impossible speed for something so huge. The great dagger-rimmed maw parted and the rifle bucked in Chavez's hands as he and Rafer blew the back of its skull out with one long burst.

"Yeah, they'll do that sometimes, bury themselves like that," Rafer said. "They gorge themselves and then they dig in to digest, I guess. I think they like the cooler sand underneath, too."

"Well, thanks for the warning." Chavez didn't rise; he didn't trust his knees quite yet, not when they felt softer than the knot in his stomach.

"Hey, what do you want from me? I can't think of everything. Why don't they tell you anything back there?"

"I think it's their plan," Chavez said sourly. "I think they figure that anybody who can survive your tutoring can outlive anything this goddamned planet can throw at them."

"I don't have to take that."

"Then ask for a new roommate. It won't take me long to pack."

"It doesn't work that way. Anyhow, you're wrong about Santer. He'd never let a rookie get himself killed before he's had a chance to make some money off you."

"I believe that. Shit. What kind of animal walks two kilometers from dinner and then lays down for a nap?"

"The kind of animal that doesn't want to be sleeping next to a bunch of bloody meat when the scavengers show up."

"You mean there's something out here that eats dragons?"

"Kid, they got stuff out in this sand that'll eat anything, or give it one hell of a try before it learns better."

Chavez looked around unhappily. "Great. What do you do about that?"

"Well, I always make sure to sit on a rock, so they can't tunnel up and—you goin' somewhere?"

"Just stretching my legs."

"Ah-hah."

That was how you learned with Rafer Stone.

They worked the long knives around the stubby spinal plates that protected the soft skin along the ridge of the dead dragon's back where the hide continued to grow and stretch as the beast aged. Most of the hide was cut free and Chavez was working on the heavy shoulder joint exposed by the peeled-back hide, while Rafer Stone struggled to separate the heavier hipbones. When that was done they would hook up the trac and use its hauling power to flip the body, letting them reach the other legs. Then they would make fast the disjointed limbs and simply pull the whole skin free of the carcass.

"These things grow funny," Rafer announced without

preamble. "Because of the way the hide grows out from the back."

"What do you mean?"

"The hide around the belly and the flanks hasn't got much give. It's all older skin. So the damn dragons can't put on any weight there. It'd interfere with their leg mobility and probably start to squeeze their guts out. So they start to store fat under the skin on their backs."

"What's there to get fat on out here?"

"Beats the hell out of me, boy. But I've seen some humpbacked wonders of dragons. Now it used to be, you'd see a real old one that couldn't hunt the way it used to, after it got pushed off its territory by a young one. They just shrivel right up; like a rotten melon. Nothing but a big old empty rind."

"There many like that out here?"

"Nah, not anymore. Santer's shipping out more hides these days, so we're killing 'em younger."

"Can't take that too far, can they? Or we're liable to run out of dragons."

Rafer Stone laughed. "Never happen. Fucking Santer without fucking dragonhides? There's no such thing. There'll always be an Eli Santer, and that means there'll always be dragons."

"And that means there'll always be clowns like us here hunting them for him."

"Yeah. Likely will be."

There was a silence then, broken only by the sound of knives cutting meat and cartilage.

"You know, I've been in the assigned labor pool since the first week I stepped off port property in this system," Rafer said.

"How'd you manage that?"

"This was where my passage fare ran out. Well, Wolkenheim was. So I walked out the gate, and went looking for work. But some First Wave type was looking for cheap help, so the immigration people decided I wasn't likely to become a productive, taxpaying citizen anytime soon enough to suit them. There I was."

"Ever since, huh?"

"Well, not all the time. You watch yourself, you can make

enough to declare solvency and they gotta let you go. But once you get in the assigned labor files, you don't ever really get out. They keep an eye out for you, and whenever the work pool looks like drying up, there they are, checking your returns."

"How many times have you been in the pool?"

"Oh, hell, boy, you stop counting. Five times, maybe six."

"This is my first."

"Won't be your last, I can guarantee you that. Shit, it ain't as bad as all that. I've seen a lot of places, done a lot of things I never would have done if I hadn't been pulled out of the pool. Jockeyed a twelve-ton harvester out in the grain belts on Wolkenheim, did two years and a piece logging over to Fricjk's Wilderness, hell, I probably graded half the groundcar track to Newtown personally."

"And now you're here."

"Yeah, well, it ain't as great as all that, either. But I'll get through this, too."

"And get hauled off someplace else."

"Most likely. But at least I know I got a next meal coming, even if I ain't sure just from where, yet. You still got them tourfaxes, Chavez?"

"What?"

"Those tourfaxes of Stefan's. You still have 'em?"

"Yeah. I didn't know what to do with them."

"Junk 'em. That's what got his ass killed."

"How do you mean?"

"Them faxes. All those plans. You don't make plans in the labor pool, boy. You don't have that much elbow room. You're where you are, and you're gonna stay there until they decide to let you go someplace else, and the world doesn't wait for you to catch up. The more that missy what's'ername—"

"Anya."

"Whatever. The more he saw her cooling off on him, the more shit backed up between his ears. They had all these plans for when he was gonna get back home, and then after a while she let go of 'em. He didn't. Hell, every other damn thing he said started with 'When I get out of this' or 'When this is all over—' Got to where he just didn't keep his mind

on the job, and there's just too many ways to get killed out
here for that."

"You make plans, though," Chavez said, after a pause.
"You bank your hide payments."

"Hell, yeah," Rafer admitted. "But that's just taking care
of business, like I said. No reason to pretend the future
won't happen. You just can't live in it. No, save for
tomorrow, boy—but keep your mind on today."

And that was something else Chavez could have learned
from Rafer Stone, if he'd been interested.

Eli Santer grinned at Tovas' discomfort.

The little man did not like Trollshulm, and had long ago
given up any pretense of contrary sentiment. He stood at
the base of *Abilene's* ramp, his back turned to the dry, dusty
hot wind and the fierce sun that burned into the nape of his
neck. His thin Wolkenheim clothing was little protection on
this harder world; Tovas could feel the ultraviolet piercing
the loose fabric with a million incandescent needles.

None of it bothered Santer. Trollshulm was his world,
man and boy, his home as well as his property. The planet
had shaped Eli Santer to itself, burning away any softness of
spirit the way it seemed to leach away the very moisture of
his flesh. It had made him into a creature of the sand who
would defend his territory as fiercely as the dragons he
hunted, and who conceived of little that existed beyond.

That was a weakness that made Lakim Tovas a necessity
to Eli Santer, Tovas knew. But Tovas's misery on Santer's
home ground made him something Eli Santer could never
respect, whatever his value. Yet in spite of that intolerance,
Santer was not a stupid man. That meant that Lakim Tovas
would have to tread the path he had chosen very carefully.

"Welcome back to paradise, Lakim," Santer said. "You
going to stick around awhile this trip?"

"By all means. I intend to stay every bit as long as I have
to. After which I mean to get back to civilization if I have to
steal this ship and pilot it myself."

Santer laughed. "You should hang on here a few weeks.
The outdoor life is good for you; it builds character."

"I have never considered heat stroke a sign of moral superiority."

"Your loss." Santer turned to the driver of his sled. "Trebig, take Mr. Tovas back to my dome. You know how it is with these domesticated specimens. You have to keep them out of the sun."

"What about you, Eli?"

Santer threw his head back theatrically and drew a deep breath, grinning.

"Oh, it's a nice cool day, Anders. I think I'll just walk back." He looked at Tovas to see what effect his jibe would have. The little man just shrugged and spread his hands.

"Mad dogs and dragonskinners, sir."

Santer laughed again. "God knows we've got noonday sun enough for both. Go ahead, Lakim. I'll be along."

Tovas had already poured himself a tall glass of insystem whiskey—with ice that would have cost a skinner a mark extra in the depot canteen, by the time Santer returned.

"So. Have you recovered your civilized composure yet?"

"Very nearly, Eli."

"Good for you. How did it go with Rodinov?"

"Not as well as we might have hoped. He wasn't interested in accommodating us."

"Why not?"

"We may have a problem here, Eli. Mr. Rodinov seems to put great store in this synthetic of Protherall's."

"It's that good?"

"Rodinov thinks so."

"Is he right?"

"I managed to secure a sample of the cloth through a cooperative second party. We owe Keppler Speculations a favor for that by the way." That was true. Tovas needed a source for his information that Santer wouldn't question. "We can give it to our people here for their own analysis. But the Zion Ring specifications are alarming enough in their own right." The Zion Ring specifications, confirmed by Rodinov's own investigation.

"This new synthetic has a great deal in common with our product. It's produced from a long-chain silicon-combination molecule, much like dragonhide. Most of the combining elements are also similar, but the exact pattern of the combination differs radically. That's to be expected, of course."

"Fine. But how does it compare to hide in practice?"

"I have the exact specifications here." Tovas held up a dataplac. "But the basics I know. Taking dragonhide and assigning it a value of one, the Zion Ring synthetic has a puncture resistance of point seven three, an abrasion resistance of point eight one, a tensile strength of point six nine, and an elasticity factor of one point nine six."

"It's junk. What about permeability?"

"It's a woven fabric, Eli. It's completely permeable, without further treatment. It also has an ultraviolet degradation factor of one point five three, again barring supplementary treatment."

"Then we have nothing to worry about. They simply haven't got the product to compete with us."

"Unfortunately, that's not true, Eli."

"Why not?"

"Because compared to every other protective fabric on the market this far out from Confederate center, the Zion Ring synthetic is superior by a factor of as much as two to three hundred percent. Conventional ballistic nylon, Kevlar, even Nemourlon simply aren't in the same class."

"Well, neither is dragonhide. We've still got the numbers on them."

Tovas shook his head. "I'm afraid we don't. The figures I've just quoted you are based on a single ply of synthetic, compared with a single layer of dragonhide."

"That's the only kind there is. The dragons only grow one skin at a time."

"But the Zion Ring synthetic is not subject to the same limitations. It's a woven fabric, Eli, not a grown skin. You can weave as many layers' thickness as you like, or you can fasten layers together much more easily than you can sew sheets of hide together. Also, if you utilize the synthetic as the stitching material, you can make a seam much stronger than you can join hides with any other fastening material. And when you compare even a two-ply layer of Zion Ring synthetic with a single layer of dragonhide . . ."

"Goddamn Ian Protherall. What's the status of the TerraCo deal?"

"Well, Rodinov has taken his quarter's option. That gives him enough time, I should think, to initiate establishment of a large-scale manufacturing facility."

"It does, does it?" Santer scowled. "Not in this colony. Not if Santer Holdings has anything to say about it."

"Santer Holdings doesn't."

"The hell we don't. We've got enough favors owed us that if we say he doesn't build, he doesn't build. We'll block his permits, keep him from acquiring property—what the hell are you shaking your head for?"

"Eli, Rodinov is TerraCo."

"And I'm Santer Holdings."

"And that means he's bigger than you. TerraCo is an interstellar corporation. That means he has an influence with the Confederacy we can't hope to match."

"What's that mean?"

"It means that there's a limit to how much pressure we can bring to bear on TerraCo before they go running to Mission House with a restraint of trade complaint. And they could probably make it stick."

"What 'restraint of trade' are you talking about? What would we be doing that we haven't done before? That any businessman in this system doesn't do? We're taking advantage of a position it took us generations to reach, nothing more."

"We aren't doing business in this system alone anymore, Eli. Because TerraCo isn't a Hansen System firm. We can't expect them to play by some unwritten gentleman's agreement between honorable First Wave citizens, and we can't look for any support from Mission House if we try to use that agreement to freeze TerraCo out of doing business in this system. The Confederacy wants open trade, not a handful of closed markets scattered between the stars. They'd never allow the precedent."

"They've allowed it so far."

"Nobody's ever competed for our market before."

"Well, what about our interests? Is Mission House going to let some outsystem bandit come in and squeeze out local industry?"

"I don't know. It's an approach to explore. But I wouldn't hold out much hope. After all, the synthetic is going to be manufactured in the Hansen System, using local labor, putting tax marks into the local economy. TerraCo might even be able to make a case that they'll be a greater benefit to the community than the dragonhide operation."

"So what do we do? Just sit here and let them choke us out?"

"I never said that. I simply say we can't stop TerraCo from establishing a manufacturing base during this quarter. After that, there are a number of approaches we might take."

"Spell them out."

"There's always the chance that they will encounter difficulties in beginning production. There could be plant trouble, quality control problems, labor difficulties."

"We could encourage that."

"If necessary. And if it can be done safely. Rodinov knows how things work in the Hansen System. And of course there is always the possibility that once they are prepared to begin production, they might not have the right to."

"Go on."

"Rodinov has purchased an exclusive option on the synthetic for this quarter only. That was all Protherall was offering, because of his own financial situation. He will not set a final price for rights to the synthetic until he knows how much he will need to save the *Flute*. And until he makes that final deal with Rodinov, the rights to the synthetic remain part of his assets—and accessible to his creditors."

"So if Protherall goes under, we could grab the synthetic right out of Rodinov's hands."

"We could at least assure that it was denied to TerraCo, yes."

"And that would leave them with all that capital tied up in financing a plant for a product they don't own. I like it, Lakim. What are the chances we could pull it off?"

"Captain Protherall is considerably more accessible to us than TerraCo. And he is in a much weaker position."

"Yes. Too weak to have tried a stunt like this in the first place."

"He saw a chance. He took it."

"At my expense. He doesn't get to do that twice, Lakim. Not to Santer Holdings. Not to me."

"No. I agree. We have to show that we are not a firm to be outmaneuvered. We must reinforce our posture in this regard."

"So Captain Protherall has to become an example."

"I will attend to it. There is one other thing."

"What is it?"

"If we time this properly, we will leave TerraCo with a plant they cannot make use of. They will be eager to recoup at least part of their capital loss. We could probably acquire the facility at a fraction of its contracted cost."

"And do what with it?"

"The Zion Ring synthetic is a marketable commodity, Eli."

"Not as long as there are dragons. Skinning made this operation, Lakim. Skinning made this world. Santer Holdings won't give that up, not while I sit behind this desk."

"As you say."

"Besides, I want Rodinov to eat that investment, every damned mark of it. I want to hurt him so badly he'll never come against me again. He's as guilty in this as Protherall, and if I can't break TerraCo the way I want Protherall broken, I can sure as hell at least bend them a little. They have to learn that."

"I'm sure they will appreciate the lesson."

Fighting Ivan Petrovitch Rodinov didn't worry Eli Santer. But he hated having to defend himself against his own family.

Eli Santer faced the rest of his family from behind his raised desk the way some beleaguered feudal baron might stare down over his parapet at a besieging host. The arrival of *Abilene* was the only occasion that sparked these clannish gatherings. The rest of the time, the family went its several separate ways, its members tending to their own affairs and leaving Eli Santer alone to run his planet. But *Abilene* meant waited-for goods, and information too sensitive for the open-access interplanetary channels—and for some, a chance to remind Eli Santer that his rule might not necessarily go forever uncontested.

Of the twenty-three natives left on Trollshulm with enough Santer Blood to have a say if they wanted one, the four who mattered faced him in his office. And of those four, there were three he knew he could discount.

Anders Trebig was safe; his job as Santer's chief head-hunter, his company cop, assured his loyalty. The power to give a direct order and see it obeyed satisfied his ambitions, even if it was a power he exercised mostly over drunken rowdies in the depot canteen and sullen skinners come short on their monthly hide quotas. He lounged back in his chair, sleek and hard-looking in his gleaming leathers, fancying himself a dangerous man, as much of a menace to Eli Santer as a fat hound by the fireside. Santer remembered the alacrity with which Trebig had jumped at the offer to come in off the sands permanently.

His hold over Thomas Markov was less direct, but no less firm. Markov captained *Abilene*, and Santer Holdings owned *Abilene*, and Eli Santer held Santer Holdings. Leave Markov his ship, leave him alone, and he would support Eli Santer in everything else. He was a square, solid man with square, solid forgettable features, the perfect spacer for hire. His profession was the source of his pliability, Santer thought. How could a man who spent his life falling through emptiness put down any kind of roots, find anyplace to make a stand of his own?

His closer kin, the last two Santers on-planet still to bear the name besides himself, were a different matter.

Martin was the lesser threat to Eli's control. The differences between Eli Santer and his cousin were graven into their very flesh. Where life on Trollshulm seemed to have kiln-fired Eli Santer, strengthening him by the unremitting harshness of its demands, Martin Santer seemed simply to have been worn thin by it, like a canvas stretched to the desert winds, worn threadbare and porous by the steady abrasion of the blowing sands. While Eli Santer ran his planet and sold the hides of the great Trollshulman dragons, Martin presided over his hatchery and seeding teams, sowing the sands with new generations of dragons to stalk the skinners and be stalked by them in turn, to provide fresh fodder for the efficient engine of predation that was Santer Holdings. If he saw an action as a threat to "his" dragons, he could become an implacable opponent; if not, it sank beneath his threshold of attention, leaving him free to stock Eli Santer's world with crawling, fanged gold.

Adrienne Santer was something else entirely.

If Trollshulm had shaped Eli Santer, it had absorbed Adrienne. She sat still as some fossil disinterred by the shifting dunes, twenty years Eli Santer's senior, spiderweb thin and fragile as garrotte wire. She watched him with the lidded, unblinking gaze of a dragon older than any a skinner had ever hunted, knowing and patient, waiting for its prey to expose a weakness.

She could have had his chair, and Eli Santer knew it. It had been the luck of the sand that her father had died under a dragon's claws while Eli Santer's father lived. Had it gone the other way, she would have succeeded to primacy in Santer Holdings, and he would have been the one sitting there, watching and waiting, barred from power by the corporate machinery of the firm. He wondered if she would have recognized him to be as great a potential challenge then as he saw her to be now. The others had appetites as well, but smaller appetites, appeased by their lives on the sands or their ships or playing with the company cops. All Adrienne Santer had was her eyes.

"We're being challenged," he declared. "Ivan Rodinov and TerraCo are trying to move in on the hide market. And it looks like they have the product to do it." He summarized Tovas' report on the synthetic and TerraCo's acquisition of it. He played heavily on Protherall's effrontery and the danger from TerraCo, hoping to fix their attention on the external enemy. It didn't work.

"This is the one danger we've always faced," he said. "The hides are the one product that *is* Santer Holdings, the bottom line of everything we are. And now the bastards are trying to take that away from us."

"So what do you propose we do about it?" asked Thomas Markov.

"What we have to. Block TerraCo's construction of the pilot facility, however we have to. Squeeze Protherall hard enough and fast enough to take the synthetic away from him, then keep on squeezing until we break him, make an example of him."

"We've decided all this already, have we?" Adrienne Santer asked. "That was quick, Eli. Just which 'we' was involved in this decision?"

"I was," said Eli Santer.

"You were. And your pet latecomer, of course."

"That's his job."

"Santers do Santers' jobs, Eli. I don't recall seeing any mention of this come up through company channels."

"It didn't," admitted Eli Santer. "We could have waited on it, of course. We'd probably have received the first interoffice memo about it just about the time Protherall and TerraCo went to final contract."

"Don't insult your own, Eli. Especially not for some latecomer."

"Who works for me."

"For Santer Holdings," Adrienne corrected him sharply.

"All right. So why don't I just call him in here—"

"Because this is family business, Eli, and a family meeting. He has no place here. You should know that."

"His place is where I want him to be. That's why I'm sitting here."

"The whole issue is irrelevant," interrupted Markov. "We have to do something about Protherall and TerraCo. What else would we do except what Eli's suggesting?"

"The issue is not irrelevant," Adrienne answered him. "This isn't a matter of what we're going to do to some tramp captain or a competitor—"

"Of course it is."

"—It's a question of how we decide what to do. Have any of these decisions been implemented yet?"

"How could they be?" Eli Santer asked. "Tovas just came in with the word on *Abilene*. He'll be taking my instructions back with him."

"*Your* instructions. That's exactly the point I'm making, Eli. There was nothing to be done about this before the family meeting in any case, but you and that latecomer had Santer Holdings's mind made up before we even knew what was happening."

"Somebody has to make the decisions."

"But not some scabby latecomer," snapped Adrienne Santer.

"Now who's insulting their own?" Eli Santer asked.

"Who came up with all these responses Santer Holdings is supposed to make, Eli? Did you? Or were they Tovas' 'suggestions'?"

"I make the decisions for Santer Holdings, Adrienne."

"That's right, you do. And so do we. Or at least we're supposed to; we're family, Eli. You can't cut us out of the decision-making process like this. Especially not for some latecomer. Santer Holdings has never been run that way."

"We've never been threatened like this before," said Eli Santer. "We need decisions, not argument."

"So that's why you turn to Tovas? Because he can't tell you 'no'?" She leaned forward. "And what about you, Eli?"

"What about me?"

"Can you tell him 'no'?"

"That doesn't even deserve an answer. He works for me, not the other way around."

"Yes. Whereas we work with you, the way you should work with us."

"The way some of you work with me," said Eli Santer. "No offense intended, but what do you contribute besides your presence, Adrienne?"

"Precious little," she answered. "You've seen to that."

"And that's really what we're discussing here, isn't it?" Santer asked. "That's all we ever really discuss. The issue is not how well I'm running the company, is it? It's how little you get to run it."

"No. The issue is, how much *do* you run this company? You're so eager to keep me, to keep us, below you, that you'd rather turn to outsiders you don't know at all to run Santer Holdings for you—"

"Damn it, I run this world!"

"Do you deny that all these plans you have for TerraCo and Protherall were Tovas' ideas?"

"They were options he presented. I decided."

"Yes, between the options *he* gave you."

"Tovas knows the Wolkenheim situation a lot better than any of you. That's why I use him."

"Yes. But do you realize he knows it better than you, also?"

"Of course. But that's all right. Because he may know Wolkenheim better than I do—but I know him better than he thinks."

Adrienne Santer subsided in her chair, not beaten—not ever—but realizing she was facing an argument she could not rebut.

"I hope that's true, Eli. Because if you don't, then you don't know what you're doing. With him. To us."

6

Chavez couldn't understand Rafer Stone's anger.

They were bound back to Santer's depot, the sledge with their month's take trundling along behind them as the little trac scuttled between the massive dunes like a beetle industriously churning through a child's sandbox. They were four hours out from camp, and Rafer hadn't said one word in all that time.

The anger had come on him gradually, beginning as they returned from their last run empty-handed. It had grown as they shared a last meal from the empty ration cartons. It had built as they bundled their eight collected hides onto the sledge that morning, and now it wreathed him around like a thunderhead waiting to discharge.

"Man, what the hell is bothering you?" Chavez demanded. "You gonna sit there like that all the goddamn way to the depot?"

"You know what's buggin' me," Rafer said, grudging each word. "At least you oughta' if you'd payed any goddamn attention to anything since you got here."

"Hey, I don't want to hear any of that," Chavez objected flatly. "If I don't know what's going on, I don't know what's going on. Now what the hell is going on?"

"Eight hides is what's going on," said Rafer Stone. "Eight fucking hides."

"So?"

"So we're behind the fucking quota, aren't we?"

"I know that," Chavez agreed. "So what? If we didn't see ten dragons, we couldn't kill 'em, could we?"

"It ain't that easy," Rafer said.

"Why not?"

"You'll see."

"Thanks for the help," Chavez said.

He pitched the bulky ration carton on top of the pile already weighting down the sledge and dogged down the clamp on the retaining strap, making the rations fast beside the drums of perimeter toxin.

Shasti Keane ticked off the carton on her clipboard and keyed the inventory into memory. "You're welcome," she said cheerfully. "Skilled supervision makes any job go smoother, doesn't it?"

"So does picking up the boxes."

"Hardly an executive function now, is it?"

"There is that. Too much like real work."

"Don't use foul words like those in front of a lady, Mr. Blackstone. Where are your manners?"

"I got sand all over them, so I threw 'em away."

"You could always draw a new set."

"For free?"

"Here?"

"Sorry," Chavez said. "I should have known better."

He leaned against the side of the trac, the metal of its body cool enough to touch in the shade of the loading dock. He was shirtless, both to enjoy the shade and because most of his clothing was in the depot laundry for the thorough cleaning it couldn't be given with the limited water supply out at the campsite. He wouldn't have thought it possible to lose weight on the carbohydrate-rich field rations, but he had, he saw—mostly water fat probably; that left him lean and angular as a mesquite branch in the Southwestern deserts he remembered from Terra North America.

"Come on inside," Shasti suggested. "I may have a few used scruples you can have, cheap."

Chavez followed her back into the geodesic, the sudden, air-conditioned coolness catching in his throat. Shasti opened the small refrigerator behind her counter and brought out two plastles of carbonated fruit juice. Chavez wondered at the cost of such luxury.

"We'll make this quick," Shasti promised. "I've never seen *anyone* get goose flesh on Trollshulm before."

"It must be the company I'm keeping."

"I know your type," Shasti said, "You only love me for my icebox." She typed a command into her terminal as Chavez unsealed the plastles. "Now let's see where we're sending you this month."

"What do you mean?"

"We'll have to assign you a new hunting ground," Shasti said. "The one you've been working is pretty obviously worked out, if Rafer Stone came in short. That's unusual; usually we have some warning of when that's going to happen beforehand, so we can shift you and keep you up to quota. We'll have to put a biosurvey team in there and find out what went wrong. In the meantime . . ." She trailed off, studying the screen before her. Chavez tried to make sense out of the pattern of scarlet dots scattered in varying degrees of thickness across the map. "Good," Shasti said. "We can give you a new area without having to move your camp. It's only another forty kilometers drive-time."

"A leisurely forty kilometers drive in the bright Trollshulm sunshine," Chavez mocked. "What could be more fun?"

"Sixty kilometers?"

"Forty doesn't sound so bad," Chavez said quickly.

"I thought you'd like it."

"Let's not overstate my joy here."

"I'm not. You're going to need all the breaks you can get if you're going to bring in six hides apiece next month."

"What?"

"Actually, we're cutting it a little fine at forty," Shasti continued, as though he hadn't spoken. She indicated several of the red telltales on the map. "Some of those are probably a little young yet for harvesting. But they should be passable."

"How many hides next month?" Chavez asked.

"Six."

"What happened to five?"

"Well, you were short this month, weren't you?" Shasti answered. "You have to make up the balance somewhere."

"What happens if we don't make six hides next month?"

Shasti stared at him. "Why should next month be any different?"

"Well, shit."

"I don't set the quotas," Shasti said defensively.

"I know, I know. There's no point in yelling at you—but shit, I've got to yell at somebody." He set the unfinished drink down on the counter and walked out.

Rafer Stone was waiting for him beside the trac.

"Well, let's go," Chavez said. "We haven't got time to waste sitting around here."

"Oh, yes, we do," Rafer said. He wore the dour, yet somehow relieved expression of a man whose worst expectations have all come true.

"What do you mean?" Chavez asked. "They upped our damn quota."

"That ain't all they've done," Rafer Stone said.

"Oh, no. What else?"

"Only eight hides between us. That makes us low team this month. That means we get to pull extra duty."

"Yeah? Like what?"

Rafer Stone spat disgustedly.

"Fucking nursemaids."

"I heard *Abilene* lifting out this afternoon," Shasti said. Lying there in the darkness, Trollshulm was almost tolerable. With the burning heat of the sun walled off beneath the horizon, the warmth of the night air was a less insistent sensation, an impression rather than an imposition. The occasional gust of windblown sand breaking around the walls of the geodesic was a papery whisper, drowned out by the rustlings of the sheets as she turned on her side beside Eli Santer.

"Yes. A hundred and fifty hides. We'll earmark them for *Northwest Passage*."

"All right." Santer's chest was warm and dry under her cheek, the skin taut over bone and compact muscle. There was no yielding in it, as though his body had been carved from some light, seasoned hardwood, contained and ungiving. "Did Tovas leave with it?"

"Yes."

"Good. I don't like him."

"You're not alone. But what's your reason? You weren't one of his finds."

"No. No, I wasn't. But I still don't like him. He makes me uncomfortable. I look at him and I have this feeling, that he would just take anything of mine that I let him have—and I would never get anything back."

Santer grinned, teeth a brief whiteness in the dark.

"No, you wouldn't. Not from Tovas. That's why I use him. I know what you mean, though. He doesn't belong to anything, unless belonging to it can get him something else he wants. Hell, he doesn't know what belonging to something means. I think he thinks belonging to anything is some kind of vice, or weakness. I know he doesn't understand why I won't let go of the hides, or why I won't come live in one of his plush First Wave towers on a world full of lakes and forests." He rose up over her on one elbow. "*This* is *my world*. Santers fought to keep it when every other family packed up and ran back to Wolkenheim. We fought to keep it when it killed us to fight. And now I'll fight to keep it when it feeds us."

Shasti looked at him, silent. This was not the first time Eli Santer had spoken to her that way; sometimes, in bed, he tried to explain himself, perhaps justify himself, in a way he would never do during the course of the day. But it was an offer she had decided from the first she would never accept. She would come to his bed because that was the nature of their arrangement, but she withheld from him any other intimacy. The sex was something he could compel, but any other involvement was something she could still control, and would control, just because she still could.

"Tovas belongs to you because he wants to use you, too," she said, changing the subject.

"Yeah. But I can accept that. I'll let somebody use me if I can use them back. That's a clean exchange."

"Yes, I guess it is."

He lay back down beside her, with the inchoate sense of refusal he often felt but could not identify after such times, and for a time neither spoke. At last she sat up and swung slim legs out of the bed, reaching for her clothes. "I'll make a note about those hides in the morning."

He watched her pull the gold tunic down over her head, small breasts pulled taut by her upraised arms, the smooth curve of waist into hips lost as she let the loose shirttails drop.

"You never stay," he said.

"I sleep better in my own bed," she said, without rancor.

"You don't have to leave."

"Are you asking me to stay?" she asked, knowing that he never would, now that she had made it a condition *she* imposed. She gave him time to answer, if he was going to surprise her, holding to their arrangement. Finally she shrugged, in the silence of the room.

"Good night, Eli."

7

"Eli Santer is not a man for half measures, is he?" Rodinov asked.

"Under the circumstances, he is right not to be," Tovas answered. "He understands his situation well enough to recognize the threat you pose, even if he will not accept that he cannot beat you."

"Then you don't think his plan will work?"

"Against any insystem competitor," Tovas said, "yes, it would. It's a sound approach, one that I at least could execute quite effectively. But he still underestimates the resources TerraCo has to hand. If Protherall is forced into receivership—and he will be; I have as great an interest in retaliating against him as Eli does—it's foolish to assume TerraCo would let the synthetic fall into the hands of any other creditor than itself."

"We are not one of Protherall's creditors."

"Not yet. But I am sure you will take steps to become one. It is a necessary protection."

"What will becoming Protherall's creditor cost me?"

Tovas shrugged. "What Eli proposes to do is force the synthetic out onto the open market again. Then he will drive the price of it up so high that it will intimidate the insystem competition, and, presumably, TerraCo as well."

"How high will he drive the price?"

"To protect the dragonhides? He will spend every mark he has and every mark he hopes to make for years to come to obtain and suppress the synthetic. It will be expensive to pursue this course; I won't lie to you about that. But you simply have more money than Santer Holdings—in the end, he will spend enough to leave him vulnerable to

69

absorption by TerraCo. You will get the synthetic plus all the assets and organization of Santer Holdings. It will establish TerraCo forever in this region."

"Forever is not a common business term."

"For a major risk, there should be a major reward. But there are steps you have to take to ensure that reward."

"What are they?"

"Santer has to believe you are fighting him as strongly as possible—that is, as strongly as any insystem firm would do. To give him that impression, we have to give him an initial success."

"Which is?"

"Protherall goes. He must forfeit his ship. That will convince Eli that he can oppose you effectively."

"All right," Rodinov said. "Then we give him Protherall. But won't that put the synthetic at risk?"

"Not if it's timed correctly. And of course, I can make certain that it is."

"I'm sure you can. But if we are to proceed on that basis," Rodinov said, "I would need some assurance of your cooperation."

Now it was Tovas's turn to be puzzled. "I don't understand."

"I will require a commitment from you, my friend."

"My survival is my commitment, Mr. Rodinov. I've explained that already."

"Yes, you have. Just as you explained to Eli Santer that he could still suppress the synthetic."

"I've outlined the entire course of action Eli will have to follow for you."

"Quite true. You've been very free with Eli Santer's confidence. So what I'm looking for is a guarantee that you will be more respectful of mine. Something more concrete than words, Mr. Tovas."

"What did you have in mind?"

"So far, the only party in this affair who stands to lose nothing whichever way it turns out is yourself, sir. Eli Santer is risking his entire world; I am risking the funds of my employer and my position as compradore for TerraCo. Whichever one of us loses, Lakim Tovas wins."

"I cannot see that you would act any differently in my position."

"Quite possibly not. But I am not in your position. And I am not prepared to put my faith in anyone who is. That is, after all, the key to Eli Santer's vulnerability here."

"Then what do you want?"

"I want you to take a side, Mr. Tovas. And I believe the only side you can reasonably take is mine. And once you've admitted that to yourself, I want you to give me an earnest of your loyalty."

"I assume you have something specific in mind."

"The harvest will be in on Hansenwald just prior to the arrival of *Northwest Passage* insystem, will it not?"

"Yes."

"I presume Santer Holdings means to make an investment in this season's pharmaceutical yields."

"We usually do."

"As does TerraCo. But under the present circumstances, I don't see why I should spend TerraCo's good money when I don't have to."

"What are you proposing?"

"A jointly financed purchase, Mr. Tovas. TerraCo and Santer Holdings. And I needn't tell you who will secure me those funds."

"That's impossible. I could never justify it to Eli."

"I don't see where you really need to. To Eli Santer, Santer Holdings means dragonhides, after all. I'm sure that you do not trouble him with every detail of every other enterprise such a large firm is involved in."

"He allows me a certain latitude."

"And this is very well known. Which of Santer's subordinates on Wolkenheim is likely to question a decision made by his chief lieutenant? None that I know of, wouldn't you agree?"

"That is probably correct."

"I'm sure you would know. So I'm certain you can see the advisability of this joint venture. I would be more than willing to protect the confidence of a partner. But a duplicitous corporate spy is quite another matter altogether."

"This is quite unnecessary, Mr. Rodinov."

"Very true. I don't have to do this at all. That I am willing
to offer you this opportunity should be taken as a sign of my
own good faith. After all, all I have to do to ensure TerraCo's
success at this point is meet Captain Protherall's terms
when he offers them. In the end, I would still win. But that
would involve ruining Eli Santer rather than absorbing
him—and in that case, what use would I have for Eli
Santer's Stonetown errand boy? So I am quite prepared to
deal with you fairly, Mr. Tovas. Provided I may expect a
reciprocal attitude on your part. And this way, I believe I
can."

"As do I, sir," Lakim Tovas said.

Rodinov extended a hand.

"Then welcome to the firm."

Chavez Blackstone would never have believed he could
feel naked in dragonhide leathers. But crawling over the
dunes, unarmed, going where he knew he was going, he
realized he was wrong.

"They're kidding," he whispered fiercely. "They have to
be fucking kidding."

"Well, they ain't fucking kidding," Rafer Stone whispered
back fiercely, "and I ain't fucking kidding either. Now shut
the fuck up."

Since raising his voice enough to argue about it would
probably have gotten him killed, Chavez shut up. But he
reserved the right to be incredulous.

"Dragons are the only exportable resource this world
possesses," Martin Santer had told them, back in the
comfortable safety of his air-conditioned, plushly furnished
geodesic. He had established himself at the farthest end of
the depot, away from the warehouse and its rising stacks of
dragonhides awaiting transshipment. He had chosen that
isolation deliberately, as a conscious gesture, to show that
his dealings with dragons were the exact opposite of his
cousin's.

"Therefore they have to be protected," Martin Santer
continued, smiling thinly. "At least if we want to go on

killing them." The smile seemed to grow warmer, slightly. On anybody but a Santer it might have been friendly. "I know you've heard this speech before, Rafer. But Blackstone here should at least know why we want him to pull such a damn fool stunt."

"Hey, don't mind me," Rafer said. "Every minute I spend sitting on my ass in here is a minute I ain't chancing getting it chewed off out there."

"True enough. The thing of it is, Blackstone, even with people always coming in under quota like you two this month, we could kill dragons faster than they could replace themselves with no trouble at all. So we have to help them along.

"Dragons are oviparous. Females can lay as many as a dozen eggs in one sitting. Out of that dozen, between scavengers looting the nests, predators while they're still young, and competition between themselves as they grow, we're lucky if one lives to be harvestable from each litter, in the natural course of events. So we help."

"How?"

"We raid the litters ourselves."

"Is that all?"

"That's all. We steal the eggs and incubate them in a controlled, protected environment. Then we distribute the dragonets in unclaimed territory."

"That's it?" Chavez asked. He stared at Rafer incredulously. "That's what you've been weeping and moaning about? Stealing eggs?" He looked back to Martin Santer. "Hell, that sounds fine to me. Who ever got bitten by an egg?"

Rafer snorted. "Tell him the rest, Marty."

Martin Santer shrugged. "There is of course the problem of getting the mother off the nest first. . . ."

The dragon resembled nothing so much as a maternal main battle tank in Chavez's eyes as he crept up alongside Rafer at the crest of the dune. It rested curled around its clutch, the eggs open to the fierce sunshine within her guard. Each egg was the size of a grapefruit, and shone like mother-of-pearl.

"She isn't moving," Chavez whispered.

"Shut up! She'll move. . . ."

Poised atop a howling gale of sand and dust, the closed-fan sled breasted the rise beyond the dragon with a banshee's wail.

Chavez had never imagined that the creature could move so quickly. As fast as the thought of it, the dragon uncoiled and lunged for the sled, which danced back, showering her with fan-driven grit. The dragon's bellow of challenge and rage was a thunder that drowned out even the shriek of the sled's straining motors.

Again the brute lunged, and again the sled skipped back, its driver familiar with the way the game had to be played. He side-slipped the sled down and to the dragon's right, as though trying to circle past her to reach the vulnerable eggs. The dragon spun and pursued him. He side-slipped again, swooping around the hollow, and the dragon followed. But this time as he rose to evade her charge, the driver withdrew slightly, descending. The dragon took the bait and pursued him. Swooping and retreating, the sled lured the enraged mother away from her nest, a few meters at a time, until the eggs were left untended.

"Now!" Rafer said, and threw himself down the dune. Chavez slid after him.

Rafer wasted no time, scooping up eggs and shoveling them into the haversack he carried.

"Move it!" he yelled. "That bitch won't be fooled for long!"

Chavez grabbed up eggs frantically, eyes riveted on the lunging, snapping monster raging at the taunting sled.

"Enough!" Rafer shouted, slinging his haversack over his shoulders.

"I've still got room!"

"We ain't got time!"

The dragon was beginning to back into the hollow, its attention and its anger still focused on the sled. Chavez scrambled up the dune after Rafer.

"Now what?" he asked, as they skidded and slipped down the dune's far face.

"Now comes the interestin' part."

"What's that?"

"Can the sled get around that dune before that bitch comes over the top of it?"

Even as he spoke the sled burst into view around the curve of the dune, banking as sharply as it could short of toppling off its fans, the driver's head swiveling as he sought them out. And even as he dove toward them the dragon surged over the crest, screaming for her stolen young.

It probably wasn't as close as Chavez remembered it afterwards. But he had a distinct impression of teeth clashing at his heels as he threw himself aboard the already climbing sled.

"Some fun," he gasped, as they climbed to a safe height.

"Nah, the next part's the real party," Rafer said. "Next, we gotta put 'em back."

"Oh, great. When do we get to play that game?"

"Soon as they want us to. They've usually got a batch ready to go whenever they can find someone dumb enough to take 'em out."

"Lucky us."

"No shit. One more thing."

"What?"

"When we get back to depot, get that bootheel replaced. The one with the toothmarks."

8

"I'm sure you can appreciate the fairness of our offer, Captain."

The Customs and Revenue office loomed over Hansen's Landing from the height of the tallest First Wave tower in City Center, with a panoramic view overlooking the Confederate Mission House and the wide expanse of the port complex on the far side of the soiled streets of Stonetown. It was a distance Ian Protherall wished like hell he'd been able to keep between them and himself. It hadn't happened.

"I'm not sure I see how Customs and Revenue comes to be in a position to make me an offer, Mr. Temple."

Bewys Temple frowned professorially, tapping the keys of his holobloc. Protherall saw facts and figures flash up in the air before him. It was almost impossible to read the backwards lettering from the reverse side of the bloc as the words and figures flickered past, but he made out *Flute* and the name of the yard that had given him the most recent estimate.

"I'm not sure you have any right to pry into my affairs like this," he said. "This isn't a C&R matter."

"Everything pertaining to the trade of this colony is a Customs and Revenue matter, Captain. Particularly when it comes down to our ability to safeguard the colony's interest."

"I've done nothing that merits your concern."

"No. But you may be in a position to assist us in our function, in spite of your present troubles."

"My present troubles are nothing any merchant captain isn't perfectly capable of dealing with."

"Perhaps not. But we have heard informed rumors, shall we say, to the contrary. To be frank, Captain, we know as well as you do the essentially unspaceworthy current condition of *Flute*."

"Then you know a great deal more than I do, sir. Or, for that matter, my underwriters."

"Who only this last month increased your premiums by almost one hundred percent."

"I can afford it."

"This time. But we are also aware that Hansen Astronautics has told you that it will cost nearly half a million standards to bring *Flute* back up to Confederate BuShip standards."

"I can afford that, too. Or I'll be able to shortly."

"Yes—by causing a major upheaval in the economic structure of this colony."

"I wasn't aware that alarming First Wave businessmen was a violation of colony law."

"It isn't. But it could well be a violation of simple common sense."

"I'm just trying to earn a living, Mr. Temple, the same as they are."

"Customs and Revenue appreciates that, Captain. But we feel obliged to suggest that there might well be a more reasonable way for you to achieve that end."

"I'm listening."

Bewys Temple leaned back, manicured fingers poised in a steeple over which he studied Ian Protherall. "You know, of course, of the colony's intention to retire *Vigilant* at the earliest feasible date."

"I've read as much in the trade press."

"Yes. Well, it is a matter of somewhat greater urgency than has been publicly admitted, Captain. *Vigilant* is almost seventy-three years old. Even with this department's continuous policy of maintenance and systems enhancement, she has effectively reached the end of her usable service life. The time is at hand when we must consider her replacement."

"That's understandable. A revenue service needs a revenue cutter."

"Very true. But even that necessity is shaped by financial

realities. No one wants to spend a single mark more than
they have to, Captain. At the same time, everyone wants
the best product they can obtain for their money. Replacing
Vigilant becomes a difficult matter under these conditions.
In the first place, for all her age, *Vigilant* is still state-of-the-
art for the local shipbuilding industry. It has not been a field
in which the Hansen System has elected to establish a
strong footing, thanks to the Confederacy's policy of encouraging the outward mobility of more advanced designs
from the established yards of the center. In brief, we could
not build a superior ship to *Vigilant* at her price, even if we
elected to. And her performance in the modern maritime
environment is already marginal. That situation is not likely
to improve."

"I suppose not. So you'll have to go to those established
yards for a new ship then."

"And spend all those millions of standards outside the
Hansen System economy? I'm sure you can see the serious
political objections to that."

"'Dear Citizens—another example of your tax marks at
work—someplace else.' I can see where that would be a
problem."

"Absolutely. So you can appreciate our need to find a
local solution to our dilemma."

"Do you think you've found one?"

"We believe we have. Her current unfortunate state
aside, *Flute* is an excellent ship, isn't she, Captain?"

"I've had good cause to think so."

"So have we. That's why we would like to hear your terms
of sale."

"I believe you'll find them reasonable enough," Protherall said coldly. "The first is that you arrange for hell to
freeze over—"

"Consider the matter from our perspective, Captain.
We've given this matter a good deal of consideration. Even
allowing for her present condition, *Flute* is worth at least six
million standards on the open market. With the additional
systems she would require for our purposes, *Flute* would
provide us with a totally acceptable replacement for
Vigilant at less than eight million standards. We could

never hope to purchase a new ship outsystem for that price."

"You can't hope to purchase *Flute* at that price either. She's my ship, Mr. Temple. I mean to keep her."

"At a cost of six million standards, Captain? We could arrange excellent terms of payment, say half a million standards a year for the next twelve years—"

"Out of which I'd have to keep up my own payments to the bank."

"Still, you would hardly be starving."

"No. I'd just be a man every captain in the system knew for a failure. You can't pay me enough for that."

"We could even assume your remaining financial obligations, at a substantial savings to ourselves and you. The Hansen System is certainly a more respectable debtor than a merchant captain; we could probably renegotiate the remaining balance at a minimum additional cost."

"How fortunate for you. But she's not for sale, however easily you could pay for her."

"Captain Protherall. *Flute* may not be for sale—but that does not mean you will be able to keep her."

"What do you mean?"

"I mean that in light of her failure of survey, *Flute's* certificate of operation is null and void. Confederate law, sir."

"I'm fully cognizant of Confederate law. You'll note that I've suspended operations pending recertification, as legally required."

"Commendable. But recertification is a difficult and time-consuming procedure—and an expensive one. The surveying authority is likely to look long and hard at any ship that has failed survey once already. They will want to make entirely certain that they are returning a fully spaceworthy vessel to operation, for the safety of her crew and passengers as well as the good of the community. I have to wonder if you are in a position to tolerate any delays or complications—whatever they may be—that might arise. Things do go wrong, sir."

"Maybe they do. But I'm dealing with the best yard in the system, and they're working from a comprehensive survey conducted by colonial authorities in accordance with

Confederate standards. What has gone wrong will be put right, sir. I mean to see to that, at whatever cost. And once it has been put right, you can be sure that I will bring any administrative foot-dragging or harassment to the instant attention of Mission House. There is an authority in this system you people are accountable to, Mr. Temple, and I will feel no hesitation in calling on them if I have to."

"I merely wished to sound a note of friendly caution, Captain."

"Then I appreciate your concern, sir. I'd be obliged if you'd make my position known in whatever circles you feel it necessary."

"I wouldn't know where, Captain."

"I'm relieved to hear that. I'd hate to think Customs and Revenue was bowing to external pressure."

"Our offer will remain open, Captain. I look forward to talking with you again."

"Please don't be offended if I disappoint you."

"You finally got smart, huh, Rafer? Got in off the sands for good, eh?"

"No chance, Willi," said Rafer Stone. "Only two things I come in off the sands for. I come in to sell my hides, and I'm gonna come in, once, to get on the boat come to take my solvent ass off this dustball." He looked around. "But I sure as hell ain't comin' in to go to work here one day more than I have to."

Willi Krupczyk laughed at that. "That's your problem, Rafer. You don't know when you got it good." He turned and looked at Chavez. "You play your cards right, kid, and someday all of this could be yours."

"Yeah," Rafer said, "'Course, there'll be less of you to enjoy it."

Willi Krupczyk certainly justified Rafer's comment, Chavez thought. He had never seen such a dog-eared excuse for a human being before.

Willi Krupczyk couldn't have counted to ten without taking off at least one boot. He brandished the back of his fist good-humoredly at Rafer Stone. It would probably have been an obscene gesture, had the middle finger not been missing, taken off cleanly at the first knuckle. Both pinkies were gone, and his hands and one cheekbone were scarred with numerous precise, paired crescent-shaped scars a good inch and a half across. The lobe of one ear was missing, and the other looked as though someone had tried to improve its shape with a cookie cutter.

"Hey, listen," Willi said. "I'd rather chance losin' something I can spare than getting the whole package chewed up in one gulp. These little farts I can handle; once they get their growth, I don't wanna mess with 'em. That's called planning ahead, ain't that right, Mister Santer?"

Martin Santer shook his head and grinned. "If you say so, Willi. Pass out the poles."

"Sure thing, sir."

Chavez took the long pole Willi handed him and tried to puzzle out its purpose.

A small wire noose dangled from one end of the pole, its lead running back inside the pole itself. There was a sliding grip on a collar about where Chavez would naturally put his left hand; he pulled on it and the noose tightened.

"You gotta hit the safety catch with your other hand to let it loosen up again," Willi explained, reaching over and showing Chavez where the button extended out from the pole. "Once you loosen that up, the little farts'll find their own way loose again."

"Which little farts are these?" Chavez asked.

"Down there." Chavez looked down off the ramp they stood on. The ramp reached out over a broad stretch of sand surrounded by a low wall. Glistening lumps, which Chavez recognized as dragon eggs, were imbedded in the sand in neat rows, dozens of them, perhaps two feet apart.

"We've got a multiple hatching coming up," Martin Santer explained. "That's why we need the extra manpower. You'll have to catch the dragonets as quickly as they hatch, or they go after the other eggs."

"Once you got the noose on the little fart, just swing him out over the wall and hit the release, drop 'em into one of the single cages there. Then we just cart 'em off and fatten 'em up for a while."

"Sounds easy enough," Chavez said.

"Sure it is," Willi agreed.

"Just hope your momma didn't waste any money on givin'
you piano lessons," Rafer added.

"Screw you, Rafer."

"How long is this going to take?" Chavez asked.

"Hatching is due," said Martin Santer. "Today is the first
day we could reasonably expect it, but certainly within the
next three days."

"Three days?" Chavez complained. "Look, Mister Santer, we have to get back out into the field. We've got hides
to kill."

"This is necessary work," Martin Santer said. "We have
to replace what we take out or there won't be hides for
anybody. It's just basic responsible stewardship."

"And it's nice, safe rear echelon work," Willi added.

"It isn't making me any money," Chavez replied.

"Well, you weren't making enough money last month,
anyway," Santer answered him. "That's why you got picked
for this job. The sooner we get it finished, the sooner you
can get back to skinning."

"And how soon is that?"

"Whenever they start hatching."

"Damn." Chavez poked disconsolately over the edge of
the ramp with his noose. "Hey. This thing doesn't reach."

Willi Krupczyk laughed. Rafer shook his head. "Them
little bastards start hatching, we won't be catching them
from up here, kid."

"Oh, no. Let me guess."

"You gotta be quick," Willi said.

"I gotta be elsewhere, is what I gotta be," said Chavez
Blackstone.

"There! There! Get that one! Quick!"

Chavez couldn't tell who yelled the instruction. He'd
already seen the eggshell fly apart as though kicked, saw
the iguana-sized dragonet tumble out onto the sand and
make a beeline for the nearest unhatched egg before it had
even straightened out.

He lunged for it, noose extended in front of him, trying
to slip it over the little monster's head as it clawed and
chewed at the egg. He had just snared it cleanly and

yanked it clear when he felt the double impacts at his ankles.

Two eggs to either side of him had hatched with almost choreographic precision and the feral infants disgorged had gone straight for his legs. They couldn't chew their way through his dragonhide boots and leathers but nobody had told them that, and they weren't about to give it up without one hell of a try.

The dragonet at the end of his pole flailed and twisted, trying to reach the unseen wire that bound it. The others pulled and tugged and writhed around his legs, shrieking like dentists' drills, Chavez was staggering wildly back and forth through the sand, fighting desperately for his footing, stumbling toward the wall and the waiting cages.

Willi and Rafer were running over to him, beating at the dragonets chewing on his legs, trying to knock them away and snare them. It felt as though half their blows were chopping right into his shins and ankles. They were yelling at him to hold still, he was yelling at them to watch what the fuck they were hitting, Martin Santer was yelling at him to get his snared dragonet into a cage. The only people in the pit who seemed to be agreed on their course of action were the dragonets trying to drag down their first meal.

Chavez swung the snared dragonet over an open cage and hit the safety catch. Then he hit it again. And again.

"It's stuck! The fucking thing's stuck!"

"Well, reach up there and grab him by the back of the head and pull him loose!" Martin Santer yelled back. "He can't bite you like that."

Idiot that he was, Chavez actually started to do just that. The dragon whipped itself around with a snap of its tail and buried twin crescents of razor teeth into the plastic of the pole, inches short of his fingers. Chavez yanked his hand back and shoved the pole forward.

"You want the little bastard, *you* take him!"

Martin Santer threw down his pole and grabbed for the dragonet. The noose slid loose as he pulled and Santer staggered backwards, trying to keep a grip on a dragonet that was doing its best to climb up his sleeve and eat his elbow.

Chavez didn't wait to see how he was doing. He grabbed

the lip of the wall and swung himself astride it. Then he swung his legs over the edge and extended them and the snarling dragonets over open cages. Kicking and scraping his feet one against the other, he dropped the brutes into their cages—along with his boots.

Standing unsteadily on bare, bruised feet, he turned and faced Rafer Stone.

"Next month," he promised him, "we *definitely* make quota."

9

Flute rested in the massive cradles high above Protherall's head, the seemingly frail vanes of her magnetic drive folded back along her blunt, cylindrical hull, as the massive cranes rose up and withdrew from the open dock, their long derrick arms flexing with articulated precision like great saurian fossils come suddenly to life.

She looked as solid and capable as she had on the day he had first taken command, Protherall thought. There was no sign of the rot in her alloyed bones, of the decay in her deepest reaches that threatened to break his heart the way it would break her back.

"Is this a final number?" he asked, looking at the invoice.

The yard boss shrugged. "Unless something's wrong that we don't know about, yeah, it's final."

"You've got the surveyor's report right there in your hands," Protherall told him. "If there's something wrong you don't know about, it's your responsibility."

"Then we ought to be all right at this price."

"Fine. Then I'll call your office and arrange the terms of payment."

"Good luck."

The yard boss turned back toward the waiting ship. The personnel doors to the dock shut after Protherall as he left *Flute* behind and went in search of a public screen.

"Mr. Rodinov? Captain Protherall. I've got your price, sir."

"You ready?" Rafer asked.

This would be fun, Chavez thought, if he was watching it

on a popcart, or listening to someone joke about it in a bar, or doing anything except standing in the middle of it.

The dozen dragonets in the bay of the van under their feet were drumming wildly against the walls of their confinement, their individual shrieks melding into one unending roar of outrage.

"Let's get it done."

Rafer looked back to where the nervous driver watched them from his hatch. "Drop!"

The driver's head vanished, his hatch slammed shut, and the van's ramp slammed violently to the ground under the mass exodus of a dozen enraged carnivores.

"Now comes the fun part." Chavez was learning to hate it when Rafer said that.

The ground around the van was a mass of tumbling, clawing, biting dragons, taking out the terror of their transportation and a thwarted territorial imperative on each other with a vengeance.

"Come on." Chavez popped the hatch at their feet and shoved his two-meter-long dragon goad down through it. There was no response; no cringing wallflower of a dragon waited for them in the van bay. The two skinners quickly dropped down into the empty bay.

Rafer banged loudly on the bulkhead behind the driver. "Button it up!" he shouted.

The bay ramp began to inch closed, the grinding of its gears lost in the snarls of the brawling dragons.

Chavez and Rafer pulled the fragmentless concussion grenades from their belts and armed them, then tossed them out over the closing door.

High explosives make an excellent attention-getter. The dragons scattered, panicked, in all directions, not to stop running until they were far enough away from each other to set up their own territories—

—except for the one idiot, there was always one idiot, who sought shelter back in the hauler.

He was halfway through the closing hatch before they realized it. Then they were thrusting at it with the charged goads, trying to drive it back. The dragonet whipped around and got its teeth into Chavez's goad, worrying at it as though the high-voltage shocks meant nothing. It was flailing around in the rampway with all the strength and weight at its command, a draconian St. Vitus' dance that set Chavez lurching and staggering back and forth across the bay at the other end of the goad, as though the beast's frenzy was communicable, conductable by the plastic of the staff.

Then Rafer got a solid purchase with the point of his goad and shoved, and the bay ramp slammed closed behind the tumbling dragon. Chavez found himself staring at a goad chewed down to half its length.

"Didn't I say this would be fun?" Rafer asked.

"Let's get back to the desert," Chavez suggested.

"Five hundred and fifty thousand standards—and thirty-five local pfennig?" Rodinov asked.

"I've been taking a certain amount of static all day," Protherall told him. "I just felt like passing a little of it along."

"Well, I'm fairly certain the thirty-five pfennig won't be a sticking point. What sort of terms of payment were you looking for?"

"The yard wants sixty percent up front. That means I will, too."

"Sixty percent? Is that customary?"

"When there are numerous parties hoping you won't be able to put it up, yes, sir, it is. At least in this system."

"I believe you do Hansen Astronautics a disservice, Captain."

"I hope you're right."

"Two hundred and some-odd thousand standards up front, against five hundred fifty thousand—and what future terms?"

"The standard Mission House royalties provisions."

"That seems most reasonable. When will you need the balance?"

"Upon completion of the repairs."

"When will that be?"

"If I'm any judge the tenor of official sentiment in this matter, probably about a week after *Northwest Passage* clears outsystem."

"Are you expecting problems?"

"You know they're looking for a replacement for *Vigilant*; they're interested in acquiring *Flute* for the job. And there seems to be a lot of quiet disapproval of my doing business with your firm, Mr. Rodinov. So, I'm not expecting problems—just a dearth of prompt and enthusiastic cooperation, if you know what I mean."

"I believe I do. Will it hurt you to miss this starliner?"

"It certainly won't help. But I'll survive it, with this deal—and the assurance that I'll be the preferred carrier for TerraCo on all future liner calls."

"I think that's an acceptable provision, Captain." He touched a key on his desk. "Authorized Agreement Update: Rodinov: TerraCo agrees that Ian Protherall, licensed captain"—he looked up and Protherall gave his Academy number—"append number given, and the Independent Commerical Carrier *Flute*, registry number as given in Paragraph One, is herewith identified as the preferred carrier of the first choice for all starliner transshipments in the Hansen System." He switched off the input and looked over to Ian Protherall. "Captain, if you're prepared to sign, we can do this right now." He sat there, waiting to give half a million standards to Ian Protherall.

"No time like the present, Mr. Rodinov."

"Excellent." He touched the key again. "Please issue one standard authorized agreement, as modified." The hardfax copy of the contract began to slide out into the tray in neat, crisp folds. The last sheet slipped free, the empty black line with his name printed beneath it waiting for his signature. Rodinov lifted the sheaf of fax and laid it in front of him.

"We'll need witnesses," Rodinov said. He pressed another key. "Miss Theriault, Klaus, come in, please."

The receptionist and Rodinov's silent watchdog entered the office. They stood by while Protherall picked up the stylus and signed, followed by Rodinov. Then they silently added their own signatures to the witness slots and left, all without a word.

The folded contract felt as solid as an armored breastplate in his tunic pocket. For the first time in a long time Ian Protherall felt safe.

"That's it then," he said. "With any luck at all, we've all got what we wanted."

"It happens sometimes," Rodinov agreed, smiling.

"Never often enough."

"I look forward to doing business with you again, sir."

"It'll happen."

"It's happened," Lakim Tovas said. "They've signed."

"Damn it!" Santer spun from the dust-blown window to glare at him. "I thought you were going to tie him up!"

"It was being done. We have been buying up Protherall's outstanding debts. When we had secured the majority of his obligations, I had intended to go to court and order a freeze on his assets pending repayment. We would have been able to force him into receivership, with a strong chance at obtaining the rights to the synthetic ourselves."

"So what went wrong?"

"The Customs and Revenue Office has been maneuvering to compel Protherall to sell them *Flute*, as the replacement for *Vigilant*. They tried to pressure him and he must have decided to act at once to forestall them. He simply outran us."

"Damn him. Damn those interfering idiots. What are our options now?"

"We break Protherall. That is still within our capacities."

"That's not an option. That's a goddamned priority, Tovas. Finish him. Now what about TerraCo?"

"The situation there is not as good. We've failed to keep them from obtaining the rights to the synthetic. Now it becomes a matter of preventing manufacture, if we can. There are no open means we can use there."

"I didn't ask about open or covert means. What can we do?"

"I will start to bring pressure to bear in the First Wave business community. If we can define this infusion of out-system money and influence as a threat to the established institutions, we may be able to gain some unofficial assistance. I will argue that this marks a change of conduct for TerraCo—where before they used to buy and sell with us, now they are entering into insystem manufacturing and direct competition for our markets. That should alarm them."

"It damned well alarms me."

"Precisely. I will also point out that the Confederate Commerce Acts apply to TerraCo in ways that they do not to a single-system firm. For instance, TerraCo cannot take advantage of the assigned-labor pool. The number of salaried jobs a giant firm like that would therefore have to open up insystem would put a serious drain on available manpower, and could well drive up employment costs for any company that sought to exist in the same markets, as well as setting an unwholesome legal precedent. It could well become an intolerable situation for all of us."

"And what will all this alarm do for us?"

"We can hamper Rodinov's efforts to buy property for the new plant. We can drive up his contruction costs. We can dry up his other transactions. With any luck, we can make it too expensive overall for him to contemplate acting in opposition to the entire business community."

"What are our chances?"

Tovas shook his head dubiously. "It will be difficult to maintain any sort of united front indefinitely. Self-interest is as great a danger to us as TerraCo in this; Rodinov can make it too profitable for some of our weaker compatriots to hold the line. But it is possible that we can maintain it long enough to stir up alarm in Mission House."

"Do you think they'll intervene for us against an inter-stellar company?"

"If they see enough worry and outrage in the insystem community over this, they very well might at least put pressure on TerraCo to let the matter drop rather than bring the issue to an open confrontation." A thought seemed to occur to him. "In fact, we could make a good case for pressuring TerraCo through Mission House to sell us the synthetic, a profitable gesture in support of a vital local economy. But first we have to stir up enough outrage to be able to use it as a lever."

"Then start stirring."

"Very well. To other business then. Now, regarding the pharmaceuticals harvest on Hansenwald: it might be advisable to invest our maximum available capital in the harvest for resale outsystem this time around."

"Now? Why?"

"Because we cannot be seen to be acting with hesitation in the face of such a public setback. We have to display a confidence we may not necessarily feel, and the pharmaceuticals are a safe enough area to make such a display. We will certainly not lose money."

"How much of an increase are we talking about?"

"At least fifteen to twenty percent. And we should encourage other First Wave firms to increase their buys, as well. That will tend to close TerraCo out of the pharmaceuticals market and demonstrate our united willingness to defend our territory."

"All right. Get on it."

"You've lost once already," Adrienne Santer said. "How much farther do you intend to take this?"

It was remarkable, Eli Santer thought. With anybody else, his two-level office and raised desk gave him exactly the dominant psychological edge it was meant to provide. But when this one old woman opened her mouth they were transformed from an unassailable bastion to a crumbling precipice whose infirmity threatened to cast him down at her feet.

"We haven't lost," he said. "Protherall moved faster than we gave him credit for, that's all."

"That's all. And now TerraCo has its option on the synthetic and Santer Holdings is stuck with a quarter of a million in capital tied up in *Flute*'s notes, capital we can't hope to reclaim until those notes come due. The notes aren't even useful as a weapon against Protherall, because he's already sold the synthetic to Rodinov."

"No he hasn't. He's sold them an option. We can still deny TerraCo the full rights, if we break Protherall fast enough."

"He's going to be tough to break, with half a million standards of TerraCo's money in his pocket and a starliner due insystem."

"That money isn't in his pocket; it's going right into his

ship. And if he isn't recertified in time to meet *Northwest Passage*, it won't matter how much he spends on his refit."

"Must we depend on his not being recertified?"

"It's a fairly safe assumption. It's no secret that the colony is looking to replace *Vigilant* with *Flute*. I'm sure it's occurred to them that they'll have less trouble acquiring title to a ship in receivership than a profitable working vessel."

"Protherall's already outmaneuvered you once," Adrienne said. "What makes you so certain he won't be able to outsmart Customs and Revenue as well?"

"Because we're going to make sure he can't."

"Another one of Tovas' little suggestions?"

"Another one of my decisions," Santer said. He stood up behind his desk. "Why do you keep challenging that?"

"Because you're putting us at risk," Adrienne said. "Put the euphemisms aside, Eli; they aren't necessary between family. There's no legal way to move against Protherall and Rodinov now, is there?"

"Are you asking me to put legal considerations before our survival?" Santer asked. "Because if you are, you're setting one hell of a precedent for Santer Holdings—or else you're playing one hell of a hypocrite."

"There's nothing more important to me than our survival," Adrienne snapped back. "That's why I don't want to see it left in the hands of outsiders."

"I'm leaving nothing to outsiders!" Santer shouted. "We're going to break Protherall. *I* decided that. *I* ordered it done."

"After Tovas suggested it? And you ordered Tovas to do it, didn't you?"

"What is this sudden obsession of yours with Lakim Tovas?"

"You've said it yourself, Eli. This synthetic is a threat to our very survival. Yet you leave our future in the hands of an outsider."

"Lakim Tovas is my man."

"He's a latecomer, Eli. He doesn't share our concern because he doesn't share our special risks."

"What special risks are those?"

"Of losing something of his own," Adrienne said. "This is

our world, Eli, not his. Yet we're becoming more and more dependent on his wanting the same things we want, and on his making the right decisions to protect them."

"Tovas has something to lose," Santer said. "Everything he has he has through me. If he wants something, it has to be something I can give him, if he hopes to obtain it. If he puts Santer Holdings in jeopardy, he risks his whole future right along with us."

"Unless he finds himself another patron."

"He won't," Santer said flatly. "He can't, and you'd know that if you understood the way things work on Wolkenheim."

"Why can't he?"

"Because he's a latecomer, just like you say he is. He could never hope to do as well without me, not with any family in Hansen's Landing. They simply wouldn't touch him. That's why he's been so valuable to me."

"Don't you think that's become obvious to them?" Adrienne asked. "Don't you think that's become obvious to *Tovas*? Now who doesn't understand the way things work, Eli? You say no family in Hansen's Landing will touch Lakim Tovas because he's a latecomer. But you've used a latecomer, and you've profited by it. Don't you think they've seen that? Don't you think they've seen how central Tovas has become to Santer Holdings? *Don't you think they know they can use that against us?* We're dependent on someone who's vital to our survival, but that survival isn't vital to him. We're vulnerable, Eli."

"You're wrong, Adrienne. Tovas is my employee, my tool. If I don't use him, he can't be used against us."

"And if you do use him, he can."

"And if I do use him, he'll stay with me to be used more, because he can profit by it," Santer said.

"Or he'll stay with you because you're so usable yourself."

"No!" Santer snapped. "I know Tovas too well for that."

Adrienne rose, her thin shoulders bowed as though weary from the strain of battling against Santer's obduracy.

"You probably do," she said tiredly. "Better than you know yourself. . . ."

* * *

"The stage has been set," Tovas announced. They were meeting this time in Rodinov's home, out beyond the greenbelt of the city. "I am supposed to be organizing united insystem opposition to TerraCo's invasion."

"So will you?" Rodinov asked. The waterfall behind him found its source in a natural spring far below the house, whose enclosed atrium had been built around the outcropping that channeled it upward. Heaters set into the sides of the pool warmed the icy water in progressive stages, from biting cold at the base of the fall to warmer than air temperature at the far end. Rodinov toweled his head again and slipped into a short robe whose shining material matched the fabric of his trunks.

"Of course. With all my energies." Tovas pulled a folded fax page from his pocket. "This is a list of those First Wave firms too insecure or too shortsighted to go along. I've included several names from Newtown. I'm sure they'd be interested to discuss such a major addition to their tax base. Also included are several firms in Hansen's Landing that should be willing to front pharmaceutical buys for you, if you find it necessary."

"Why should that be necessary?" It troubled him to find Tovas venturing into areas where Rodinov already had plans in motion.

"I may be more successful than I expect with the others. They could very well crowd you out of the market, at least this time around. Understand, I have to be seen to be doing my utmost to confound you."

"As long as you don't succeed. Now what about the other matter?"

"I've persuaded Eli to increase our own buy this season. As far as our records will show, we're increasing our buy by fifteen percent."

"And us?"

"I've diverted funds for a thirty percent increase. The remainder will go to our joint purchase. You'll have to make the buy under your own name."

"What sort of protection have you arranged for yourself?"

"I should be able to bury the shortfall in our profits as a

result of the increased buys all around, driving up the purchase price from Hansenwald and lowering the selling price against the export market. I'll just log the discrepancy as a second 15 percent purchase after the price increase, instead of a 30 percent initial buy."

"That will work?"

"Since all inquiries will have to come through me, there is no reason it shouldn't. After all, it will only be a question of a couple of percentage points."

"All right. We're set then."

"I believe so." Tovas stood to leave. "I trust all your arrangements with Protherall are finalized."

"They are."

"Good. Because the time has come to expend him."

Rafer Stone died the way he taught: sloppily.

Their trac crested a dune and started down the opposite slope—directly onto the back of a burrowing dragon. The little machine was tossed into the air and Chavez landed heavily on his back. His sight blurred from the impact, and cleared just in time to see the massive jaws close on Rafer.

Rafer Stone never screamed; he never had time. The dragon just shook its head, once, and he came apart like a gory sausage-filled mannequin.

The great, blood-flecked head swung toward Chavez. His rifle was nowhere in sight. Chavez clawed the heavy, useless knife from his belt. He'd asked Rafer Stone what use a knife was against a dragon and the dead skinner had told him, "if one corners you, cut your throat." He raised the knife over his head, clutched point-down in both hands, hopelessly. Now, he heard someone screaming—himself. It was a low, despairing groan that built and built as the dragon started toward him—and then spasmed on the alien poisons hidden in Rafer's flesh.

It was several long minutes before the beast finally died from the tainted meat that had been Chavez's partner. And it was an hour more before Chavez could bring himself to start skinning it.

10

His mouth tasting as though he had bitten the Archbishop of Canterbury and half the other, lesser demons of hell and forgotten to spit, Moses Callahan tried to sit up. He couldn't. Further investigation established that he was strapped to his bunk, the emergency zero-g restraint webbing securely fastened. Behind his head he could hear water running in the cabin's washbasin. Craning his neck, and detonating a traitorous cramp he had not realized was waiting back there, he saw the hem of an old orange bathrobe swaying in and out of view.

"Good morning," he said, flinching at the sound of his own voice, which reminded the little man with the hammer to start knocking his sinuses out from the inside again. "Oh, I must have had a good time last night."

Maureen O'Shaunessy came into his line of sight, albeit at a peculiar angle. "It sounds as if you did, from what the policeman said."

"Oh, dear. Do I want to remember anything of this?"

"I don't think so. It was mostly anticlimactic after the cab driver declined to press charges."

"Ah. That was civil of him, now."

"You didn't help matters by offering to shove his other bumper down his other fan duct if he didn't."

"Did I say such a quarrelsome thing—the *other* bumper?"

"And didn't he try to charge you twenty marks for a six-mark trip? You weren't that drunk."

"I'm never that drunk."

"Anyway, the port police didn't appreciate the way he was trying to gouge you, and told him he'd be in more trouble for hacking without a permit than you'd be in for the vandalism charge, so he just composed himself and scraped away into the night."

"And who was this sterling guardian of the public good? I must do something nice for him some time."

"You certainly should. You can't spend the weekend in the drunk tank and make the run out to *Northwest Passage* at the same time."

"No, I can't. Although the way I feel this black morning, I'm tempted to pass it up."

Maureen's expression grew serious. "You can't afford to be doing that. Especially not now."

Her sober tone cautioned him. "Why not? Whatever's the matter now?"

"You'd better come and see for yourself." She reached down and undid the webbing. "Come along with you."

He stood unsteadily, grasping at the mug of hot coffee she handed him, and followed her down the corridor.

The primary personnel lock cycled open—

"What in the hell is *that*?"

There was a building in the middle of the dock area that hadn't been there the day before. He knew it hadn't been there. He might see things that weren't there when he was in the grip of the archbishop, but he never didn't see things that were.

It was there now, though, a squat and ugly congeries of boxes grown up instantly and inexplicably among the horizontal needle shapes of the grounded freighters and lighters. Quite aside from the impossibility of its being there in the first place, it was the stupidest place to put a building that Moses had ever heard of.

Unless . . .

"That's not a ship," he muttered. "That can't be a ship."

"That's a ship, Moses."

"What do you mean, calling that thing a ship? The brute wouldn't fly if you stuck a tactical nuclear device under its arse and gave it a good swift kick into the bargain."

"You wouldn't have to go quite that far," she said. "All you'd have to do is push a button. That's the A.S. *Albatross*, formerly of Proxima Centauri."

"The A.S.—?"

"Antigravity Ship."

She nodded at his expression. "They finally perfected the external grid field. According to the news reports, she has more than four times the hold space of any ship in port and she operates at maybe one-third the cost."

"God help us. How is she on performance?"

"*Northwest Passage* is still three days out for us. That thing got here in nineteen hours. She has a total enclosure drive field, acceleration limited only by duration."

"Bigger than any four ships," Moses said quietly, "as cheap as any three, and faster than the lot of us put together. Ah God, doesn't that change everything now. Doesn't that change everything, indeed."

Protherall stared at the x-ray prints with all the horror in his eyes of a condemned man staring at his writ of execution.

The surveyor stood by his scanning gear; he had simply walked off the ship and called Protherall without bothering to go back to his office.

"This is some kind of joke," Protherall said coldly, forcing himself not to give free voice to the panic and rage welling up within him. "This is some kind of bloody, horrible joke, isn't it?"

"The x-rays don't lie," the surveyor said.

"No, they don't. But the man who took them can, damn you."

The surveyor held the scanner pickup out to him. "You want to go through and check it yourself?"

"I wouldn't know how," Protherall said. He stalked stiffly over to the man. "But you're going to. You're going to put fresh film in that damned machine of yours, from a factory-sealed packet, and then you're going to go through the ship all over again. And I'm going to be right beside you, every step of the way."

"There's no point," the surveyor said. "It's all there. Those lighter spots inside the reinforcing beams are voids, Captain, irreparable structural flaws. I flashed every beam Hansen Astronautics welded into this ship, and at least eighty percent of them are not fit for use. It's that simple, and I'll swear out an affidavit to that effect."

"No," Protherall said. "No, goddamn you, it isn't that simple. You don't ruin a man with one look, just like that." Almost without realizing it he was advancing on the man, crowding him back against his equipment. "Now you reload that gimcrack of yours, *now*. We're going back into that ship."

The surveyor stepped back and shrugged, and pulled a packet of film still in the wrapper out of his carryall.

"You're paying for the film," he warned Protherall. "But hell, it's your money."

The captain's laugh was a ghastly noise.

Ian Protherall sat in the understated conference room, the two sets of prints splayed out on the obsidian tabletop in front of him.

The Hansen Astronautics lawyers sat facing him, in their loose First Wave robes of gray and black. They looked like two eunuchs in mourning, Protherall thought.

"We don't question your grievance in the slightest, Captain. This is an entirely deplorable circumstance and Hansen Astronautics fully intends to make equitable restitution."

"Well you goddamn should. Eighty percent defective structural materials! Eighty! What the hell kind of quality control program do you run around here?!"

The second lawyer cleared his throat. "I think a point needs to be made here before discussions go any further. Our quality control procedures were identical in every respect to the recommended industry standard. One beam in every five was selected at random and x-rayed before each lot was accepted from our subcontractor."

"Yes, and out of an eighty percent defective batch you managed to select only the twenty percent that were still structurally sound for your spot checks? Do you seriously ask me to believe that?"

"Our control procedures were both lawful and thorough, by any accepted standard. Please be assured, we are thoroughly investigating this lapse on the part of our subcontractor. We've already issued a warning to every ship that's had structural work done in our yard with their materials in the last three years. You may have done us a considerable service, Captain."

"I'm so glad to hear that. Now what are you going to do for me?"

"We will of course remove the defective members installed, at no cost to yourself, Captain. We have already diverted fresh members from a project subsequent to yours—at considerable inconvenience, I might add—to finish our commitment to yourself and *Flute*."

"Not more pot metal from the same source?"

"Every piece being used will be scanned individually this time, by an independent surveyor, to assure that it meets Confederate BuShips standards before it is installed. If you wish, we will be happy to arrange for you to approve each member yourself."

"I may want to take you up on that."

"Our estimate is that you will be able to complete this refitting with less than a fifty percent cost overrun on our original estimate—"

"A fifty percent *what*?"

"We will be perfectly happy to complete the refitting for the cost of our labor alone, Captain."

"The cost of your labor? You idiots packed my ship full of garbage, and now you expect me to pay more for the privilege of getting what I paid half a million standards for in the first place? Are you insane?"

"We understand your anger, Captain—but after all, the *work* we did was fully up to standards. We have a copy of the surveyor's affidavit here—"

The second lawyer recited a quotation from a fax-sheet on the table before him: "*The welding itself was flawless, considering the garbage it was holding together.*"

"The work you paid us to do was done correctly, Captain."

"But my ship is still unserviceable!"

"There's a saying from the medical profession that seems relevant here: 'The operation was a success, but the patient died—and give the bill to his wife.'"

"My ship and my future are on the line here—and you

make jokes?" Protherall stood, leaning on the tabletop, shoulders arched pugnaciously. "I'm not paying for any cost overruns. I'm not paying one mark more than I've already paid. You agreed to do a job on my ship and that work wasn't done."

"We cannot agree. The work was faulty through circumstances not within our reasonable control. We are not liable here."

"You want to prove that in court?" Protherall challenged.

"It would be to everyone's benefit not to have to," the second lawyer said. "We would have to contest a claim of this magnitude, Captain. Such a contest would be very time-consuming, very expensive, and not at all likely to be resolved in your favor. Those are three considerations we hope you will take under advisement."

"Now if you do wish to initiate legal proceedings," the third lawyer suggested, "you might be much better advised to take action against our subcontractor."

"Be assured, we intend to," the first lawyer said, completing the rotation.

"You would almost certainly be able to recover both your materials costs and your additional labor expenses."

"Sure I would," Protherall said bitterly. "About three years after I went into the damned labor pool. This is an unacceptable situation, gentlemen."

"We regret that, Captain. But we've stated the position of Hansen Astronautics. We hope you'll see the validity of our stance."

But Ian Protherall couldn't see the validity of the stance. Because the bottom line was, he didn't have the quarter-million standards he needed to see things their way. . . .

"How can I help you, Captain?" Rodinov asked.

"Some complications have arisen in the refitting of my ship," Protherall told him. "Nothing insuperable, but there's been a quality-control screw-up, and we have to pull out about a quarter of a million standards' worth of work and have it redone."

"Unfortunate."

"And embarrassing. And inconvenient. Because we're

talking about an *additional* quarter million, over and above the half million initially invested."

"The half million TerraCo paid for the Zion Ring synthetic."

"Right."

"It's lost to you?"

"No, but it's going to be tied up in court getting the damages recovered."

"And what has this do do with us?"

"I need some way to refinance another quarter million for the short term, to get my ship legally navigable again."

"From TerraCo?"

"I'd thought we could arrange some sort of terms, an advance against my royalties on the synthetic, or on my shipping services for future starliner calls." He shifted nervously in his seat. "After all, we're talking about some very real assets here."

"A quarter million standards' worth of reality would have to be an extremely substantial entity, Captain. I wish I could agree we had such a thing here."

"But of course we do."

"I don't see where. You talk about royalties against the Zion Ring synthetic, Captain—but we haven't even got the pilot production program initiated yet. Such royalties are months, if not years, down the line."

"But you know they'll be there."

"I'm confident they'll be there. But TerraCo has already expressed that confidence to the amount of half a million standards. Another quarter million is a bit extreme, on top of such a sum. This is assuming we could dedicate that much capital to the project at this time. But with *Northwest Passage* insystem, and the pharmaceuticals harvest coming in on Hansenwald, we are obligated to keep a substantial cash reserve liquid to respond to market conditions. As for debiting it against future starliner arrivals, that's a great many trips to a great many starliners, Captain, and the same need to keep the funds free applies. I'm afraid I don't see where we can help you here."

"You can't, can you? I've given you this system on a platter, by God."

"It's appreciated, believe me. And we will strictly honor

our agreements with you as defined to date. But we simply cannot afford an additional commitment to you at this time, when there's no immediate return to be had. I'm sorry, Captain. I wish we were in a position to do something for you. But it simply isn't viable now. . . ."

"Sit down, Captain," said Bewys Temple.

"I thought this was a bank," said Ian Protherall, "not a customs stall."

"System Trust Limited has an excellent relationship with colonial authority, Captain. They are well-informed of our interest in *Flute*. And we in turn are well-informed about your current troubles."

"Which Customs and Revenue can't help me with."

"That's not entirely true, Captain. Your present financial difficulties—"

"Are not going to be solved by selling *Flute*. I need money to save my ship, not forfeit her."

"I understand that," Temple said. "But you will not secure the financial support you need here."

"Then I'll go to another bank. Or another."

"Perhaps I have not made myself clear. You will not secure the financing you need here. You will not secure it at any lending institution in this colony. They are aware that we propose to put your ship to good use in the best interest of the colony—which is something you are not at present capable of doing, or are likely to do at any time in the forseeable future."

"I'll get my ship certified again."

"Captain Protherall, as we speak *Flute* is sitting in a bay at Hansen Astronautics, piling up a steadily increasing docking charge. No work is being done on her, not without payment. Even if work were to begin today, you would not be certified spaceworthy in time to meet *Northwest Passage*. Even if you were, you would not have the funds to secure a cargo. Even if you did, you have another quarterly premium due less than two weeks after *Northwest Passage's* departure. And when you do not make that premium, the colony will be legally justified in condemning your ship. If *Flute* is condemned, you will be fortunate to realize two million standards in involuntary sale, as opposed to the six million we've already offered. Can you possibly want that?"

"You get it all ways, don't you?" Protherall asked bitterly. "I can sell you the ship by choice, or you can condemn her and buy her with all the weight of the law behind you. It's so neat, so cut and dried. Tell me, Mr. Temple: What kind of price did you offer Hansen Astronautics to convert *Flute* for your uses after I have to sell her?"

"I won't even dignify that with an answer."

"I don't need one. But I'm surprised. I thought you'd at least want the pleasure of a good gloat."

"Captain Protherall, we are agents of colonial law. Do you really think we go skulking around planting defective structural members on honest citizens so we can steal their livelihoods out from under them?"

"It sure seems to have worked out that way, doesn't it?"

"If I didn't take note of your agitated state and the fact that you're addressing me in my official capacity, I would consider your accusations slanderous."

"Oh please, feel free. I'll be spending enough time in court, it seems. Another couple of visits one way or another should hardly prove an inconvenience."

"This confrontation is pointless, Captain. You know what your situation is. You know what you can expect from us. The longer you persist in this useless recalcitrance, the worse off you'll be. Show some sense, Captain. It's for your own good."

"Is it really, Mr. Temple? Well, I'm sorry, but my own good is my own business. So if you don't mind, I think I'll see this thing through to its conclusion."

"You're destroying yourself."

"That," said Ian Protherall, "is my prerogative."

Shasti Keane looked up as Chavez entered the commissary. She started to grin as she recognized him; the grin faded as she noticed his expression.

"What's the matter?" she asked.

"Close up here," Chavez said, "I need someone to drink with."

She smiled again, uneasily, uncertain whether she under-

· SKINNER · 105

stood his mood. "I'd like that Chavez, but I really don't think Eli—"

"No," Chavez said, very quietly, very firmly. "I really don't want to hear about Eli Santer right now, all right?"

Shasti looked at him for a moment, then nodded. "All right, Chavez."

The canteen was as bare-bones stark as any of the skinner's huts. But it had all it needed. There were tables. There were chairs. There was liquor. And when a skinner came in off the flats, he didn't care if the chairs rocked, or the tables were dirty, or that the canteen charged three times the Wolkenheim rate for its liquor. They were there.

Shasti sat across from him at a table in the corner of the low room, sipping sparingly at her drink. Chavez had already finished his second and was starting on his third.

"Tell me something," he said. "Just how many people ever do get out of here?"

"I couldn't say for sure," she answered. "I've only been here a year and a half, myself."

"What happened to whoever was here before you?"

Shasti shrugged. "At any rate, since I've been here, I've seen maybe four skinners leave. Of course, one of them had no legs."

"Oh well, that's just wonderful," Chavez grumbled.

"Chavez." He looked up from his brooding at the tone in her voice. "You can get out of here," she said. "Most of them around here have accepted the way things are. They've accepted the debts and the labor pool and always being behind. You don't have to, I think. I really believe you could hold back enough money to get away from here in a year or so."

"You do, huh?" Chavez swallowed half his drink. "Is that another service of the management? Another free speech, courtesy of Santer Holdings, Limited?"

"No," she said, stung. "No, I meant it."

"Oh." He filled his glass again. "Rafer Stone's dead."

"Oh, no. When?"

"A week ago. I just brought him in."

"After a week."

"Nobody was interested in coming out to get him. Hell,

they said, he wasn't going anywhere. I had to wait on the regular run."

"That was wrong, Chavez. That shouldn't have been."

"No, maybe not. But I don't see the heavens trembling with righteous indignation. Anyway, I went over to accounting to take care of his effects and all; nobody else seemed interested. Do you know how much he needed to declare solvency and lift out? Twenty-five hundred marks. Maybe five good size hides, on half-shares. Well, the clerk just looked down at that, and he pushed a button, and pffft, it was gone. Straight into the company coffers. Indentured laborers don't have estates, you see.

"Do you know how he died? He fell on top of a dragon that he never knew was there, and it committed suicide trying to eat him. Just plain bad luck all around. He didn't know the dragon was there; the dragon didn't know any better. Just bad luck that they ran into each other." He finished his drink and went to pour another, then disgustedly set the bottle back down. "He even warned me about just that trick, too. He *told* me about it. He shouldn't have gone that way. So maybe I can get out of here, even if he didn't. I don't know. I do know I'm not going to knock myself out trying. There's too much luck involved."

"And you don't trust yours?"

Chavez stood and reached into his pocket. "Do me a favor, will you?"

"What?"

"Get rid of these." He dropped the small packet of bright, worn tourfaxes on the table and left.

11

"I've never seen anything like it," Klepper said. "The market's going wild."

"The *Albatross* is making its mark," Moses agreed.

The captain of the new agrav ship was honoring system custom: He had brought no cargo down from the liner on his incoming voyage. And to most of the established captains' unabashed relief, *Albatross* had refrained from turning right around and charging back out with the later waves of ships going out to meet *Northwest Passage*. Which was a blessing for all concerned, because the new ship could have made three full trips in the time it took the Hansen System freighters to make one. They would have arrived to find empty holds and returned with empty pockets.

But to Moses Callahan's dismay, the *Albatross* was far from idle. No sooner had she learned of the pharmaceutical harvest on Hansenwald than she began offering space to speculators who wanted to get in on one of the few sure bets in the colony market.

"I swear to God," Moses said, "grandmothers must be emptying pfennig out of cookie jars to get in on this. I wouldn't have thought there were this many entrepreneurs in the whole Hansen System."

"Where were they when you needed them?" Klepper joked.

"Where are they when I need them now?" Moses answered. "I'm making the run because the colony's paying my operating costs, but for all this buying and selling, it's no business I've been able to do at all. They're rushing to

Albatross like so many lemmings. I'm tempted to invest in the infernal nostrums myself, just to fill my holds."

"Don't do that, youngster," Klepper warned him.

"And why not?"

"Because this is too good to last. I've seen this happen before—in other systems. Never on this scale, but then there's never been a ship like that out here before. And that's only going to make it worse."

"Make what the worse?"

"The bust. They're having the time of their lives down here. People are speculating in the insystem market who've never been able to before, because the expense of shipping kept costs up and volume down. And they're getting prices and shipping quantities out of Hansenwald like there's no tomorrow. But there's someone who isn't going to be surprised by this at all."

"And who's that?"

"Them. Up there on the *Passage*. Don't forget, they've known *Albatross* was coming since the day she locked on. They've had time to work out for themselves what's going to happen—what is happening—once she gets here. And do you know what's going to happen when all these stampeding salesmen get out to those very well-prepared buyers?"

"My God. A price war."

"It's going to be a fiscal Balaclava. Huge quantities of pharmaceuticals, from dozens of sources, all competing . . . They'll pound the export buying price right down through the floor. The labor pool is going to look like a Westsea beach on a summer day. You're lucky, youngster. At least the colony's paying your operating costs. But you stay the hell away from those pharmaceuticals."

"I hear you, indeed. But what shall I do on those long hours flying my way to a place where no one wants to do business with me?"

Klepper grimaced. "If I was you, youngster, I'd put that time to good use studying charts and reading atlases. I think some of us are going to have to look for a new home."

"We may have a problem," Lakim Tovas said.

"What problem?" Santer asked.

"Protherall is finished," Tovas answered him. "The defective structural members saw to that, and would have even if Customs and Revenue hadn't decided to take advantage of the situation. It is only a matter of time before he loses his ship."

"That's fine by me. Now what's the problem?"

"We're meeting some resistance from the buyers aboard *Passage* over our hide price."

"They're resisting? They want dragonhide, they pay the going rate. Where's the potential for resistance?"

"TerraCo."

"What?"

"Rodinov has been pushing the synthetic heavily in all his contacts, promising to be in full production by the end of the year at the latest. Some of the buyers are trying to use this to lever our price down."

"Let me get this straight, Lakim. They're trying to bully us into cutting our prices now with the threat of some competition that might present itself in a year?"

"Essentially."

"Well, you have to give them credit for trying, I'll admit that. But they're going to have to give me credit, too. I know how to deal with arm-twisting. Is our outgoing consignment ready on Wolkenheim?"

"Yes. Fifteen hundred prime hides, earmarked for Lebensraum, Houri—"

"Good. Sit on them."

"I beg your pardon?"

"Cancel the shipment. Not one hide goes out on *Northwest Passage*. If they don't want to pay our price, let them find someplace else to get the supply for their demand."

"These shipments are expected, Eli."

"That's right. They're expected from *Northwest Passage*. Let them explain why they can't meet their commitments to their clients."

"I have to counsel against this," Tovas said. "We will be hurting ourselves."

"Nonsense. We can afford to miss one shipment. The hides will be there next quarter."

"I am not so sure we can. Our cash flow situation is not

particularly favorable just now. The uncertainty in the pharmaceuticals market is making it difficult to sell at a price we might accept."

"Damn it, Lakim, it was your idea to increase our buy this quarter—"

"The *Albatross* was an unpredictable element, Eli. No one was prepared for its arrival."

"Are you telling me we can't afford not to sell these hides?"

"I am saying that it is not wise to let our profit ratios fall too far below a certain point just now."

"I still won't let myself be strong-armed, Lakim." Santer leaned back, scowling at his desktop, then leaned forward again, sharply. "All right. We hold back the hides."

"But Eli—"

"If we can't guarantee our income, we'll just have to do something to minimize our expenses."

Chavez squatted in the shade of the stone outcropping, staring out over the sand with eyes as flat and unreadable as the gray rock behind him. The constant desert wind swirled and eddied around the outcropping, drifting the blown sand around the boulders and his ankles. He ignored it; his attention was fixed on the dunes and hollows before him.

It was three weeks since he'd brought Rafer's remains back to the depot. Since then, he'd killed three dragons, alone. He'd lost a week, waiting for the supply sled, and when it finally had come, it had not brought the replacement Chavez had expected. So he had taken what was left of his partner back and returned to the desert, and gone off into the dunes to hunt dragons, alone.

Today he would kill his fourth.

He had driven up onto the spoor of a dragon kill, still fresh, the burrowing scavengers just beginning to writhe up through the sand around the ruins. Chavez jockeyed the trac on around the carcass and drove on, knowing the dragon could not be far off, knowing it would not allow itself to lie down and sink into the bloated sleep that followed a kill, not while the feared sound of humans and their machines pursued it. He picked up the dragon's spoor leading away from the torn sands around the kill and followed it, kicking the trac down into a lower gear and racing the engine, so it would whine loudly enough to carry and be heard, and force the dragon onward.

Chavez pushed on along the dragon track, to the full distance a dragon normally withdrew after a meal and beyond that, twice as far again. The dragon would be confused now, torn between its inherent biological need to sleep and digest its kill and its instinctive need to flee ahead of the keening whine of motors it associated with its hunters.

He had driven the creature perhaps six kilometers when he heard it, the thin, defiant bellow in the distance as the beast's confusion turned to rage and it turned to confront its attacker. Chavez guided the trac up off the spoor and up the face of the dune, to give himself a line of sight ahead of his course.

The tangled net of dunes smoothed out up ahead, merging into one wide arroyo that turned sharply off to Chavez's right. He studied the maze before him, searching for some trace of the position the dragon had chosen, until he was rewarded with a gout of dust, dirt, and grit flung up by the angry flailing of the dragon's tail as it set itself to face its tormenter.

His plan had worked, Chavez thought. That was the one thing wrong with being the prime predator in any system: At the top of the chain, a dragon was not used to being hunted, could not accept that there was anything capable of menacing it. A month ago, the realization might have given him satisfaction. Now it was just an observation, one more datum to be noted as Chavez got on with the mundane business of dragon-killing.

He felt none of the excitement he would once have felt as he eased himself down into the arroyo and began to move toward the dragon from behind. Behind him, the trac's engine raced, the transmission in neutral, its whine sounding out down the gullies to hold the dragon's attention.

That excitement had been born as much of plain simple fear as anything else, fear of ending up between rending teeth or beneath a crushing paw. But that was a fate to be feared only when there was a hope of avoiding it, and that hope he had renounced.

The dragon bulked enormous in the mouth of the arroyo, at the end of the web of gullies, facing back the way it had come. Twenty-seven feet from nose to tail, it flailed its tree-trunk-thick tail from side to side like an infuriated alleycat, baring its serried fangs in a continuous, rumbling snarl of challenge, not realizing it faced something *really* danger-ous: a wiry little human who didn't give a fuck.

Chavez stepped out into the middle of the arroyo, thumbing his safety off. Then he roared a challenge of his own, a throat-tearing scream carrying all his pent-up anger at the dragons and Trollshulm and Eli Santer and his own goddamn stupidity. The dragon whirled and charged before his shout had even begun to echo from the arroyo walls, to fall dead, impaled upon a spit of sliverfire. Chavez stepped back from the corpse, popping the magazine from his rifle. Four rounds.

He walked back and brought the trac forward, then bent to the awkward task of single-handedly skinning the dragon. Alone, he might have expected to be twice as long about it as he would have been, partnered; in fact it took considerably longer even than that, since he spent most of his time trying to support the massive, lifeless limbs and cut through the shoulder joints at the same time. But it didn't matter. He had nothing else to do, nowhere else to be, so he worked and sweated under the fierce glare of Hansen's Primary, which seemed to prick at each exposed inch of skin with tiny needles of fire. He levered and cut and levered and cut again, withdrawn into the single eternal moment of the routine present he had chosen for his retreat.

He baled the hide and wrestled it onto the sledge with all the indifference of a leather-clad automaton, and followed his own trail back to the hut, indifferent to the time he wasted in the simple retracing, ignoring any shortcuts he could have chosen to get him in off the sands quicker. He was on Trollshulm and once you were on Trollshulm you lived with the sand and the heat and there were no shortcuts past that, not really.

The door to the hut was open, just as he'd left it. The

sand had blown a six-inch drift in through the door in the nine hours he'd been gone. Later, when night fell and he wanted the door shut, he would carelessly shovel the bulk of it back out again. But the fine patina of dust that overlaid everything in the hut he left undisturbed, out of indifference or some subconscious acknowledgment of his surrender to the barren realities of his position.

Come the evening, he would crack open his last carton of surplus field rations, and wolf down a packaged meal, uncooked, indifferent to the pasty texture of the unnatural nutrients. Then he would lay back on his dusty bunk, staring at the curved roof of the geodesic as the wind vibrated the hexagonal plastic panels, just staring, until sometime, he never noticed when, sleep came and made his oblivion official.

Chavez's new partner dropped off the supply sled the next morning, along with the word that Santer was paying twenty percent less per hide. He should have taken it for the omen it was.

Duncan Joubouline was a short, stout man with a round face and prominent teeth that he showed in a constant, nervous grin. His partner had lifted out with his legs gone a month ago, and it had been decided to consolidate the two teams rather than add to expenses by bringing in extra men. He was extremely voluble, whether he had anything to say or not, with a quick, high voice. Chavez soon learned to tune out his constant speaking, much in the fashion he might have tuned out a dull popcart program in the background as he went about his day's work. It was a necessity. Otherwise Joubouline's adenoidal chatter would have driven him to wring the man's neck in a week.

"Been here three years," he was saying. "Doing pretty damn good for myself, too, if I say so myself. Another three years and I'll be out of here—that is, if they don't decide we have to work for nothing instead of twenty percent off, right? Hey, right?"

"Right." Chavez wondered where the pudgy little skinner was getting the wind to keep up his monologue as they trudged along the long face of the dune. It didn't matter what he said in reply, Chavez suspected, but if he didn't say something the little ass would just keep on trying to get his attention.

"Damn right. You know—"

"Quiet." There were sounds coming from farther up the transitory dune they were following, deep whoofing and chuffing noises.

"Dragon hunting," Chavez said.

He unslung his rifle and scrabbled up the side of the dune to the crest, squatting when he reached the top to make less of a mark on the horizon. Ahead he could see great gouts of sand being flung high into the air around the curve of the dune. He could not see the dragon itself, could not see the direction it faced. In its turn, the beast was too busy pursuing his prey to pay attention to its surroundings. Otherwise it would probably have heard the babbling Joubouline half-a-kilometer back.

Chavez slid back down the slope to the little man standing in the middle of the wash, nervously shifting his weight from foot to foot and fingering the stock of his rifle. His gaze was locked on the direction of the dragon sounds.

"I found it, but I can't see how it's facing," Chavez told him. "There's a branch about a hundred meters back that looks like it rejoins this hollow here just past the dragon. You go that way, then at least one of us should be able to get into position without being seen."

"Yeah. Right." Joubouline didn't move. Chavez was suddenly aware of the sweat beading heavily on the little man's forehead.

"Hey, are you all right?" That would be all he needed, he thought sourly, to lose a kill because Joubouline decided to go and get heatstroke now instead of during one of his cross-country monologues.

It was a moment before Joubouline seemed to hear him. "Huh? Oh, yeah, I'm all right, fine."

"You're sure?"

"I'm sure, I'm fine."

Joubouline turned and started back the way they had come. Chavez watched him until he moved out of sight, then began to move down the long depression between the dunes.

The dragon had captured its prey, a many-legged bur-rower, species impossible to determine after the gory ruin wrought by teeth and claws. The dragon was not quite facing him, but he had a clear quartering view down its entire flank. He set his rifle to his shoulder and took aim.

There was a roar of gunfire from beyond the dragon. It reared up and whirled, and as it turned Chavez could see Joubouline, his face a blind, ghastly mask of fear, his rifle at his hip, firing at the beast on full automatic, hosing it down with ineffectual slivers up and down the length of its body. He wailed and spun away as the dragon lunged forward in pursuit.

Chavez cursed and snapped a burst into the creature's flank, but it had an enemy already in sight before it and would not be diverted by such a feeble sting.

He slung his rifle and clawed his way up the side of the dune again. He sprinted across open ground toward the path he hoped Joubouline had taken. If he was wrong, the man was dead. If he was right, Chavez would have to put himself square in the path of a charging dragon.

There was a roar, and then another, closer. Chavez shifted direction by the sound, racing to cut man and animal off. Rifle in hand, he practically ran off the face of the dune. He slid down its face, lost his balance, and rolled, coming to his feet just as Joubouline and the dragon rounded the bend. Joubouline yelped as he saw the leveled weapon and threw himself aside. The dragon had neither the agility nor the inclination to do the same. The murderous mouth opened and Chavez fired.

It was too close. There was nothing for Chavez to do but keep firing but the dragon was too close. It wasn't going to stop. It wasn't going to fall—

—The impact of that enormous skull against his chest threw him into the dune with a fountain of sand all his own. He slid down like a wad of sacking, half-buried.

The last thing he remembered was a gleaming great body crashing down in a cloud of dust.

12

The stink of rotting dragon flesh jarred Chavez awake like a faceful of ammonia. He lay where he had fallen, half-buried by a wave of sand dislodged by his fall, lacking the will or the strength to rise against the gentle weight of it upon him. The carcass of the dragon sprawled at an impossible angle, seemingly imbedded in the face of a vertical cliff, a deceit of his supine perspective.

It was the movement around the dragon that goaded Chavez into motion at last. The sand around the body rippled and heaved with the unseen passage of scavengers swarming to the feast Chavez had provided them. Even as he watched, the flank of the dead giant bulged and writhed as a carrion-eater burrowed in under the obdurate integument to reach the succulent meat underneath. Chavez knew he had to get up, had to get moving before they turned their attention to him. His tainted human flesh would doubtless prove as lethal to the scavengers as Rafer Stone's had been to his dragon, but there would be no satisfaction in that if Chavez didn't outlive their learning it.

The spilled sand slid away easily as he lifted first one arm and then his shoulders. The real resistance to any movement came from within his own body, a treacherous wash of pain that drew red curtains down on the wings of his vision, threatening to bear him back into unconsciousness.

He hurt *everywhere*. In his legs, where knees and hips protested the strain of the unnatural posture in which he had lain for uncounted hours. All through his belly and ribs, where the dragon's great cask of a head had struck him. In his neck, strained by the press of the sand against his head. And his face, that part of it the sand had left uncovered, had reddened and blistered under the fierce light of Hansen's Primary.

He rolled over clumsily and sat up. One eye wouldn't open; the alien sand had clung to the sweat of his brow, caking into a deathmask over half his face as it dried. More had found its way into his mouth and up his nose and down his collar. It chafed viciously beneath the waistband of his pants and in the tender hollows of his elbows and armpits. And he was suddenly thirsty—or rather, he suddenly identified the choking mass of cotton that seemed to fill the whole of his mouth and throat as thirst. It was a parching beyond anything he had ever known. His throat was so dry that it was difficult even to breathe, almost impossible to swallow the water he craved so desperately. He suckled urgently at the plastic neck of his canteen, draining it dry without thought for later. The water seemed to disappear even as it touched his swollen, dessicated tongue, without easing the constriction in his gullet in the slightest, but as he lowered the canteen Chavez no longer felt as if he was about to strangle on a mouthful of cobwebs and dust, quite.

He lurched to his feet, and saw his rifle lying where he had flung it in his fall. It had stabbed into the sand like a high-tech javelin and toppled. The barrel was hopelessly plugged; the magazine well, open after it had ejected the spent sliver-box, had admitted dust and grit to the deepest parts of the action. It was useless as a weapon, too light and fragile even for a decent club, but all that Chavez could think of in his numbed, suffering state was that he had paid for it, and that he would not discard anything he had paid for. He picked it up and slung it over his shoulder, and started off up the wash for where he and Joubouline had left the trac.

He stared at the empty patch of sand as though it was too awful a joke even to merit outrage. There was no trac, no sign that there had ever been a trac. During his unconsciousness the wind had even filled in the tread prints, so completely that a three-foot stretch of curved track sheltered in the lee of the dune was the only evidence left of Joubouline's desertion.

Chavez looked up from the empty gully toward the hills on the distant horizon, his only landmark in an ocean of sand. The dunes rose and fell like waves in the shimmering, heated air rising from their flanks. Broad patches of "devil's water," the teasing, mirror-slick mirages of the desert that mocked a desperate man's thirst, danced in the distance on all sides. In all that vast landscape there was nothing else that stood upright as he stood on that murderous skillet of a desert, so open to the unremitting assault of the sun.

The pain returning with each stiff-legged step, his empty canteen slapping him in the butt like a fool's pig bladder, Chavez stepped down onto the face of the dune and began the twenty-five mile walk to his hut—to the nearest place a man might live.

Shasti Keane looked up at Eli Santer uncomfortably. She was never less at ease with him than on these rare times when he came to her at work. The quartermaster geodesic was her one last hiding-place; surrounded by the stores she dispensed, the records she kept, the shelves she arranged herself, it was the final place in her world where she retained some illusion of privacy and control in her own life. It was perhaps the one lie Shasti Keane still allowed herself, and there was no room in that lie for Eli Santer. But it was Eli Santer's hut, bought and paid for, just as she was Eli Santer's indentured employee and mistress, bought and paid for. It would never occur to Eli Santer to stay away from his own property, and before the assurance that ownership granted him it was the lie that gave, every time he walked through the door, to be patched together a little less solidly, a little more threadbare and transparent each time he walked out again.

"We'll have to cut the hide price by another twenty percent," Santer told her.

"Can we do that?" Shasti asked.

Santer looked at her. "What stops me?"

"It's going to make a mess of things here," she said, gesturing at her terminal and the invisible ranks of files and accounts it fronted. "The skinners can't put any money back into the system if they're not earning it to begin with. And there's only so far that we can cut what we pay them before we have to start financing their supplies and outfitting out of other earnings."

"They can still pay their own way on a twenty percent cut."

"They can," Shasti admitted. "But they won't like it."

"I'm not asking them to like it," Santer said. He straightened up in annoyance from the counter he'd been leaning against. "I'm not asking them to like it. *I* don't like people trying to tell me how much I can charge for my own goods. That doesn't seem to stop them trying. But if I won't stand for it from my buyers, you'd better believe I won't take it from my employees."

"I'm not saying you should, Eli. But there has to be some step or steps we can take to minimize discontent among the skinners, if only in the interests of keeping them efficient."

"What do you suggest then?" Santer asked. "We can't cut our supply costs. We're paying rock bottom on staple stores already. Our shipping costs are fixed—and hell, for that matter, I'm running *Abilene* at a loss with no hides going out. That's another cost I have to cover, damn it. Tovas tells me we're taking a rocking in the markets on Wolkenheim. And I am not going to let those bastards on *Northwest Passage* knock my price down. If I let them get away with it once, they'll chip away at me forever. So I don't have any money coming in this quarter, and I have a hell of a lot of money that has to go out. That means you have to find me some money I don't have to spend. And I can't see where else it's going to come from, do you?"

Shasti Keane couldn't. But what she couldn't see, either, was what she could do to keep Eli Santer out of the skinners' pockets—his skinners, she reminded herself, his pockets—or what he would allow her to do. The second question was the more important: If Santer was prepared to strip the skinners, how far would he tolerate Shasti's trying to minimize the damage, if it meant disagreeing with him?

And how nearly did she dare to approach that limit? How much risk to her own situation was she prepared to take on the behalf of a pack of strangers? Not much, she admitted.

And how much did that reluctance make her as much a user of the skinners as Santer himself?

"No, I don't," she admitted. And then she committed

herself as far as she dared. "But there are things we can do to make it go down easier."

"Why?"

"Why make it any harder on them than we have to? That would be bad for business."

For a moment, she thought Santer would dismiss even that appeal to hardhearted pragmatism. Then Santer shrugged slightly, as if such petty mutiny wasn't worth the effort to suppress.

"What do you have in mind?"

"Extend credit."

"We did that for the last cut."

"Extend it further. Raise the debt ceiling, maybe cut the interest—"

"No cuts."

"No cuts," Shasti agreed quickly, to forestall further refusal. "At least keep it at the current level."

"I still won't have any money coming in."

"This kind of debt's almost as good as money for your purposes. After all, they aren't going anywhere until they've paid it off, are they?" Santer stared at her, expression unreadable. "It lets you balance out your stores expenses, Eli, and it will keep the skinners in line. It cancels out your major expenses, and that's what you wanted, isn't it?"

At last he nodded, a single bob of his head with no satisfaction in it. "All right. Set it up that way if you think it's best. But you'd better remember something—this situation is going to get worse before it gets better, and there's a limit to what I'm prepared to give away. This is my world. I'm going to keep it."

"I know that, Eli," Shasti said.

"Yes, you do," Santer agreed. He seemed to relax, and Shasti permitted herself a small feeling of triumph, far enough back that it could never show to the man before her.

"Will you come by later?" Santer asked.

And just like that, the triumph was gone, extinguished by Santer's casual reassertion of his ultimate control.

"If you want me to," Shasti said neutrally. She never said

anything else. There was nothing else she could ever say, while she lived on Eli Santer's world.

"I'd like that," Santer said.

The night wind broke softly around him as the geodesic's door banged shut behind Eli Santer. The domes and warehouses of the depot rose up all around him, featureless black silhouettes against the paler darkness of the night sky, squatting there in sullen defiance of the slow erosion of the blowing sand. The solidity of those buildings, that he had put there in the face of all the desert's power, appealed to Santer, reflected the confidence he felt in his confrontation with TerraCo. He would beat Rodinov. The compradore had studied in too soft a school to challenge a man who had been shaped by sandstorm and dragons. He could see what he fought for, touch it, shape it to his will. That gave him an edge over any water-fat executive who fought his battles on the immaterial terrain of electronic spreadsheets and accounts ledgers. Santer's world was real, and it would sustain him when all of Rodinov's intangible power deserted him. And he would show Adrienne; he would prove to her that what he decided, happened, that he ran Santer Holdings because he was strong enough, smart enough, and hard enough to deserve it.

He started off up the street, the thin panels of the geodesic flexing quietly in the wind behind him.

The desert jumped up and hit him in the face again. It wasn't the first time Chavez had fallen in the past hours, and it wouldn't be the last. Not yet, although with each new fall the urge to give in to his thirst and exhaustion—*just rest a bit, just a little while longer, what could it hurt*—grew stronger than it had the time before, the prospect of forcing himself upright and resuming his automaton's stagger that much less bearable. Even the pain conspired to encourage his relaxation. In the course of his march the protests of his body had come to choreograph themselves with each plodding step he took. His foot would slap down and the pain would vault upwards, through the strained muscles of his legs and his aching joints, through his bruised gut and wrenched neck to burst in a fresh pulse of misery in his head. It had become his clock, his metronome, as steady and predictable as his heartbeat or the effort he made to draw each new breath. It wasn't much to look forward to, Chavez thought wearily, seduced by the yielding warmth of the sand, tempted again toward the immobility that would kill him.

Then he smelled it, a pungent reek of ammonia and ketones, spoiled dragonmeat and a dozen more objectionable substances rolled into one. Perimeter toxins, the repellent chemical mixture the skinners ringed their camp-sites with to keep the burrowing scavengers out. The fumes were strong enough at ground level to bring tears to his eyes. Chavez wouldn't have thought there was moisture enough left in his body for tears, but the fumes swirling and burning around him drew them forth.

He rose up on hands and knees, blinking furiously to clear his eyes, and looked up.

The hut was just where it should have been, not thirty feet away from him, shining softly by the light of the lamp within, and Chavez suddenly realized that he could not remember the last time he had actually thought of a direction to his wanderings, a goal to be reached.

Duncan Joubouline lurched up off the edge of his bunk as Chavez heaved through the doorway, and the yell he let out as he saw him was a fair repeat of the way he had screamed at the dragon. The empty rifle dropped from Chavez's hand as he started toward Joubouline for a step and a half before he got his appetites in order and lunged for the vapor still, where he drank down more water than he ever thought he could possibly have held. Then he turned to Joubouline with upraised fists, and managed to get in at least two solid punches per hand before the floor spun out from under him and he passed out again.

It was daylight when he woke up again.

Evidently he'd been right about how much water he could keep down. He awoke lying in a treacly puddle of his own vomit. His head said all manner of rude things to him as he dragged himself to his feet and lurched over to the radio on legs that had converted yesterday's pain into a planklike, joint-locking stiffness.

The depot infirmary surgeon was a model of the type. Was Chavez coughing up blood? No? Then internal injuries could probably be ruled out. It sounded as if concussion was a strong possibility, though, so if Chavez began to feel drowsy, he should call in at once—what? How long was he unconscious? That long? And he regained consciousness? Well, yes, obviously he'd regained consciousness, no, the doctor didn't think it was a goddamned single-sideband ouija board.

"You'll probably be all right, then," he said.

"An expert opinion I will cherish forever."

"I doubt there's any point to your making an extra trip in, but if you want to stop by on your next supply run, feel free," the doctor said.

"I'm glad you can find the time to see me."

"Ordinarily, I'd ask you to come in immediately—"

"—but you just finished feeding the leeches, I know. Thanks," Chavez said, and signed off.

Through all this Duncan Joubouline sat on his bunk, staring at him miserably through blackened, puffy eyes. Chavez set the microphone down and turned, looking at Joubouline as though just noticing him for the first time.

It surprised him that he couldn't dredge up more than mild anger at the little man. It was as though all his rage had sloughed off him with the dead skin peeling from his sunburned face and hands.

"You still here?" he asked.

"Where the hell was I going to go?"

"That didn't seem to be a problem yesterday."

"Yeah."

Chavez drew a mug of water and rinsed his mouth out, crossing to the hut door to spit it out onto the sand. He was abruptly, intensely aware that he stank; between the dried sweat soaked into the inside of his leathers and the puke down his chest it was impossible to stand still. His own stench assaulted his nostrils with all the ferocity of a full drum of perimeter toxin as he tried to stagger away from his own smell.

He stepped out of the hut and stripped. His feet had swollen so badly, it was almost impossible to get his boots off. He spread the leathers out to dry in the sun; he could scrape and sponge them down later, after more important business had been taken care of.

Joubouline hadn't moved when Chavez reentered the hut. Chavez went back to the still and poured himself a fresh mug. His stomach rebelled when he tried to swallow it but he forced it down, knowing he had to have it, that thirst was an unreliable guide to dehydration. He lowered himself to sit stiffly by the still, facing the man who had abandoned him.

"Start packing," he said. "I'm putting in for a new partner. You're going out on the next sled."

"I'm afraid not," Joubouline said, sounding as if he really was.

"You are, huh? Why not?"

"Because there aren't going to be any new partners, not for a long time. Word around the depot before I came out here was that Santer's hurting for money—that's why the cut in hide prices. He's not going to bring in any new men when he can't afford to pay the ones he's got. So it looks as if we're stuck with each other, my friend."

"Oh, well, that's just wonderful," Chavez said, slumping back against the wall. "Christ. I can't believe you've lasted three years out here. Did you ever *see* a dragon before?"

"Not a moving one, but the one time."

"Then where have you been getting your hides?"

"We used to—my partner and I, his name was Zuongsi Cheng—we used to wait until they'd gorged themselves feeding and dug in to sleep it off. Then we'd dig down to their heads and get 'em through the eyes, right up close."

Chavez was impressed in spite of himself. "That's not a bad idea."

"Mister Cheng was a very inventive fellow. And it was a very good idea indeed, except for the one time it didn't work. Either we started digging too soon or this particular dragon was a light sleeper."

"It woke up."

"It woke up, and that was when friend Cheng lost his

legs. I never hoped to see anything like that again—and then you went *looking* for it. . . ."

Chavez nodded. "I see." He understood the little man's panic now. He didn't regret trying to break his face, but he understood him.

"Well," he said, "if I'm stuck with you, I'm going to work you. I'm out here to skin dragons, 'friend,' and that's what we're going to do. Just one thing: if you ever run out on me like that again, I'll kill you. All right?"

"Yeah." There was nothing else he could have said.

13

The trouble with trying too hard to keep others from betraying you, Ivan Petrovitch Rodinov thought, is that eventually you end up betraying yourself.

He had overreacted, he had to admit that. He had become so used to thinking of Lakim Tovas in terms of treachery that he had taken Tovas' warning that he might succeed in organizing a pharmaceutical harvest shutout against TerraCo as being cut from the same disingenuous cloth as the line he knew Tovas must be feeding Eli Santer to explain their failure to thwart TerraCo. So he had taken the list Tovas had given him of First Wave firms who might cross the line and made substantial buys through almost all of them.

And then *Albatross* had come insystem, and kicked the very foundations out from under the structure of interplanetary economics in the Hansen System.

Now Rodinov found himself sitting on top of pharmaceutical stocks far in excess of TerraCo's normal needs. In the usual course of events he could have sold off the excess to smaller speculators, once the season's initial spurt of buying spent itself. Market conditions would then, with any luck, have escalated the price per pharmaceutical unit to a point where Rodinov could dispose of his surplus at a price high enough to assure a modest profit, yet low enough to remain less costly that shipping in fresh stocks from Hansenwald.

But *Albatross* had arrived, bringing with it all the good fortune one might have expected from such an infelicitous naming. This time around, everybody already had excess stocks, even the smaller firms that usually bought from the big importers, even the firms smaller than those, who

normally shied away from off-planet speculation. No one
was going to need more, particularly not when the sharp
buyers up aboard *Northwest Passage* had taken full advantage of the glut to drive the price per unit down below what
Rodinov had paid in the first place.

He was facing a substantial loss, not a dangerous one—
yet—but sizable and embarrassing, Rodinov thought, and
he was facing it because he could not trust Lakim Tovas. So
he saw no reason why Tovas should not make amends for
the inconvenience he had caused.

He called up the joint purchase Tovas had secretly
financed with Eli Santer's money. To sell the stocks jointly
would do neither of them any good. Both Santer Holdings
and TerraCo would realize a loss at the going, deflated
price. But not if the proceeds weren't split, he told himself,
staring at the numbers in the holobloc. Not if someone took
the only pragmatic, reasonable course of action. After all,
there was no reason both parties should suffer, especially
when one of those parties didn't dare protest. Bending to
his keyboard, Rodinov authorized the sale, directing the
whole of the proceeds into TerraCo's accounts.

"Hey, Admiral!"

Moses Callahan turned quickly and a little unsteadily at
Klepper's call. The older captain quickened his pace to
catch up to him on the deserted street leading to the port
gate. The two bored port cops waved them through
unchallenged.

They walked out across the broad, level expanse of
permaplast between the grounded ships. The alloy hulls of
the lighters and intrasystem freighters shone like jade in
the gentle green light of Hansenwald overhead, beautiful
and fragile and every bit as ornamental in the presence of
the blocky mass of *Albatross*, hulking over the field like a
mocking cubist tribute to planned obsolescence.

"What are you doing out at this ungodly hour, hey,
Admiral? And indulging in strong drink, as well. That's no
way for a captain to behave before a flight."

"You've the right of that," Moses agreed. "It isn't. But
who are you to be pointing this out, chasing me back

portside at such an indecent hour as you were?" He sniffed.
"And unless I'm greatly mistaken, you're more than a little
fermented yourself, now."

Klepper laughed. "Maybe just a little, ya. But my
business is finished, youngster. I've made my last run out to
Northwest Passage this trip." He looked up at the angular
bulk of *Albatross*. "Maybe my last, ever. That great bitch
will be going out to meet the *Natchez* when she calls. God
knows what she'll leave for the rest of us." Then he forced
himself to lighten the tone of his voice. "But you've got a
steady contract, youngster. Neither rain nor sleet nor the
gloom of Hans Joseph Klepper will keep the *Irish Missed*
from her appointed rounds."

"No, they won't, at all," Moses agreed sourly. "But that
cow there will."

"Hey?"

"The colony has evaluated the subsidized run to Hansenwald," Moses said. "In light of the arrival of *Albatross*. And
the good men and true of the PanDistrict Council have
decided it is cheaper and therefore more cost-effective to
pay me to keep the *Missed* grounded and buy space aboard
that scow as need arises."

"Oh, no. . . ."

"Needless to say, the chances of their continuing to pay
me not to fly after this contract expires are less than
reassuring."

"Well, damn them all."

"Indeed."

"You know, youngster," Klepper said. "The more I think
about it, the more I think I'll be taking *Brunhilde* up and
hitching a ride outsystem when *Natchez* comes in."

"You wouldn't."

"Why not? What's left for me here?"

"You've done business in the Hansen System for fifteen
years, Hans. They know you here, you've got a place
here—"

"No," Klepper said. "No, I've got a *function* here,
youngster. They've got a use for me, and for you—or they
used to have. Now, though—" He gestured at the hulking
antigravity freighter. "Whatever they think to use us for, it

won't be the use you and I selected for ourselves. And I don't intend to wait around and see what it is."

"Nor do I then, I suppose."

High up on the flank of *Albatross* a diminutive rectangle of light appeared, a viewport or hatch opening. Moses squinted up at it, trying to make out whoever stood up there.

"Do you know, I've never met anybody off that scow in all the time it's been here?"

"Neither have I," Klepper said. "I expect they're embarrassed to face us."

"And well they should be." Moses raised his voice, still glaring at the light. "Well you should be, you avaricious bastards! Taking food from the mouths of honest men and women with your gadgetry and gimmicks! Shame! Shame!"

The light shone on, unperturbed by Moses' outrage.

"Where's the justice in it?" he demanded, and by now his anger was only half feigned. "I ask you that. A man can spend years building something for himself, and then along comes the likes of them, to make the whole of it worthless."

"Don't blame them for that, youngster."

"And why not?"

"Because you can't. You have no right to. You and me, we had chances. We saw them, we took them." Klepper shrugged. "Now whoever masters that bitch sees a chance of his own, and he's taking it."

"To our ruination."

"It happens. One man's golden opportunity slams a door in another man's face."

Ian Protherall sat down behind *Flute's* command board, and wondered if he'd ever get to do that again.

The boards were lit up and functional before him; it would have been more trouble than it was worth to shut down *Flute's* main core when so much of the yard's lighter work could be done using ship's power. *Flute* had a hot drive; but for the weakness in her bones he could have lifted off and gone back into business right then and there. But for the weakness in her bones, and the bastards who'd sold him junk for structural members, and that other bastard Rodinov and those *real* bastards at Customs and Revenue. . . .

If they had their way, *Flute* would never lift out again, not with Protherall in command. Every day that *Flute* sat on the ground was a victory for the whole bastard lot of them, while his yard costs mounted and the shipping business went to hell in a handbasket all around him.

The tapping of his fingers on his keyboard almost surprised him. The monitors blinked and flickered, telling of power being diverted from the main plant to dormant magnetics, of polarities slowly building in the vanes folded back along the flanks of the hull.

It certainly surprised the yard security desk. There had been no way yard security could legally deny him access to his own ship, but having *Flute* come to life in their laps was a different matter, too much to be tolerated.

"*Flute*, this is yard security. What's going on down there?"

"I just wanted to see what else you clowns might have ruined when I wasn't looking."

"Shut down at once," came the order. "This is not a drive-cleared zone."

There would be consternation down there, Protherall knew. Urgent screenings, pleas for instructions. Hesitation.

"Negative, yard. Cannot comply. Suggest you keep your people at five hundred meters clear. The secondary leakage off these old vanes can get pretty nasty." That would hold them for a while, he thought, while charges built toward lift-point and he dialed up life-support and sensors and got a *ship* around him again.

He wasn't broke. He wasn't helpless. Not if he refused to play their games. He'd probably lose his up-front money— probably, hell, it was gone, write it off, pissed away into this sorry hole of a planet. But that still left him a good two or three hundred thousand, more than enough for a new stake in a new system, where an old bird like *Flute* would be valued for the work it could do more than for its compliance with some damned bureaucratic standard.

And *Northwest Passage* was waiting to take him there, sleek and fast and beyond colony law.

All he had to do was *go*. It was a mad act, impossibly

sudden, but Ian Protherall had had his fill of being the last reasonable man in the Hansen System.

The numbers were there on his screen now. The vanes were charged. Nothing would stop him.

He keyed in the command and the lateral vanes extended, port and starboard, flexing lightly as the planet's magnetic field pawed at them.

"*Flute*, this is yard security. Lock your vanes back and cut drive at once."

"Sorry, yard. Can't do that."

"*Flute*, be advised that the yard intends to seek legal restraint in this matter." They must have awakened the lawyers.

"They're going to need a fast judge with one hell of a long arm to serve it," he said.

"*Flute*, cut drive immediately."

That sounded like an order, Protherall thought. We've got a real take-charge guy out there.

Movement caught his eye through the forward ports. A long, girdered arm was slowly coming into view, followed by the bulk of one of the enormous yard cranes, looming up over *Flute* like a one-armed mantis. A take-charge guy, all right. Protherall wondered who they'd found to activate the cranes at such an ungodly hour. Then he laughed. They were going to make a race of it.

He keyed in lift. The plant fed power to the magnetic drives, and the broadswept vanes did their best to push the planet away.

Flute's weight came off the cradles with a groan like straining timber. The groaning continued for a long moment, then ceased as old frames found a new alignment with each other, tired old beams and flawed new work alike. Protherall wondered which had protested the more loudly. Screw it, he decided, as penurious shipmasters had decided throughout history, the hell with metal fatigue; this old girl's got *heart*.

Flute lifted gently out of the dock, risen now a whole foot or more above her cradles. Magnetic drive was nobody's choice for a quick getaway—but then the ponderous yard cranes were hardly anyone's idea of a fast pursuit vehicle, either. The distance between the top of the hull and those reaching derricks narrowed with all the speed of dinosaurs brawling in a tar pit. Protherall ordered up lateral vector, trying to visualize the relative positions of the cranes he could not see, crawling toward the widest opening left to him.

The gap between the crane-arm and hull shrank—and then disappeared altogether. Protherall heard a sickening rasp of metal on metal, diffused by intervening bulkheads, as the yard tried to trap him beneath that pinioning limb. But the altimeter showed steady climb and the boards showed no damage. A close scrape indeed . . . but a clean escape.

"Yard, this is *Flute*. Inform your legal people that I'm contemplating charges for this shocking assault." He wondered if the yard security boss had deployed the cranes on someone's higher authorization. He halfway hoped not; let the bastard get fired. To hell with them all.

Flute was clear of the dock now, rising free above the port. Protherall deployed his ventral and dorsal vanes and energized them. *Flute* redoubled her mollusclike pace.

Now the port authorities were jamming his comm-lines. Them he had to talk to; Protherall had no intention of punctuating his declaration of independence by colliding with some grubby little lighter bringing a load of exotic lingerie or whatever down from *Northwest Passage*.

"*Flute*, this is port flight direction. You are making an unregistered departure. Please state your purpose."

"Port control, this is *Flute*. My departure is unregistered and final. My purpose is survival."

"Say again, *Flute*."

"My purpose is survival. I am seeking transport aboard *Northwest Passage* outsystem."

When the port voice came back there was a puzzled, personal note in it, as though the operator was taken aback by this sudden change in one of the disembodied voices he dealt with every day.

"This is a little sudden, isn't it, *Flute*?"

"There's no law against sudden, port."

"*Flute*, Hansen Astronautics is reporting an unauthorized lift-off from a no-drive zone. They claim damage to their facilities."

"Port, Hansen Authorities attempted to unlawfully detain my vessel and my person. Any damage they suffered was in the course of that attempt. I deny liability. In fact, if I was going to remain here, I would consider prosecution." Let them chew on that.

A new voice came on line. "*Flute*, port, this is Customs and Revenue."

"Hello, Bewys."

"Be advised that we have information to the effect that *Flute* is engaged in conspiracy to violate Customs and Revenue ordinances and is operating in violation of Confederate BuShip standards. We request that *Flute* return to port immediately."

"That's a damned lie," Protherall snapped. "And to hell with that."

"Be advised, *Flute*. Serious measures are contemplated."

"Then take them. Port flight direction, will you give me an outbound course or should I just pick one at random?"

There was a pause. "How much is up there for me to run into, port?" Protherall pressed.

"Stand by for course feed, *Flute*."

Protherall set up a safe hold for the data burst before accepting it. He didn't want any unverified programs running around loose in his navcomps.

He clucked his tongue in surprise as he studied the readback. They'd played it straight with him.

"*Flute*, this is port. Be advised that Customs and Revenue are threatening to lodge a complaint with Mission House."

Protherall was not about to be bluffed. Not this late in the game. "Let them. I'd love to see the charges Mission House files against *them*. Restraint of trade, conspiracy to defraud, interference with interstellar commerce. Go ahead, tell them I'd love to see them in Mission House, if they can afford it. *Flute*, out."

The bright lights of Hansen's Landing were a tiny nebula behind the ship now, as *Flute* rose into the night sky and freedom.

14

There was a blip where no blip should have been, closing on *Flute* from out of nowhere.

Vigilant. There was nothing else it could be, sweeping in from an angle where no ship could have been expected. *Northwest Passage* was ahead of *Flute*, still a good two days' flight off. The few ships still trading this late in the call were ahead or behind him, Protherall knew. There was nothing out beyond this intruding blip but vacuum.

His guess was confirmed a moment later, when *Vigilant's* call sign crackled in his speakers, and a demand for his own identification. Why not, he thought. It wasn't as if they didn't know who they challenged. There couldn't be that many rogue freighters on the loose in the Hansen System. He sent his I.D. code and sat back to wait while the signal crawled across the distance separating the two ships.

While he waited, he thought, studying the figures his screens gave him on *Vigilant's* speed and angle of approach. He felt oddly calm as he contemplated the matter at hand, soothed by the quiet mutter of ventilators and chiming telltales. *Vigilant, Flute* and *Northwest Passage* could be drawn as endpoints on a vast triangle, hundreds of millions of miles on a side. Very nearly as much distance separated *Flute* and *Vigilant* as divided *Flute* and *Northwest Passage.*

And *Vigilant* was not matching his speed. Not yet.

It all came down to acceleration, to cold equations of mass versus thrust. Laden, *Flute* could never have beaten the revenue cutter into *Northwest Passage's* zone of influence. But he was running empty holds, driving less weight than *Flute's* designers would ever have called for when they wrote up her specs. He could accelerate as no one might expect, and he had an edge, however slight, in velocity.

And once he was in range to negotiate with *Northwest Passage*, the cutter couldn't touch him.

He straightened in his acceleration couch and keyed in full power on the drives. The hull groaned again as this new load was imposed on it; not in years had he ever given the order for full throttle. It wasn't cost-effective. It wasn't prudent. The acceleration pressed him back briefly against the couch before aging compensators caught up with it. *Flute* leaped forward again, challenging *Vigilant* to follow.

It was still a race.

Lakim Tovas was furious, but he dared not let it show. It would not do to have Eli Santer asking him what the matter was—not when the matter was that Tovas had just lost thirty thousand Confederate standards of Eli Santer's money, fraudulently invested with TerraCo.

Thank God this one time for Trollshulman heat, Tovas thought. It let him turn as livid as he wanted without arousing suspicion of anything worse than imminent heat-stroke.

"I need money, Lakim," Santer was saying as they walked away from *Abilene* in her cradle.

"Well, you're certainly not going to get it from the pharmaceuticals harvest this year."

"That bad?"

"And it will probably get worse. This is the first time in anybody's memory that the price per unit has gone down the further we get from first harvest."

"Damn it." Santer kicked at the sand, throwing a small geyser of dust ahead of them as they walked. "What went wrong?"

"*Albatross.*"

"We've had new ships come in here before."

"Not like this. This isn't just a new ship, Eli. It's a whole new order of technology. It changes the very nature of the way things work. There's always disruption whenever that happens."

"That isn't much consolation when you're caught in the middle of it."

"Perhaps not."

"No perhaps. But what I've got to do now is survive it. And that takes money. I've got no hides going out, and the pharmaceuticals are a write-off. What about our other investments?"

"Other investments? You haven't that many, Eli. At the risk of sounding like an 'I told you so,' you've never diversified as much as you needed to."

"The Santers sell dragonhide, by God."

"When people will buy it."

"They've bought it before. And they'll buy it again. Now how long can we hold on until they do?"

"It's hard to overstate the seriousness of the pharmaceuticals situation," Tovas said. "The whole of your other Wolkenheimen investments barely suffice to cover that loss. You'll have consumed the last of this year's profit within twelve weeks at your current rate of expenditure. After that, you'll be eating directly into capital."

"Twelve weeks? Then we should be all right. That's well into the start of the next quarter, and *Natchez* should be through by then—what?"

Tovas was shaking his head. "Eli, *Natchez* is running on a five-month cycle now."

"What?"

"She took over two systems from the old *Wanderjahr* network, and Peng's Paradise in the Arcadian Worlds has come into the export market. So they've had to extend their circuit."

"When the hell did all this happen?"

"The word came in with *Northwest Passage*."

"First I've heard of that," Santer said.

Of course it was, Tovas thought sourly. Any news that wasn't bound in dragonhide was of no interest to Eli Santer.

"So what happens if we just try to tough it out until it does arrive?" Santer asked.

"You mean simply liquidating assets as needed to meet operating costs?"

"Why not? We've survived without all this diversification before. All I need is the dragons, Lakim."

"By the time *Natchez* arrives, you will not have them. The pharmaceuticals market can only get worse. Our losses in that area will only mount. It's impossible to unload what we've purchased already. *Nobody* is buying insystem anymore, and most of the exporters are cutting each other's throats to sell anything to the buyers on *Northwest Passage*, at any price. And a crash of this magnitude has major reverberations. It puts a damper on almost any investment and speculation. We could not realize anything like our assets' full worth—and not enough to meet our operating costs. To eat, here on Trollshulm, you would have to sell interest in the dragonhide operation."

"No way in hell," Santer said flatly.

"Then you must cut your costs still further."

"How?"

Tovas turned and pointed back to the grounded *Abilene*.

"For a start, you cannot afford to operate a ship."

"We need the transport."

"Not now. The expense does not justify it. You aren't exporting anything this quarter, Eli. And paying the full costs of operating a ship just to import food drives your costs up ruinously."

"Then what do we do?"

"Ground *Abilene*. Buy space on an independent ship."

"The *Albatross*?"

"I doubt we could commit for enough of their capacity to interest them at this stage. I had another ship in mind, the *Irish Missed*."

"Why them?"

"Because they were on the colony's subsidized run to Hansenwald, prior to *Albatross*. But the last thing the colony wants now is more pharmaceuticals coming in. So they've been paying the *Missed* to stay on the ground and running the mail and courier work to Hansenwald on *Albatross*, since it's been making the run anyway. I believe I can get them to let the *Missed* resume the subsidized run, but to Trollshulm instead."

"We've never had a subsidized run before."

"We've never needed one, and they've never had one paid for that they could not use. Why shouldn't somebody get the benefit of it, especially when that somebody is one of the most prominent First Wave firms insystem?"

"All right. Arrange it, if you can."

"There will have to be more, at this end."

"This end is mine," Santer said. "I'll do what has to be done here."

Later, alone in his cabin aboard *Abilene*, Lakim Tovas thought of what he would have to do when he reached Hansen's Landing.

He would make the arrangements to use the *Irish Missed*, as promised. *Abilene* would deposit him and then return to Trollshulm, where dockage would be no extra expense. But his own troubles would take some more effort.

He looked up as the door to his cramped little cubicle slid open and Adrienne Santer stepped in, stooping to clear the low sill of the cabin hatch, fitting herself into the limited space of the cabin as carefully as a praying mantis arranging itself on a twig.

Tovas started to get up. "Madame Santer—"

"Don't waste our time with courtesies neither of us believes in, Mr. Tovas." There was no anger in her voice; it was as if she wasn't even willing to waste the energy necessary to rage at him. "It's past time we talked."

"About what, madame?"

"Please, she said. "Let's just take it as given that not every Santer is prepared to play your disingenuous little games, shall we? We have to talk about what you're doing to Eli Santer—and Santer Holdings."

Somehow, Tovas managed to keep the sudden stab of panic that struck him from registering on his face. "Please explain that, madame."

"It's very simple. What you've taken from us, I want back."

"And that is?"

"Santer Holdings."

Tovas spread his hands, palms upward. "I don't understand this, Madame Santer. I work for Santer Holdings. I work for Eli Santer."

"You mean you work *on* him. You really don't understand, do you?" Adrienne asked. "You really don't understand what you've done to us. This is our world, latecomer. We've held it for ten generations now, while every other family that ever landed here either died out or packed up and ran. We've fought with it and for it, bled and died on it, changed to fit it. Santers did all that, Mr. Tovas."

"You should be proud, madame."

"Well, I can't be." She leaned down over him, and her eyes were the eyes of a stooping falcon. "Because that's what you've taken away. We're not all blinded by some need to cling to power, Mr. Tovas. We can see who's really in charge of Santer Holdings these days."

"As can I," Tovas answered. "Eli Santer."

The relief he felt beggared description. For one vertiginous moment he had been certain that his treachery had been discovered, that Adrienne Santer had come only to bait him with his own damnation personally before taking the truth to her cousin. Instead it was nothing more than another First Wave family squabble, foolish and inward-looking, which could not threaten him.

"Eli acts on the information you see that he gets, Tovas. He chooses from options you lay out for him, and thinks he's still in charge because he makes the choices. But we both know better."

"So what do you want from me?"

"I want Santer Holdings back in Santer hands, Tovas. I want you gone."

"But that I cannot help you with," Tovas said, in mock regret. "I work for Eli Santer and Santer Holdings. Whether I stay or go is entirely his decision, in any case. If Eli Santer tells me, 'Stay,' I should be foolish, given my natural standing in the Hansen System, to refuse him. As a good and loyal employee, I should never wish to.

"And, of course, if I did wield the power you ascribe to me, I should be very foolish indeed to ever allow him to reach that conclusion—shouldn't I, madame?"

"My God," Adrienne said quietly. "I thought I was ready for this. But your arrogance still astounds me."

"Was there anything else you wished to discuss, madame?"

"We're hardly finished with this topic yet."

"On the contrary," Tovas said pleasantly. "I think we've said all that needs to be said."

* * *

"Good evening, Thomas."

Santer found Markov in *Abilene's* master stateroom. The captain sat back from his terminal and looked up as Santer stepped in, wondering to himself how spacers could tear themselves away from the alleged confinements of planets in search of the vastnesses of space, and then consent to being bottled up in these cramped metal coffins.

"Eli," Markov said. "I was just about to go looking for you."

"Why? Any trouble here?"

"No," Markov said. "None. We'll be ready to lift out come the morning, on schedule. All I need now is your shopping list for stores and spares, and we'll be all set."

"There isn't any list this trip, Thomas," Santer said.

"What? Why not?"

"Because you won't be doing any buying."

"I don't understand."

"I'm grounding *Abilene.*"

"No," Markov said, grinning. When Santer let the silence stretch longer than that one word could fill, he added, "You're joking."

"You'll make this last run back to Hansen's Landing and drop off Tovas and any pool releases. Then you'll travel back here in ballast and put the trip into dock."

"Eli, what the devil are you saying? You've got to have a ship—"

"I know. But I can't afford one. We can't afford one. Not our own. We're hurting for cash, Thomas, hurting badly. If I ground *Abilene* and arrange to have the colony switch the *Irish Missed's* subsidized run over to Trollshulm from Hansenwald, I can save the whole of *Abilene's* operating costs. I haven't got a choice."

"*You* haven't got a choice!" Thomas exploded. "Damn it, Eli, what the hell kind of choice are you giving *me*?"

"This isn't permanent, Thomas. We'll probably be able to resume service once *Natchez* comes insystem."

"You mean when *Albatross* is available to make runs out to the liners?"

"That won't make any difference. We have to have our

own ship here, Thomas. We have to be able to guarantee our own transport."

"So you're grounding me."

"I can't afford you! Not now, at any rate."

"If you can't afford *Abilene* now, you'll never be able to afford her again, will you?" Markov stood. "We're expendable, right?"

"This is for the family, Thomas," Santer said.

"*I'm* family," Markov snapped. "*Abilene's* a family concern. You can't just cut me out like this, Eli. I'm not some damned labor pool latecomer you can dictate terms to. I won't stand for it."

"You'll stand it a damn sight easier than you'd stand seeing her sold, won't you? That's what it comes down to, Thomas. Santer Holdings can't afford to run its own ship right now. If we can't hold out until *Natchez* comes through, we may not even be able to afford to own one."

"Then let *Abilene* work for her keep. We can carry cargoes outside the family—"

"Where? Between *Albatross* and the market glut, where are you going to find these cargoes? The government can't even find enough cargo to justify running the *Irish Missed*. What are you going to do, Thomas?" Santer asked.

Markov swayed before him, fists balled helplessly at his sides. "Then at least let me make this last supply run."

"I'm sorry. I'm going to use our supply needs as a lever to push the Council into giving us the subsidized run immediately."

"That's nonsense," Markov snapped. "If you need supplies, you need supplies. You're just wasting half-a-run's hold space. Look," he pleaded, "at least get the subsidized run switched over to *Abilene* from the *Missed*."

"There's no chance of that," Santer said, although he had intended to use just that as his opening request to the Council, to make assigning the *Missed's* run to Trollshulm seem a reasonable alternative. "They're contracted with the *Irish Missed*. They won't break contract with Callahan and they're not about to start paying for a second ship when they haven't even got any work for one. *Abilene* just isn't necessary to them."

"Or to you," Markov said bitterly.

"*Abilene's* necessary to me," Santer said. "I need the money taking her out of service represents—to save the hides, Thomas. To save our world. If I can't do that, then *Abilene* isn't worth a damn to me. Nothing is."

"So I see."

"You're not being thrown aside, Thomas," Santer said. "There's work for you here; you know that. And we'll get *Abilene* back into service. That's a promise."

"Sure it is," Markov said. "Until the next time it suits *you* to ground her—or sell her off."

"You keep harping on that—"

"Yes, I keep harping on that! Damn you, Eli, I was master of this ship when you were still running around on the sands waiting for your father to die. I made this ship work for us; half the growth we've seen in this company came because we controlled our own shipping! I don't like having all that treated as an inconsequential sideshow! *I* don't like being treated as an inconsequential sideshow!"

"Well, that's too bad, Thomas," Santer said quietly. "Because you *are* a sideshow, and you are disposable. *Everything* is, as long as it lets us hold onto the hides. And if you could see your way past your own damned self-interest, maybe you'd be Santer enough to understand that!"

He nearly bowled Adrienne Santer over as he stormed from the stateroom. He glared at her angrily and she matched his stare without flinching.

"What are you doing here?" Santer demanded.

"I was talking to an employee of Santer Holdings," she answered, and Santer realized that Tovas's stateroom was down the corridor behind her. "Why? Do you have some objection to that?"

"It's your privilege," he said sourly.

"I'm glad we agree on that much," Adrienne said. "Now, what was going on in there?"

"Why not?" Santer said. "You'll find out soon enough. I'm pulling *Abilene* out of service to cut out her operating expenses. She's going to make one last run to Hansen's Landing and then she's grounded. We'll be sending our latest batch of pool releases out with her. Perhaps you'd care to go along?"

"Don't try to be clever," Adrienne said. "This is as much my world as yours, Eli. So you've made another one of your lightning decisions, have you? And of course there was no time to consult the rest of us about this."

"What would you have said?" Eli demanded. "We can't afford to keep *Abilene* in service and you can't argue your way out of that." He pushed on, letting his anger run freely. "Of course, if you can find the money in this tub to keep it running, I'll be glad to hear about it."

He shoved past her before she could answer, out the airlock and back onto his familiar sands.

Adrienne Santer looked after him as the heavy lock door cycled shut between them. Maybe she wouldn't find the money to keep *Abilene* running, she thought . . . but she decided she would at last find something she needed.

Rodinov had not even had the grace to dissemble about his treachery.

"I don't see what your objection is," he had said, urbane and unruffled behind his expansive desk. He hadn't even bothered to offer Tovas a chair. "What are partners for, if not to help one another?"

"Apparently, they are to be stolen from."

"Not at all," Rodinov said. "Not at all. After all, how can one steal stolen money? That is what's bothering you, isn't it? You were willing to hand me Eli Santer's money, but now you're getting nervous. That money was a sign of your good faith, Tovas. Once you committed it, it was mine to do with as I please. As, in fact, are you."

"What do you mean?"

"You have ceased to be an independent agent. You are dependent upon me now, to protect you in the event that you are discovered or that we fail. I do not anticipate failure, so your only fear is discovery. And since, if I win, Santer Holdings is mine, no one is likely to try very hard to discover you without my consent. Thirty thousand standards is a small enough price to pay for that protection, isn't it?"

"You can't do this to me."

"Of course I can. I always could. You have no power in

this community that does not come from Eli Santer's money. But you grew too used to using that power to remember that, especially when Santer made it so easy for you by staying up in his wretched sandbox with his lizards. But all *you* are without his favor—or mine—is an arrogant, duplicitous little latecomer thief. I'm not foolish enough to count on your loyalty, so I'll assure your subservience. I think you have the wit to recognize that you will give me that."

Tovas recognized it, all right. But he wondered how confident Ivan Petrovitch Rodinov was feeling now, when the news channels and comm-links were crowded with accounts of Ian Protherall's mad bolt for *Northwest Passage* and escape from the Hansen System. What would happen now, he wondered, if Protherall managed to get away? What would happen when Rodinov's initial option on the synthetic process expired without renewal? He had invested enough in the synthetic and the pilot plant project already to hurt TerraCo very badly indeed in the Hansen System. Badly enough that he might want to lash out at someone, anyone, who could take some of the onus off him for the loss.

Tovas would have to protect himself. He had originally dealt with Rodinov from a position of strength because he had something Rodinov wanted: an inside line to Santer's reaction to the challenge of the synthetic. Now he was in a position of weakness because Rodinov had something he needed: protection from Eli Santer. So the way back to strength called for Tovas to find something Rodinov needed—or the means to deny him that something.

In the shaky economy of the Hansen System as it stood, there was only one thing Rodinov needed above all else: money.

And in the shaky economy of the Hansen System as it stood, there was one sure way to deny him that money.

Abilene touched down at Hansen's Landing, and Lakim Tovas began buying. The sudden surge of activity in the pharmaceuticals market was regarded as a momentary aberration, that disappeared almost as soon as it began.

15

Duncan Joubouline never ran out on Chavez Blackstone again.

That was the good news.

The bad news was that Chavez could never be sure he wouldn't. So he never gave him the chance.

Duncan Joubouline ran the camp. He pulled maintenance on the trac, generator, and still, cleaned out the hut, and cooked. He freshened the perimeter toxins whenever called for. He drove the trac out into the hunting fields, and helped skin the kills, and carted them back.

But Chavez Blackstone never, ever took him on the hunt itself. The supply sleds would land, dropping off their stores, and Chavez would then and there take Joubouline's ammunition and add it to his own. Then he would let Joubouline drive him out and drop him off, to stalk the great carnivores alone, and trust to his sharpening skills and chance not to get him into a corner he couldn't get out of. Joubouline knew better than to protest this treatment. The one time he had objected, for pride's sake, Chavez had fixed him with a stare as blank and pitilessly indifferent as dragon's eyes, and Joubouline never finished the sentence.

Then Joubouline picked up a new trick. He had brought a bottle with him when the sled first dropped him off, just like the bottle in the back of Chavez's locker. By the end of the day Chavez beat him up, it was empty.

The next sled to come in dropped off a case. Whiskey fetched more than forty marks a liter back in depot. A case lasted Joubouline two weeks—in the beginning—a two hundred and forty mark a week habit. But he improved. After a month he could knock a case off in a week flat.

At first Chavez tried to talk to him about it, tried to point out that at a thousand marks a month he was putting himself so deep in the hole that he would never get off Trollshulm. Of course, there was no reasoning with a serious drunk. He knew what his money situation was: He kept track of it with all the diligence of a wino hoarding up his loose change for a pint. He knew what he was doing, goddamnit, so just leave him the hell alone.

Chavez would have been happy to, but in a one-room hut in the middle of a desert that wasn't easy. The hut quickly took on the sickening smell of drunkard's sweat, a stink bad enough to have forced Chavez off the bottle for weeks at a time on those occasions when his own drinking had built up to the point where he could manage that choice exudation himself, back in Stonetown. He took to leaving the hut door open at night, even to physically pitching Joubouline out onto the sand when the odor became intolerable.

If there was any positive aspect to trying to live with a drunken Duncan Joubouline, it was that between watching him get drunk and the increasing price of whiskey relative to his wallet, Chavez was drying up in the best behaviorist fashion. It didn't seem fair, though, to kick the habit just to have its most distasteful aspects imposed on him from the outside. But Joubouline was right; requests for new partners weren't even being answered. So all Chavez could do was endure it, blowing up uselessly whenever Joubouline grated on him particularly badly. For the rest of the time, he lapsed into a sullen, self-contained silence that expanded until it seemed to be the dominant facet of his character and his world. But this time he saw it happening, and welcomed it for the wall it built around him.

He was going to make it, Protherall realized.

Northwest Passage was centered cleanly on his screens. The equilateral triangle that he once could have formed between the starliner, *Flute*, and *Vigilant* had stretched and distorted into a right triangle whose base lengthened with every passing kilometer. His initial velocity advantage had been enough after all. The revenue cutter had been unable to beat his unballasted acceleration, and he had drawn farther and farther ahead of them until now they were conceding defeat, initiating their turnover and braking maneuvers to get back on station. There was no way they could reach him before he passed the nav-beacons marking the limits of Hansen System space, and once he passed those, no colony law could touch him.

The speakers on his boards crackled with the warning hiss of an incoming message.

"*Flute*, this is *Vigilant*. Please respond."

He couldn't resist. "*Flute* to *Vigilant*. Packing it in, constable?"

"Making an appeal to reason, *Flute*. We're trying to save your life."

"So am I," Protherall said.

"You've picked a damn funny way to do it, Captain. Are you aware of the thrust vector you've picked up?"

"Somewhat larger than yours, I believe."

"That's right. And now you've got to shed it before you can dock with *Northwest Passage*. You'll never do it, Captain. You're flying a structurally defective ship. You try to pile on the deceleration you'll need to make rendezvous and she'll come apart around you."

"I don't think so."

"This isn't a contest of opinions, Protherall! We've seen the plates they shot of your hull. It's a miracle you haven't come apart before now."

"There's nothing miraculous about it. This is a good ship. But then you might have heard that already."

"Captain, please. We don't want to see anybody dead."

"*Flute*, this is *Northwest Passage*." A new voice came on. "Are we hearing this correctly? If you are in difficulty, please stand clear of our ship."

"*Northwest Passage*, this is *Flute*. My difficulties are purely political and I've just about outrun them," Protherall answered. "I would like to begin negotiation for passage outward."

"We've got the space, *Flute*, if you can make it this far."

"I'll be there," Protherall said. "Sorry, *Vigilant*, but I just can't pass up such a polite invitation."

The voice that came back from his speakers had the resigned tone of someone who has realized a terrible mistake is about to be made, and is helpless to stop it. "Right, *Flute*, good luck. One last piece of advice. If you possibly can, keep your deceleration vector down below point three seven gees."

The irregular precision of the number caught at Protherall's attention. It was either sincere advice or a nice, authentic touch of misdirection. He called up the turnover and braking equations, and plugged that factor in. It worked; it would let him reach *Northwest Passage* without overshooting, but it would have to be implemented quickly.

He set the braking software up on the board and confirmed a course correction for his rendezvous with the starliner. Then he slaved the drives to the software and gave the ship her head.

The vibration began almost at once, slowly but building quickly to match anything he'd felt on the outbound leg. The groaning went on and on, as the vanes dug in against the magnetic lines of force in the system and sought to check *Flute*'s headlong flight. It showed no sign of letting up, no sign that the spars were reaching new and harmonious alignment as they had after previous applications of thrust. But the boards were still green and his screen showed velocity coming off as nicely as one could ask. Protherall sat back, allowing himself to relax. Once the deceleration was complete it would be nothing but a slow, easy coast up to the waiting starliner and freedom—

He had time perhaps to raise an eyebrow at the percussive sound of a structural member shearing before he died. The girder broke across cleanly, supported only briefly by the flawed sistering beam the yard had welded into place. The girder was one of the set that made up the crucial box section amidships that braced the hinges and servomotors for the long magnetic vanes. As the box section twisted under the sudden failure one of the vanes flexed out of position with power still on. More girders flexed and yielded; the vanes had no support now at all, and tore away wildly. Hull integrity vanished instantly as the girders sprung plates. Bulkheads tried to close but their frames, distorted by the twisted hull around them, would not seal, and *Flute* was wreathed in a white mist of air and water vapor as she tumbled wildly out of control.

And the magnetic drives, their insulation ruptured, poured out a wash of killing electromagnetic radiation uncontrolled by the directing grids lethal as the most potent maser. Protherall scarcely had time to realize the ruin he had made of his ship before it killed him.

The broken-backed hulk of *Flute* missed the waiting starliner by more than fifty kilometers, still following the cautious, deceptive bearing *Northwest Passage* had given her.

"Cut the hide prices by half," Santer said. "Again."

Shasti Keane stared at him in disbelief. "How in the world am I supposed to do that, Eli?"

"The way you did it last time. When they bring in hides, you pay them less. That seems easy enough."

"The last time, that still left them something. This won't leave them anything at all."

"It leaves them with food in their bellies."

"And no way to pay for it."

"Then let them have some more credit, and pile up some more of that fancy debt you keep telling me is almost as good as money. They're lucky I can still afford to pay them that."

"I don't think it will work a third time."

"Make it work. This is the way it's going to be."

"There's a limit to what the skinners will stand for."

"Is there? Then maybe they'd better start worrying about my limits. Because I've reached them. I've given up everything I'm going to give, to them or anybody. I've got people telling me I'm running out of money, I've got people telling me I'm running out of choices, and I'm telling you I'm running out of patience. Cut the price, cut it by half, and do whatever you have to do to make it work!"

"The skinners—"

"The hell with the skinners!" Santer shouted. "I don't owe them anything more than I've already given them! Hell, I don't even owe them *that*! The only reason they're here is because they can't hack it anyplace else! I'm not going to jeopardize everything my family's ever worked for just to win their approval—or yours. They work for me, lady. You work for me. And that means you're going to do this because I want it done!" He drew a breath, forcing calm. "I'm running out of room. This isn't a question of a quarter's profit anymore. It's a question of keeping my world. There's nothing I'll put above that. Nothing."

He left her then, in the suddenly quiet dome, among all the racks of goods she'd been instructed to sell to people who couldn't afford to buy them.

This was going to be brutal. The one thing that made Trollshulm tolerable to every indentured worker on the planet was the prospect of working their way clear and leaving, however unlikely that was. It was something to cling to, a lie to tell each other and themselves over glasses of overpriced liquor whose cost trapped them there that much longer. Now they wouldn't even have that, as they watched the debt they had to incur for the basic staples of life they had to buy mount higher and higher, every mark of it a boulder on their shoulders, pinning them to the sands of Santer's world forever. She wasn't ready to be a witness to that. And she was scared witless of having to live through it.

Eli Santer had told her what he wanted done, and she would do it. But she would have to do something more, as well—if there was anything to be done at all. . . .

The night wind softly rattled the panels of the commissary geodesic as Shasti Keane sat in front of her screen, unaware of the time, conscious only of the persistent, unacceptable answer the idiot machine insisted on presenting her.

"I hope you're putting the company's equipment to good use at such a late hour, Miss Keane." Shasti started and spun in her seat at the sound of Adrienne's voice behind her. The older woman stood between the stacked shelves that opened onto Shasti's private corner, half-hidden in shadow, lit only by the back glow from Shasti's desk lamp and terminal.

"Oh. Good evening, madame. I didn't hear you come in." She turned back to stare at her unhelpful terminal again. "It's company use, yes, but I'm afraid it hasn't been a good use at that, no."

"What were you working on?"

"Just a rather annoying accounting problem—"

"Miss Keane. I may have to tolerate my cousin trying to put me off, but I really don't have to take it from an employee."

"No, I don't suppose you do. Excuse me." Shasti sighed. "I'm trying to find some way not to have to implement the hide-price cut Eli's ordered."

"I see. Have you had any luck?"

"I'm afraid not. We truly don't seem to have the money to get by without it. Not in the Trollshulm accounts, anyway, and they're all I can access."

"That's too bad." Adrienne moved forward to look down at the screen over Shasti's head. Shasti felt her presence at her back uncomfortably. Adrienne was a Santer all right, she thought: She had Eli's knack for crowding right in on a person's guard without ever consciously realizing she was doing it.

"Has Eli asked you to do this?" she asked.

"No," Shasti said. "No, this was my idea, for all the good it's done."

"Then why should you bother yourself? Your employment isn't dependent on the price you pay the skinners, is it?"

"No, I suppose not."

"Then why go to all this trouble?"

"Because I really don't want this price cut to go through."

"Why not?" Adrienne asked. "Eli wants it."

"Yes, Eli wants it," Shasti said. "But Eli isn't the one who has to tell the skinners. That's my job. Eli can set the price for hide as low as he likes. He doesn't have to watch their faces when they hear it."

"And that bothers you?"

"Yes. Yes, much to my surprise, it does bother me. Look, ninety-five percent of the skinners are indentureds from the labor pool. They're here because they were sent here, not because they want to be, and even at the normal hide price it takes them a bloody long time to buy their way free again. Some of them never do. But I could work in a situation like that, because that's the way things are, and that's how they would be whether I was here or not. But these price cuts—*I have to do that*. I have to make things worse for these people."

"You don't make those decisions."

"I make the announcements. I make it real for them. And I hate it. I hate feeling as though I'm using these people."

"That's a peculiar sentiment for someone in your position."

"I thought so too, at first," Shasti said, "when I was still trying to talk myself out of it and just get on with my job. But it isn't, really. My arrangement with Eli is my arrangement. I made it, for me. I don't think I could make it for somebody else, though." She laughed, ruefully. "I'll whore willingly enough, but I make a lousy pimp. And that's what this feels like. I don't know. I guess I just lack your proper First Wave assertiveness."

"I suppose you do," Adrienne said. "Excuse me."

She leaned down past Shasti and reached out to the terminal. Words and numbers printed out as she typed.

"What are those?"

"Access codes to our main accounts in Hansen's Landing."

"What am I supposed to do with those."

"I should have thought that was obvious. Keep looking."

"That's what I thought you were going to say. But I damned well had to hear it first. Why are you doing this?"

"Because you aren't the only one who's unhappy with the way Eli Santer is handling our problems. And because you're a latecomer, like Tovas."

"Like Tovas," Shasti repeated, uncomprehending.

"If Eli Santer can use latecomers against his own blood, I don't see why I can't return that favor."

16

Rodinov was scared, Tovas thought. Protherall's death had shaken him badly, or he would never have agreed to see Tovas at his home again. Well, Tovas would just have to frighten him some more. It was time to redefine their relationship one more time.

The compradore of TerraCo stood waiting for him by the waterfall. "So you've heard."

"No one who owns a screen insystem hasn't," Tovas said.

"No, I expect you're right. Damn the man! Damn him! Do you know what this does to us?"

"To you, certainly. You are in very serious trouble, I should think."

The glare Rodinov turned on him would have withered thorns.

"You should think. Yes, you very well should think. Here I am, with millions of standards' worth of land purchased for a pilot plant and a design for the plant itself approved, even some of the construction contracts let—and that infernal man goes and kills himself before I have a chance to extend my option on the merchandise. Do you know what kind of position this puts me in?"

"As a matter of fact, I do," Tovas said. "One where you need me again."

"Where I need you?" Rodinov laughed. "What I need, latecomer, is funds. Funds that will give me half a chance at purchasing the rest of the rights to the synthetic when the colony puts Protherall's estate up for sale. That's what I need. Can you give me that?"

"After a fashion," said Lakim Tovas.

It was gratifying to see how eagerly Rodinov stalked

toward him, to see the hope he tried to suppress behind his eyes.

"What does that mean?" Rodinov demanded. "Explain yourself."

"What it means, Mister Rodinov, is that I took our last talk very much to heart. You were quite right, you know. All that I am, I do owe to Eli Santer's wealth. So I decided to take advantage of that.

"I went shopping, Mister Rodinov. You see, it occurred to me that the more I spent on pharmaceuticals, the lower I could drive the value of the stocks you held . . . if I so chose."

"You little swine."

"Little but necessary, sir. At least to you. Because any time I choose, I can now cost you millions. And your future is already doubtful—if you lose the synthetic. You might have survived never getting involved with it; and you might yet survive paying an enormous price for it. But you cannot survive paying an enormous price for it and then losing it, on top of a catastrophic misinvestment in another market. I can at least prevent that second disaster—or bring it on. It's really up to you."

"What do you want?" Rodinov asked hoarsely.

"What I always wanted. Santer Holdings as part of TerraCo, myself in a position of power—my own power—in Santer Holdings, and a partner I can trust behind my back. I've got that now, at least."

"Yes. Just as if you planned it that way."

"Very nearly." Tovas shrugged. "Of course, we never planned for Protherall to actually try to fly his ship once the faulty structural members had been detected, but I don't think Eli will complain. And it certainly does me no harm. But the important thing now is to make sure that I do you no unnecessary harm either, Mister Rodinov, and I believe I have outlined the terms under which I can guarantee that to your satisfaction."

"Perfectly."

"Very good. Good day, sir."

* * *

"That's it," Hans Joseph Klepper announced. "I'm leaving."

The small bar off Mariner's Hall was open only to masters and their crews. Klepper was at the center of the crowd gathered at the bar—a long section of old magnetic vane set in plastic and fed just enough of a charge to suspend it above the floor.

"Where for?" Moses asked.

"Anywhere outbound," Klepper said. "Anyplace that hasn't had time to get as fat and greedy as these bastards. Anyplace where a First Waver is still somebody plowing a field."

"You'll lock on with *Northwest Passage*, then?"

"As soon as I can lift out."

"Ah, you're in that much of a rush, are you?" Moses said. He shook his head. "I'll miss you."

"Don't miss me, youngster. Follow me. There's nothing for any of us here, anymore."

Moses stared down into his glass, divining a world in which he was paid not to fly, where no one needed him or his ship except as a convenience.

"I'm thinking you may be right. . . ."

Eli Santer stared at the data plac uncomprehendingly. "What is this?" he asked.

"That's your last chance, Eli." Adrienne Santer stepped up onto Santer's podium and moved beside his desk.

"How do you mean?"

"That's a notarized, signed and sealed statement by Thomas and Martin, putting and seconding the motion that you be deposed by majority vote of the family stockholders, and myself installed as new chairman and president of Santer Holdings."

"My God," Santer said. "So you finally worked up the courage between you, did you? I wouldn't have thought they had it in them."

"What did you expect, Eli? You drove Thomas to it; *you* grounded his ship. Did you expect him to take that lying down?"

"With you around? I shouldn't have," Santer admitted.
"How did you rope Martin into this?"

"Martin's very rightly concerned, Eli, that once you've
finished gutting the day-to-day operations of the company,
you'll start in on the long-term programs next. He's
protecting his dragons."

"Of course. And you're helping him. Well, fine, then,"
Eli said grimly. "If you want this fight now, let's have this
fight now. When do you want to convene the family for the
vote?"

"When? I don't want to convene the family at all, Eli—at
least not just now."

"Why not? Don't you think you've got a chance, even
with Thomas and Martin?"

"A chance?" Adrienne laughed grimly. "Eli, with the
exception of the four of us, every voting member of the
family is a skinner. How do you think they feel about you
right now? You certainly haven't got their support, and
their shares added to Thomas's and Martin's at least cancel
out yours and dear Trebig's. So, it seems to me, the
deciding vote is mine."

"If that's so, and you want the job so badly, why don't you
just take it?" Santer asked.

"Because I *don't* want it, Eli. Not just yet. All I'd be
taking over right now would be your problems, and I prefer
to let you bear the burden of solving them."

"And if I do?"

"If you do—" Adrienne shrugged. "Then that plac is
worthless and I'm back where I started. But if you don't"—
and she leaned down over his desk—"or if I decide your
solution is liable to do us more harm than good, then you're
finished, Eli. I'll break you so completely that I swear the
family will never even remember you existed."

She straightened, and stepped down off the platform and
walked toward the door.

"You're out of running room, Eli. You only get one more
mistake."

"What the hell do you *mean*, six hundred marks?"
Joubouline squealed. "We're bringing you six prime hides!

Are you trying to tell me you're paying a lousy hundred marks a hide for prime?"

"That's the new rate," Shasti said.

"Well, to hell with that! I won't take it! *We* won't take it! We're not going to take it, are we, Chavez?"

"I don't see anyone else making us an offer," Chavez said.

"There, you see? He understands," Shasti said. "Look, Duncan, we can't pay you with money we haven't got. It's a bad deal, I know; but if you're tight we can open up a line of credit for you. No interest until the prices go back up."

This time it wasn't working. Duncan Joubouline had just had his whiskey economy shot to hell, and he couldn't see beyond that. He turned from the counter and practically ran from the accounts office. Chavez sighed and signed over the hides.

Since he couldn't afford to drink anymore, the first thing Joubouline did was rush to the canteen and buy a bottle. Chavez caught up with him there.

He had settled into a steady rhythm by the time Chavez came in, tossing off shots of whiskey and muttering "goddamn it, goddamn it, it isn't fair, goddamn it," while he refilled.

"Well, that's sure going to help," Chavez said. He was past making allowances for Joubouline's failings.

"Oh, ain't nothing going to help," Joubouline said. "They got us right where they want us. We gotta take what they feel like giving us, that's how they figure; and *if* they ever decide to raise the price again, we'll be so far in the hole we ain't never gonna get off this mudball."

"So buying that dishwater won't help."

"At this point, friend, it can't hurt."

Chavez had made his token effort at reformation; his conscience was clear. He turned away from Joubouline and nursed his own beer.

He was brought out of his reverie by a blurred afterimpression of sudden movement at his side and the sound of breaking glass as Joubouline smashed the empty bottle against the back of the bar.

"Goddamn it, it ain't fair!" he screamed, and bolted from the canteen. There was an embarrassed silence as the few occupants of the canteen stared at the bits of broken glass on the shelf.

Then they heard the shots.

Everyone rushed outside. The scene was surprisingly normal. There was no panic; there hadn't been time. No one was sure yet which direction to panic in. Everyone in sight around the depot was frozen where they stood: a cluster of skinners where they had been talking by the trac-train loading dock, looking around themselves, another crouched immobile over the bundled hide he'd just wrestled off his trac, still gripping the baling hooks thrust through the cording. Then came the tearing-canvas sound of high-cyclic automatic weapons fire, and the street cleared in a mad scramble of bodies. Sprawled in the doorway of the canteen, Chavez then saw the crumpled bodies of two men before the sliver-ripped door of the accounts office and one of Santer's private guards slumped against the wall of the commissary, staring at the bloody mess Joubouline's skinning knife had made of his gut. Then the gun fired again and Chavez rolled to safety as slivers gouged the permaplast above his head.

The siege of Duncan Joubouline was three hours old.

As sieges went, it worked both ways. Of course, Eli Santer's pack of headhunters had swiftly ringed in the commissary, but even so, the knowledge that Joubouline had several windows and a Kalashnikov-Kern with a full, thousand-sliver drum magazine kept most people from going about their business unless they could do it under solid cover.

The two bodies in front of the accounts office had been removed. The headhunter sprawled by the commissary door had been left there and had finally died about an hour after his stabbing. The headhunters held that job because they had proven more adept at killing men than dragons; that was not the qualification that spawned the sort of camaraderie that would lead one headhunter to risk himself for another in a situation like that, in spite of the fact that Joubouline had called out to them several times and told them that they could pick the man up safely.

The headhunters didn't really know how to handle this situation. At first, when Joubouline was still firing, still working on his booze-fueled rage, the appropriate response seemed simple: grab a corner or a trac fender to hide behind and shoot back. That had stopped when Anders Trebig, the headhunter captain, had realized that most of the stuff in the building they were blowing the hell out of, up to and including Shasti Keane, was Eli Santer's property. Then they had tried saturating the building with bass stunner fire, again until Trebig compared the expense of that tactic in exhausted enerpacs with the probable results through a layer of permaplast. So the salvo was reduced to an occasional potshot or three.

Then somebody had struck upon the bright idea of sending in Chavez. After all, he was the man's partner; he should be able to talk him into surrendering. And if he couldn't, well, that was one less stomach on the budget. Eli Santer was fast reaching the point where that was a valid consideration.

It was an awful long walk across the empty street between the massed guns of the headhunters on the one hand and Joubouline's uncertain reception on the other. Chavez halted ten feet from the door to the commissary.

"Joubouline? Duncan? It's me, Blackstone," he called out. He flinched as a bass stunner's fringe effect brushed him and the wall of the commissary shook under the impact, and braced for the shock of a sliver-burst in return. When it didn't come, he turned and bestowed a vicious glare on the assembled headhunters. One of them offered him an upthrust finger in reply. Chavez shook his head and looked back at the commissary.

"Duncan? I'm gonna come in. I'm not carrying." He had no rifle. He pulled his knife from its scabbard and laid it down carefully on the ground, then opened his shirt to show that nothing was concealed there. "I'm clean, I'm coming in, all right? Duncan?"

There was no answer. Chavez waited. So did Joubouline, apparently. Chavez turned and looked back at the headhunters' positions again. He could see Anders Trebig and a new face, Santer himself, watching him impassively. He shook his head and started forward.

Duncan Joubouline was leaning against one wall as Chavez entered. He didn't look at him. Broad patches on every wall that opposed a window had been chewed up by sliver-fire; and one shelf had been shot to scrap, its contents, some kind of canned foods, dripping stickily down the wall.

Shasti Keane was sitting huddled in a corner, knees drawn up. There was a triple-thud as another volley of stunner fire struck the walls. It wasn't so bad through the permaplast, not more than twice as painful as sticking your head inside a bass drum, but Shasti curled in on herself as though she'd been electrically shocked and the muzzle of Joubouline's rifle swung through a foot-long arc. As she straightened up she mumbled something foul in fluent Pushti.

Joubouline was no longer drunk, at least not violently so. The flesh seemed to hang slack on his face, as though the task of maintaining any expression wasn't worth the effort to him any longer. His eyes were bleak, haunted by a fatal certainty.

Chavez looked at him, and had no idea what to say, at first. He felt terribly clumsy and conspicuous standing there in the doorway, so he moved inside and out of sight of the waiting headhunters and, parenthetically, out of the line of fire.

Joubouline did him a favor and broke the silence first. "Well," he said. It was a sentence in itself. "I guess we've got us a problem here."

Chavez repressed the urge to say that *he* didn't. "Yeah. I guess so."

"Yeah. I suppose they sent you in here to talk me into surrendering."

Chavez suddenly felt sick at what he was being asked to do. "Yeah, but that's crap and we both know it. Man, you crossed Eli Santer; you caused him trouble. You can stay in here, or you can come out with me; either way you're dead. He won't let you get away with this."

"No, I didn't really think he would. I *had* to do it, though," he said. "I had to, Chavez. Them robbing us like that; I never would have caught up again, you know? I'd never have gotten home. And now I'm stuck in here." He smiled, as much as he could without moving his face. "I'm always stuck somewhere."

A sudden wave of identification washed over Chavez. He couldn't see Duncan Joubouline anymore; he didn't see him leaning wearily against the wall there. He saw himself, Chavez Blackstone, and he knew he was seeing truly. Maybe not very soon, maybe not that year, or the next, or the next after that, but he would be there, with the same slack, beaten expression, destroyed as utterly as the little man in front of him by his complacent acceptance of his domination by others out to further their own ends regardless of what happened to him.

He would not let that happen. But in the meantime there was something he had to do, the only thing he'd really hoped to do when he entered the commissary.

"You're dead, man," he said, and if it was possible to say something like that sympathetically, that was how he said it. "But there's no reason to get us killed with you. At least let the girl and me out of here before they come in after you."

"All right." It clearly made no difference one way or the other to him.

Chavez helped Shasti to her feet and moved toward the door. He cautiously extended one arm into the opening and waved, calling out—

—before he finished the first word his arm was thrown violently back at him, numbed by the first shot in the thundering volley of bass stunner fire that seemed as though it would jolt the building right off its foundations. As he threw himself down, dragging Shasti with him, he could make out the thin, whistling sound of high-velocity slivers threaded through the basso detonations that shook the air. The room filled with a powdery cloud of shattered perma-plast. He looked up and saw Joubouline thrown against the wall by the impact of a sliver-burst.

Duncan was still on his feet when the first of the massed headhunters burst into the room, his shoulder ruined and dripping blood, staring stupidly at the rifle he still gripped by the barrel. Evidently that was a threatening-enough gesture; the lead headhunter shot him again point-blank through the chest.

Then the room was full of headhunters, crowding them

so closely that they couldn't stand up, so eager to make sure
that they were all right that none of them noticed that they
kept stepping on Chavez's numbed arm.

Santer and Trebig watched dispassionately as Duncan
Joubouline was carried from the commissary. Chavez and
Shasti followed the headhunters carrying the body.

There was an odd light in Shasti's eyes, a strange
expression on her face that couldn't entirely be explained
by the prolonged stunner bombardment. Or perhaps it
could, at that.

Santer looked down at her and grinned as she walked up
to him. The grin went away but the teeth stayed very much
in evidence as she snapped her foot straight between his
legs. Trebig grabbed belatedly for her arms as Santer folded
and she went for his eyes.

Chavez felt a prickling on the back of his neck, like you
would feel in the air just before a thunderstorm on a humid
day. He looked up to see the pregnant knitting-needle
shape of the *Irish Missed* drifting down out of the sky on
magentic drive.

He looked back just in time to see Shasti's head snap back
under the back-hand follow-up to Santer's first slap. Then
his own anger and leftover fear found a focus and he was
charging forward.

He hit Santer somewhere in the chest, carrying him clear
of the circle of headhunters with the force of his attack. He
hit Santer once, the shock of the impact running straight up
his arm, and had actually drawn his fist back for a second
blow by the time the headhunters piled on top of him and
brought him down. The last thing he remembered seeing
was Eli Santer's boot descending toward his face with
regrettable finality.

Eli Santer had found something that puzzled him.

He could understand being attacked by TerraCo. He
could understand skinners who ran amok, driven by their
own frustration and weakness to suicidal violence. He
understood a world so unremittingly harsh that it took all a
man's strength and will to survive there.

But he could not understand being attacked by Shasti Keane at all, and said so.

"I know you don't. That's the part of this that outrages me the most. You bastards were shooting at me!"

"There was an armed lunatic in there. He was killing people."

"I was in there!"

"We had to do it. I had to do it. I couldn't let him get away with that."

"No, you couldn't, could you? Nobody ever gets away with anything on Eli Santer," Shasti said. "And you don't care what you have to do to keep it that way, do you? You killed him, you would have killed Blackstone, you would have killed me, wouldn't you? And it wouldn't have mattered. You'd have used or sacrificed anybody to get Joubouline. And I'm not prepared to be used."

"This is a new objection," Santer said. "You've never complained about being used when it got you a nice easy inside job that kept you off the sands."

"No, I didn't," Shasti admitted. "But being used never almost got me killed before. And even if that wouldn't change my mind, I've never had to help you use people the way you're using them now. You've cut the prices so low these people can't even pretend they're working their way out of the pool anymore. How long do you think it's going to be before you've got a whole desert full of Duncan Jouboulines out there?"

"That'll never happen. This place isn't that hard. I grew up in it, doing everything they do—"

"And look what it's done to you. Look what it's done to me. I went along with you. All this time, I've helped you use these people and used you and let you use me because it got me something I wanted. . . . I've become too much like you, Eli. This world has made me too much like you; you've made me too much like you. It's time I stopped."

"You'll stop all right. If you're all of a sudden too moral to use people I'll be happy to send you someplace where there's no one around to use."

Shasti shrugged. "I know you will. I've given the speeches often enough. I should be able to survive."

"Well, you'll get the chance." Santer's frustration boiled

over. "Damn it, you knew what you were doing. It was a fair exchange."

"Yes," Shasti said. "And that's all it was. Nothing left on either side. I don't want that anymore."

"Then don't expect me to offer it. Because you're right. I'll give up everything and everybody to keep this world my own."

"If that's what you want," Shasti answered him. "I'm sorry it's too late for that, though."

"What do you mean?"

"You aren't going to win, Eli."

"The hell I won't—"

"*You've lost already.*"

"What are you talking about?"

"When you came to me this last time, and told me to cut the hide prices by half," Shasti said, "I didn't want to do it. I patched in a satellite relay to our main files in Hansen's Landing. I was trying to find some way to keep from having to cut the price to the skinners. I thought maybe if I could find some savings that would have been made somewhere else, you'd lessen the cut." She looked at him. "I was lying to myself, of course. You'd have taken whatever I found and still ordered the cut."

"What else did you think I'd do?" Santer asked. "You know me."

"Oh, yes."

"Besides, you'd never have broken our security programs."

"I know. I was reaching. And I couldn't break them. But I did find something."

"What?"

"It was in a general work file. I guess someone stored it there temporarily and forgot about it. It would have been erased eventually. I just got to it before someone decided to dump the file."

"What did you find?"

"A thirty thousand standard pharmaceuticals purchase."

"So what? Believe me, I know we've bought too damned much pharmaceuticals—"

"You don't understand. The buy was made with your money, Eli, but it wasn't made in your name."

"Tovas has been making joint buys. On my orders."

"I checked this one. I tried to inquire about buying pharmaceuticals from the company named. They claim they're one of the few companies who've bought no pharmaceuticals at all."

"They lied."

"Why?" Santer had no answer. "That thirty thousand was all I could find, Eli. I couldn't access the rest of the system. But go ahead, save your hundred marks a skin, pile up those standards. Because somebody down there is spending them faster than you can ever hope to make them up. I'll go draw my leathers now."

"Wait a minute," Santer said. "You can't just leave it like that."

"Yes I can." She didn't look back. "I've got no use for this."

The depot didn't have a jail. There had never been need for one. There was little enough to steal on Trollshulm and nowhere to run with it, certainly nowhere to hide. If a skinner got too disorderly, he was simply pacified with a gunbutt or bass stunner and dropped back at his camp on the next sled out.

They had thrown Chavez into a disused storage hut, for safekeeping until it was decided what, if any, special treatment Santer would call for. That was where Moses found him.

He pulled the door ajar to the limit of the chain securing it.

"Ah, there you are. Come to your just deserts at last, are you?"

Chavez tried to grin. But his face had to move for that and his face hurt too much for movement. "It seems that way."

"Well, it's lucky for you that Santer Holdings boasts an enlightened penal system," Moses said. "Come on, I'll stand you to a little moral reinforcement over to the canteen."

"I'd like to take you up on that, Moses. But I have sort of a prior engagement here."

"So I can see. But there are exceptions to every rule." Moses hauled back on the door and the chain slid free as it opened, to show the unlocked padlock dangling from its end.

"I'm in a position of rare privilege these days," Moses told him. "If they want their dinner, they have to be nice to me. Come along."

The prevailing mood in the canteen was dry and depressed. Several of the skinners sitting about cast frankly envious looks at Moses as he brought the bottle back to the table where O'Shaunessy and Chavez waited.

"I'll tell you now," he said, setting the bottle down, "when I saw you in there, Chavez, I thought his highness the premier had caught up with you at last."

"Not quite," Chavez said. "Although he's all I need to make this place perfect."

"This is the second time you've brought that up," O'Shaunessy said. "Whatever are you talking about?"

"Ah." Moses shrugged. "It's Chavez's past indiscretion, isn't it. It's up to him to do the telling."

"Is that so," Chavez said. "Well, as you can see, I haven't learned much since I came out this way. But I've learned enough to let past indiscretions remain discreet, thank you. My present ones are trouble enough."

"Isn't that the truth, now?"

"And aren't the both of you doing this just to frustrate me?" O'Shaunessy complained.

"So frustrate him back," Chavez suggested.

"Thank you for that," Moses grumbled. "She's liable to do it. This whole bloody system is falling apart. Promising young ship captains not getting the respect they deserve, bastards like this Santer press-ganging honest folk right and left and the government going right along with it, mind you; it's getting to the point where a man can't even hold on to what's his anymore."

"Yeah, well, there's a lot of that going around, Cap'n."

"Don't I know it. Why on my last run from Hansenwald, some swine of a customs officer demanded a bribe to clear my hold invoices! Demanded! The sonofabitch didn't even wait for me to offer it."

Chavez nodded. "It's definitely time to be moving on, I think. Those of us who can."

"Sure and it is, but how are we to do it? You can't get out of here until you've credit to your name again, and that's never going to happen, the way things are now. And I'll never make a stake for speculation on Council contract work, even if the Council doesn't go after the *Missed* the way they went after Protherall."

"Is that a possibility?"

"Once *Northwest Passage* heads outsystem, there won't be much else to choose from. Honest men such as ourselves can't win, my friend."

Chavez thought about that for a moment. "No, they can't at that, can they?" He drained his beer. "On the other hand, Cap'n. . . ."

17

Dragonleathers didn't suit Shasti Keane.

She seemed lost inside the bulk of the heavy garments, even though they were the smallest size stocked. She toiled up and down the dune faces with the strenuous effort born of inexperience, and she clutched at her rifle as though she expected dragons to come leaping out at her from all sides.

But when her first dragon did rear up and charge, she leveled her gun muzzle and knocked it down before the beast took three steps.

Later, she would claim that she didn't remember firing.

"That's all right," Chavez assured her. "At least if you panic, you panic pointed in the right direction."

Shasti proved to be quite a good dragonskinner. She was careful about choosing her positions and placing her shots, but not so cautious that she wouldn't hold her place and fire until she dropped her kill. And in the skinning-out itself she excelled. She would wade—literally—right in, working the heavy knife and muttering to herself in a steady monologue of Pushti, with an occasional Anglic "sonofabitch" thrown in. Chavez doubted that her mind was entirely on her work.

They were escaping. Gradually.

For every two hides they turned in at depot, they had another buried in a cache at their camp. Into other hiding-places went the stray slivers they hoarded from depleted magazines, the canned and concentrated foods they stashed away a can or a packet at a time. But perhaps their most important resource wasn't one that could be so easily concealed, but only contained. It was anger, anger reserved for Eli Santer, for getting them shot at and taking money from their pockets to pay his own bills, anger that fueled their plans for burning him right where he'd feel it most.

Right in the wallet.

It was the first time in years that Lakim Tovas had not known what was going on.

The two *Abilene* crewmen had appeared in Santer Holding's Hansen's Landing offices without any warning. Tovas hadn't even known the freighter was back in service, much less making runs back to Wolkenheim. It was a decision by Eli Santer that Tovas hadn't known about—worse, that he hadn't made for him. Tovas' plans were still too vulnerable to such unplanned factors for Tovas' comfort . . . particularly when they invited him aboard *Abilene*. That should have been the captain's responsibility, when dealing with a senior official of the firm that employed him, and he should have conveyed the invitation personally. But something in the bearing of the two crewmen suggested that if he didn't accompany them on his own two feet, he could expect to be dragged.

But what Tovas hadn't expected was Eli Santer aboard the *Abilene*, millions of miles from the world he *never* left, his face like the unyielding stone of Trollshulm's mountains as he stood to tower over the latecomer Terran in the cramped wardroom.

"Where's my money, Lakim?" Santer asked, and the door slid shut behind Tovas like a falling ax blade as Santer came around the table.

Eli Santer stalked through the hologram pillars of the Warrens and the pale merchants infesting them like some great saurian predator returned to stride among his lizardly descendents, a hard thing of weathered skin and dragonhide among scuttling creatures of soft flesh and cloth. Nobody sought to hinder him as he sought out door thirty-seven and TerraCo's offices beyond it.

They tried to stop him there: The silent Klaus appeared

the minute he stepped into the receptionist's anteroom.
Santer sized him up and dismissed him with a look—
muscle he bought and sold on his world for three meals and
a bottle. He looked back to the receptionist, who seemed to
be maintaining her composure solely by the thickness of
her cosmetics.

"Rodinov," Santer said.

"He's not—Mister Rodinov isn't in, today, Mister? . . ."

"You tell him Eli Santer is here, if he isn't listening
already. He can see me or not, but he'll know I'm here, one
way or another, soon enough. You go ahead."

"There's no need," Rodinov told her, as he came out of his
office. He looked over to Santer. "Eli."

"I know about Lakim Tovas," Santer said.

"I don't see what—"

"Shut up," Santer said, almost calmly. "Just listen. I know
about your deal. I know about the pharmaceuticals. So I
think it's only fair that you know what I'm going to do with
them."

Rodinov knew with sickening certainty what he would
hear next. It made an unflattering epitaph.

"Right now my brokers are unloading every ounce of
pharmaceuticals Tovas bought with my money onto the
market. At whatever price the buyers care to offer."

"My God," Rodinov said. "You'll crash the entire
market."

"Wrong," Santer said. "I'll crash your market here. Not
mine."

"You'll fall with us."

"No I won't. Because you know what I'm going to do with
the proceeds? I'm going to buy *food*. And then I'm going to
go back to my world and hunt dragons until *Natchez*
arrives. Then I'm going to sell my hides, and when the
colony starts taking offers on Protherall's synthetic I'm going
to bid on it and win. Because you people down here are
going to lose everything trying to cover your losses."

"So will you." Rodinov pressed on, emboldened by his
desperation. "You'll lose every asset you have on this
planet."

"And I'll still have the dragons. Who'll be able to afford to
take them from me? Who'll have the cash to pay for the

expensive lawyers and the years of litigation?" He pointed
out the door. "I could go back out there right now and *tell*
every one of my creditors that Santer Holdings will meet its
obligations when *Natchez* comes in, and they'll accept it
because they have to. Right about now Santer Holdings is
the economic power of the Hansen System, Rodinov. And
I'm going to use that power to make sure TerraCo knows
there's no place for it here—and who arranged it. You tried
to take my world from me. So now I take your markets from
you. And your future."

"You *can't*—"

"I already have." And Santer turned and went back out
onto the Warren floor amid the torrent of falling numbers
he had set in motion, lost within the panic he had created.

So much sand, Tovas thought dully.

Abilene was descending on Trollshulm, but it was no part
of the world Tovas had ever seen before.

The dunes stretched away unbroken to the very horizon,
nothing but sand reaching to embrace the sky in the
distance, half a world away from even the rough sustenance
of Santer's depot.

The ship touched belly to the sand with a gentle shudder,
most of its weight still borne by the charged vanes.

The airlock's inner hatch cycled once behind them as the
two crewmen left, unwanted witnesses. Now there was
only Tovas and Santer.

"You wanted my world so badly," Santer said, "I'll give it
to you, then."

The blow should not have been a surprise. But he still
felt a shock of astonishment as Santer struck him hard
between the shoulder blades and then he was falling down
the curving face of the hull. He landed heavily, wrenching
his back. Gasping with the pain, he rolled over to stare up
into the pitiless face of Eli Santer.

"It's yours now, Tovas," Santer called down, coldly. "Do
what you want with it."

Tovas tried to protest, to plead, but all that came out was
a keening moan of fear and pain. And as the ship rose up,

Tovas' cry lost in the humming of the vanes, he knew that those would not matter for long.

The *Irish Missed* rested in her cradle at Hansen's Landing, towering over the older, smaller ships, dwarfed in turn by the angular mass of *Albatross*. Moses Callahan sat deep in his couch in the crowded control deck, surrounded by his screens, which repeated in digest the information displayed on the panels around the bulkheads.

He touched the intercom stud. "Lady Macbeth, are you with me?"

"The name is O'Shaunessy, sir. I'll thank you to remember it." Maureen O'Shaunessy was probably the only person in the Hansen System who could *sound* redheaded, even over a tiny intercom.

"Listen, O'Shaunessy, ship's engineers are supposed to be Scottish. I'll not be breaking an honored tradition just for the sake of such as yourself, ma'am. Now by any chance might our drives be ready?"

"They're readier than you deserve."

"Now, how can that be? I deserve the best." Prudently, he switched off.

Moses threw several switches and murmured into the microphone hung in front of his face.

"All set, Captain," the answer came. "Control confirms your course and acknowledges ETA Trollshulm one four four hours Greenwich."

Well, it'll be a shame to disillusion them, but that'll do for now, Moses thought happily.

He pressed a final button and the atmospheric drive hummed into life. The *Irish Missed* twisted gently in her cradle, then began to rise gracefully as the drive gripped the magnetic flux lines of the planet and tried to push them away.

So slowly at first, and then faster and faster, she climbed away from the docks and groundside law. The scream of rushing air began to penetrate even the insulated control room, then just as quickly faded away as the *Missed* rose serenely above the complaining atmosphere.

"Legal distance," O'Shaunessy called out.

"Lady Macbeth, you can light your candle."

Pale fusion fire blossomed behind the *Missed* and she continued to accelerate at a constant one gravity.

"Moses, how long before *Natchez* reaches the earliest possible rendezvous point?"

"On our current timetable?" Buttons punched. "Nine days Greenwich."

"Very good, Captain Callahan. Steer on."

Moses grinned. "Aye aye, sir."

"It's been a disappointment," Shasti admitted.

They were sitting in their little plastic hut, nursing drinks poured from a bottle she had found in the bottom of Joubouline's locker. It was night; the only sounds were their voices and the muted buzzing of the generator outside. The single light-plate in the hut was never intended to provide full illumination, but it did cast a warm, rather subdued light, oddly well-suited to drinking and talk.

"I didn't exactly come here because I wanted to," Chavez was saying. "I mean, to the Hansen System."

"Then why did you?" Shasti asked.

"I guess you'd call it a labor dispute."

"A labor dispute that sends you clear into another solar system? What on earth"—she had the good grace to flinch at her own unintended double meaning—"did you do?"

"Actually, it's more what I didn't do, and who I didn't do it with."

"Oh?"

"I had me this job, hell of a good job. I was a third mate on a waterborne yacht for the chairman of the Greater Pacific Co-Prosperity Sphere."

"Sounds like fun."

"Oh, yeah. Good money, and I liked the traveling. All the way from the Indian Ocean to Hawaii. Working conditions weren't too bad, either. His Excellency Premier Ling Shen-Jo doesn't—didn't, I guess—believe in roughing it. Nothing but the best for old Ling. Unfortunately, that went for His Excellency's daughter, too. And she decided I qualified."

"How flattering of her."

"Flattering my ass—you should excuse the language." Chavez shook his head. "You know the Sphere mentality. Mao's thought welded to the best Tokyo hard charging. I could handle a Madame Butterfly, but the Gang of Four combined with a Manchurian tigress in heat was way out of my depth."

"Too much woman for you, hey?"

"Too much for me and any two relief gigolos of your choice, in any sense of the term. The lady was about half my height and twice my width. And she wasn't used to accepting rejection gracefully. I guess it runs in the family. By the time the captain got all the screaming stopped the two of them had me cornered right up in the bow, with boathooks."

"She had a friend?"

"She had a father."

"The Chairman of the Greater Pacific Co-Prosperity Sphere—"

"—was helping his buck-named blimp of a daughter chase a pantsless sailor around the deck with a pointy stick, right. For a great statesman, he sure as hell had the common touch. Anyway, between the captain and the shop steward, I survived long enough to get off the boat . . . but I figured it was time to go someplace where His Excellency wasn't likely to catch up with me."

"He certainly isn't liable to catch you here."

"Not unless they dig him up, no. I figure that was about fifty, maybe sixty years ago, objective time."

"Really? You certainly age gracefully. What's your secret?"

"Bad timing," Chavez said. "I came out on one of the first generation translight ships, back when they still had to run up to a pretty good fraction of lightspeed to build up enough phantom mass for the jump. Of course, by the time we got here, they'd refined the hardware, the colony was hip-deep in scruffy latecomers like me off the second-generation ships that got here before us, and the labor pool was in full swing." He shrugged. "Well, at least it solved my problem with His Excellency . . . just like *this* place solved my problem with Councilor Thorson."

"Do you make a habit of such drastic solutions?"

"Not if I can help it. Didn't somebody once say that history repeats itself, but the second time as farce? I think the joke is starting to wear a little thin, in my case. Not that I seem to have much to say about it. Her Excellency, Junior, got her glands fixated on me without my encouragement. They rebuilt the stardrive and set up the labor pools when I wasn't looking. Hell, seems like my whole life has been getting bent out of shape by things going on around me that I had nothing to do with."

"I didn't come out here on my own, you know," Shasti said. "I was sent. The government came to our village and told us that we'd have to contribute so many people to the colonization program if we were to qualify for any government assistance. So we did, and of course the little half-Anglo bitch got chosen to go along.

"So, we all wound up on Ramayana Three, and then the plague hit, and when it had run its course, the survivors were scattered all over colonized space. I wound up on Wolkenheim, looking for work; and I didn't find it in time, so I wound up here."

She paused to sip at her drink. She could be nearly as talkative as Joubouline had been sometimes, but Chavez found that it didn't bother him. She never talked to hear the sound of her own voice; if she said something it was because she needed to say it. And Chavez found that he wanted to listen.

"It's a disappointment, though," she finally said. "I always thought I was worth more than one-eighth of a tractor; I'd hoped my price would run a little higher out here. Guess it doesn't, though."

Not realizing what he was saying until he'd said it, Chavez said, "I guess that would depend on what the buyer thought he was buying, wouldn't it?"

Shasti looked at him. "Yes, I suppose it would, at that."

Chavez flushed. "Oh, hell," he said. He sprang to his feet and fled the hut, grabbing his rifle as he went through the door.

Baffled, Shasti got up and followed him.

He was sitting on a rock just inside the perimeter toxins. His weapon was broken open across his lap, and he was running a degaussing rod down the barrel.

"Chavez, what's the matter?"

He didn't look back at her. "What happened is Chavez Blackstone's just been an idiot again."

"How?"

"'That depends on what they thought they were buying.' That was a stupid damn thing to say. I lay out my whole sob story just like it matters and then I make a stupid joke like that about yours."

"That's just how you are," she said, smiling.

"Yes, it is. That's just how a dumb, beached, slum-dwelling ex-sailor is."

"Well, you don't sound like a dumb slum dweller."

"É, *puta*, you come talkin' down you throat at me, I say bang in your head. I don't talk like that because once you do, you start thinking like that. Then you're stuck for sure." He shook his head. "Not that my best effort is any improvement."

"At least it's an effort. That's something by itself. I can't remember the last time anybody felt obliged to make an effort around me." She moved around in front of him, kneeling to meet his lowered gaze. "How are we going to work this, Chavez?"

"How are we going to work what?"

"I've been here longer than you have, you know. And the one thing I've noticed is that every time we've paired up men and women skinners, they wind up bedmates." She looked around. "It's not as though there's much else to do out here, is there?"

"I guess not. How does that usually work out?"

"Some of them stay together. Some of them ask to be split up. Some of them try to kill each other. About the way it usually works out. But I want to be sure how it's going to be between us, before the situation arises."

Chavez slapped the degaussing rod back down the barrel. "You could have phrased that better."

"What do you mean?"

"Forget it. I guess they don't have double entendres in Pushti. You sound as though this is expected of us."

"It's the way it works."

"Maybe. But don't you get tired of behaving according to expectations all the time? I'd think you were a little tired of

acting as you were expected to. After all, that's how you
wound up out here."

"I've thought about that. And what I think is that doing
something just because it's against somebody's expectations
leaves them just as much power over you as going along
with them. If someone else's expectations dominate your
decisions, then the decisions aren't yours. You aren't
making choices, you're taking something offered to you. So
I'm not going to insist on celibacy, just because they don't
expect it. But if we do wind up sleeping together, it's going
to be because I want to, not because it fits in with someone
else's notions. Present company excepted, of course."

"Yes, I was going to say. A certain cooperation on my part
might be useful."

"I don't understand why you need all this explanation.
From what you've told me, it's never been necessary
before."

"I know, and look what's happened. I've been run off a
planet once, stuck in the labor pool the second time. If I
screw up again—excuse the expression—there's nothing
left but to feed me to the dragons."

"I'll keep it in mind."

The *Irish Missed* drove on toward the binary worlds
Trollshulm and Hansenwald, silent and graceful. Even
within her, the loudest sounds were the ventilation fans and
the muted burbling of the fusion flames in their magnetic
pinchbottles.

Moses Callahan was proud of his ship, in spite of her age.
All right, so perhaps fusion-and-magnetics hermaphrodites
were not very economical next to an agrav freighter, but she
was sound and faithful, and Moses wouldn't have traded her
sweet lines for one of those boxy newcomers if you'd
threatened to shoot the Pope-In-Absence. It was the same
feeling, he supposed, that the sail captains must have felt
while they were losing the seas to steam, or the dirigible
masters as they watched a clunky trimotor blunder past.

Progress was a spiteful mistress, however; and sooner or
later her more faithful suitors would emerge from their labs
and classrooms and factories to elbow Moses aside for her

affections once again. It was as good a time as any to be
moving outward, he decided, to another world where the
Missed would still be competitive.

By that time Trollshulm had grown to a distinct, brassy
sphere in their screens. Green Hansenwald could just be
seen as an emerald crescent beyond it.

"Come on up, Maureen," Moses said, "it's time to send
our message."

He picked up the slender cassette and slipped it into the
transmitter.

A recorded voice rasped out of the monitor, interlaced
with carefully added static:

"*Mayday, Mayday—IF Irish Missed, Mayday . . .
pinchbottle failure in starboard fusion unit . . . captain
injured and unconscious. Mayday, Mayday. . . .*"

There was a lapse of some forty minutes, the signal
patiently repeating itself, before the first reply reached
them from Wolkenheim.

"*IF Irish Missed, IF Irish Missed*, this is Wolkenheim
Control. Transmission acknowledged; what are your inten-
tions?"

Moses quickly cut the tape, as O'Shaunessy leaned past
him, jacking in her own headset, keeping the transmission
frequency tuned just the least bit off to maintain the static
fuzz.

"Wolkenheim Control, *Irish Missed*. This is Maureen
O'Shaunessy, engineer. I've assumed command due to
Captain Callahan's incapacitation. I still have magnetic
drive. I intend to make for Trollshulm under reduced
thrust. I will set down there and obtain medical assistance
for Captain Callahan. Over."

This time it was a scant five minutes before a reply came.

"*Irish Missed*, this is Eli Santer. You keep that ship the
hell away from my port. I haven't got the facilities to
delouse a hot drive."

"*Irish Missed* to *Mister* Santer," O'Shaunessy snapped.
"Sir, I don't believe Captain Callahan will last without
treatment. I'm setting down on Trollshulm if I have to land
in your rose garden. Out."

"That's telling 'em, love," Callahan said. "You're a stout
and loyal crew, you are."

"I'm just so devoted," O'Shaunessy agreed. "Do you think Mister Santer will take kindly to be argued with?"

"I hope not. It'll be a pleasure robbing him, won't it?"

"If Blackstone can pull off his end of it."

"I think he can manage. Let's just be there when he does."

The sled heaved again and almost tore off a chunk of ridge.

Gord Horvath cursed and hauled at the twin-stick controls of the sled, pulling it back away from the rock as much by force of will as by any extra power he fed the drive. But that just put him right back out in the wind again, where the dust swirled and blew with such maddening irregularity that sometimes he could see for hundreds of meters ahead through a pocket of absolutely clear air, like bursting through the side of a well-shaft, solid behind him and to the sides and straight ahead, but absolutely empty in between—and then it would close right in, impenetrable, to where the goddamn front of the *sled* would disappear and leave him piloting by memory. "Dragondust," they called it, the meanest air on the planet named after the original meanest animal. Horvath had been way the hell out at the tail end of his run when he first saw it welling up on the horizon, but he had figured he could at least finish the outbound leg before it caught up with him. He had figured wrong.

Now the sled was lurching and bobbing in the corkscrewing gusts of wind, engineered perfectly to carry heavy loads but built square and flat-bottomed, with an incredible amount of exposed surface if the wind ever caught it at the wrong angle. He had dropped a new monopole generator/still unit at the last camp he'd visited before the storm caught up with him, a heavy, bulky thing that had weighted down the sled and made it handle like a thrown brick. He missed its ballasting weight, now.

He knew he was somewhere near the Blackstone camp, for it lay right at the base of the ridge he was following, the ridge that threatened to claw him down with every fresh surge of wind and was his only clue as to where the hell he

was. There was a sudden swirl of killer dust and then the air
was clear, and it seemed to Horvath as though he could just
make out the shape of a skinner's hut, *there*, just inside the
new edge of the murk—

—the sled skidded past a slick patch of rock, a vertical
face on the ridge, smooth as paper and slick as oiled glass. A
gust of wind struck at the base of the rock and was
channeled directly upward, just as Horvath was correcting
for another gust up at his level. The sled flipped up
sideways and slashed down at the ridge.

He didn't remember what he did then. All he could
recall afterward was a sudden expanse of blurred rock
heaving up before him and a desperate heave-and-stomp
action at the controls, as much an unvoiced protest of the
impending crash as anything else.

The flank of the sled crumpled as though clutched in an
enormous fist at the first impact with rock, and the sled
pivoted around the point of impact and spun away from the
rock face. It thudded in again, beyond the rock, and sent a
shower of sand and stones tumbling down the ridgeside.
The sled went with it, as Horvath cut lift to the minimum
and concentrated merely on keeping the craft upright.

He touched down and immediately cut his power, letting
the vehicle's weight anchor it, the sand already piling up
around its sides. He was in luck. He recognized where he
was, not fifty yards from Blackstone's camp. Reassured of
nearby safety, he took a moment to examine the damage to
his sled. Remarkably, it still seemed airworthy. The starboard forward quarter was a mess of crumpled steel, but
the damage seemed to be limited to the hull. The lift-and-
thrust fans seemed undamaged. Horvath powered down
the sled and started off in the direction of Chavez's camp.

An object stopped him, square and bulky and set solidly
in the face of the ridge. Puzzled by its unnatural symmetry,
Horvath approached it. Then he realized what it was.
Wrapped and bundled hides, perhaps a dozen. They had
been buried, and only the freak slide caused by his crash
had revealed them.

He hesitated. There was no sensible reason for anyone to
bury good hides. Blackstone and Santer's woman had to be
up to something Santer wouldn't like, and whatever it was,

Gord Horvath wanted no part of it. But whatever it was, the dust was worsening again, too. He moved on toward Chavez's hut.

Huddled in their permaplast hut, there were certain things Chavez and Shasti had learned to expect from a dragondust blow.

Callers were not one of them.

Chavez pulled the door open and Horvath staggered in with a gout of dust and wind. Grit filled the air as Shasti slammed the lids down on the "pack rat" stew they had cobbled up from several packaged rations.

"Man, what the hell were you doing out there?" Chavez demanded.

"Sled run," Horvath told him. "Got caught out trying to beat the blow. Had to ground the sled about a hundred meters back."

"You lucked out," Chavez said, offering him a cup of still water.

"Don't I know it."

"You got your kit?"

"Back on the sled."

"You should have brought it."

"Yeah, I should have. But man, all I wanted was in out of the blow. I guess I wasn't thinking past that."

"I guess not. Well, hell, we haven't got anything we can spare you, so let's go get it." He started knotting a kerchief around his neck, fitting it so it passed easily over his nose and then snugged down.

"No, that's okay," Horvath said quickly.

"The hell it is. There's no telling how long this is going to last. If you want anything off that sled, you better get it before it's buried clean."

"Shit, it ain't worth it."

"Yeah, it is. Come on." He picked up his rifle and slipped out into the storm. Horvath had no choice but to follow him.

He caught up with Chavez where the young man was standing over the exposed hides, looking from them to the grounded sled, to Horvath, and back to hides, his hands working on the stocks of his rifle—

* * *

"We could have killed him, Chavez."

"Yeah," Chavez said. "We could have." The sled was a small bright sliver in the distance, still shrinking.

"He's going to report the hides. You know that."

"He probably will."

"They'll come after us."

"Maybe not. Maybe not soon enough, anyway."

"If we'd shot him, they wouldn't ever know. They'd think he went down in the storm. And we'd be clear."

"But we'd have shot him."

"It might have been worth it."

"Santer would have thought so."

"Yes, he would."

Chavez started for the trac. "Let's go to work."

"Yes, let's."

Eli Santer paced back and forth in the communications shed where he'd spent most of the last nine hours. Refusing the *Missed* landing permission had been an unpleasant decision, and one that could have serious legal consequences; but damn it, between the load that had been held back from *Northwest Passage* and the hides that had been brought in since, he was sitting on top of a cargo that would put him right back in the pink of fiscal health as soon as it was locked away in *Natchez's* holds. There was no way in hell that he was going to risk a crippled ship falling on it before then. And now he had a man and an expensive sled missing as well, in a sudden dragondust blow.

"Sir," the operator said, "there's a call from Horvath."

"Well, put it up on the screen, damn it." The picture scrambled and faded in. Horvath looked out at him.

"Mister Santer, there's something strange going on out at Blackstone's camp," he said.

"What do you mean?"

"Well, I got forced down by that dust blow just outside his camp, and I landed kind of rough. When I hit, though, I uncovered something that had been buried there."

"What was it?"

"Hides, sir, a good ten or twelve, I'd say."

"Hides?" Santer stared at his screen uncomprehendingly.

"Yes, sir, hides."

"What the hell is he playing at?" Santer wondered. "Is the sled still operational?"

"Yes, sir, just a little dinged up."

"All right. Get back here." He switched off. "Wonderful," he said. "Just goddamn wonderful. I've got a hot ship falling in my lap and now a crazy skinner goes burying fifty thousand standards—oh, god *damn* it!" He stabbed a finger at the comm operator. "Punch up security, fast!" The screen hashed out and cleared as the operator punched in a new combination.

"Security," Santer said. "Get me Trebig. Blackstone and the whore are trying to run some hides."

Six sleds were drawn up in front of the headhunter barracks. A dozen men emerged, carrying Kalashnikov-Kerns with full thousand-sliver combat drums, their belts heavy with spare magazines. This was a serious hunting party. They climbed into the machines and flew off to the west.

As was so often the case after a serious dust blow, the air was remarkably clear that day. So it was that Shasti saw the tiny, brilliant motes of the closed-fan sleds, shining brightly in the late afternoon sun, as they coursed along the ridge in the distance. She turned back to Chavez, who was wrestling a fresh hide onto the bed of their trac.

"Chavez, you'd better see this."

Blackstone gave the bloody skin a final shove and joined her, looking off in the direction she pointed out. The sleds were circling above their camp now, hovering in indecision. Finally one of them cut away from the milling pack and dropped down out of sight behind the dunes.

"What the hell is going on there?"

"That's our camp."

"I know that."

"I think they found us out."

"Oh, Christ."

"Any ideas as to what we do?" The sled had climbed back to rejoin its brothers; after a moment's immobility they scattered and began to peel off out across the desert.

"Get caught, I suppose."

"I was hoping for something a little more creative."

"Get in the trac."

It was a *long* ride. The trac was capable of perhaps forty, fifty kilometers per hour in a flat-out, adrenaline-induced panic, but such frantic speed would have thrown such a splendid roostertail of sand into the sky that every headhunter within a hundred kilometers would have been on them inside of an hour. So they crawled across the terrain at a maddening ten or fifteen kph, the fine sand that threatened to reveal them at any moment quickly blowing over and eradicating their treadmarks behind them. They could see the headhunters' sleds quartering the desert all around them, not on them yet, but drawing closer. The tracs were all painted a bright orange to aid in the location of distressed vehicles, but this one's flanks were thick and dull with dust. Even so, the sleds wouldn't have to get too much closer for one of them to spot it.

They found the gully Chavez was looking for. The trac lurched over its lip and slid down with a rasp of protesting gears as Chavez downshifted. He slid the trac under the opposite face of the ravine, which canted out over the ravine itself and left an area of several yards in shadow.

Chavez and Shasti relaxed, until they saw their treadmarks across the floor of the gully. They were sheltered from the wind there, and the marks stood out like a roadsign.

Chavez moved quickly but Shasti beat him to it. She jumped down from her seat and ran out into the wash, peeling off her tunic and using it to brush away the treadmarks. She finished one, then the other, ducking back under the covering just as a sled whined overhead.

There was a moment's quiet as they listened to the sled moving off. Then Chavez looked at Shasti. She caught his look and managed to get back into the bulky tunic without seeming to move.

"That was fast," Chavez said approvingly.

"Yes, and I covered those tracks up pretty quickly, too," she said, managing to grin briefly. "What do we do now?"

"Not much we can do," Chavez said, "The *Missed* won't be landing for another day and a half. All we can do now is wait for dark and then try to get back to camp for the hides."

"They'll be waiting for that, won't they?"

"Yeah. . . ."

They stood warily in the shadow of a large boulder, looking across the clearing at their dark hut. Behind them, out on the flats, an occasional bar of light stabbed from sky to ground as the sleds kept up their search. It had taken them two hours to get that far across the sand, but the few yards ahead of them were the most dangerous. Chavez sighed and edged out of cover, working around the edge of the clearing toward the hut. There was no one in sight. He found out why.

He stepped into the hut and something cold pressed against the back of his neck. "Don't move—"

The headhunter had made a mistake in getting that close to Chavez, who jerked to the side and slammed the butt of his rifle behind him even as a burst of slivers cut past his ear. He turned and kept clubbing as the headhunter folded, dropping his weapon, trying futilely to cover up under the constant, brutal pounding—

He never saw the second headhunter where he'd lain sleeping in the corner. The man put a shoulder into him and stumbled past out the door.

Chavez saw him running, weaponless, across the clearing. He shot at him and missed, then took off in pursuit, losing sight of his man behind a rock.

He cut around the boulder; and the headhunter, standing by a sled hidden in the rocks, caught him glancingly with a burst from a bass stunner pulled from a seat scabbard. Chavez's left side went numb, and he flopped forward onto the ground. He felt the pressure of a stone against his ribs and knew that that would hurt when the feeling came back. He heard the headhunter saying, "Mister Trebig, Mister Trebig, I got him, sir, I—" and then there was a short, nasty

sound, like a tearing handkerchief. He twisted around and
saw the headhunter slumping down limply against the side
of the sled, a microphone dropping from his hand. Shasti
ran past him into view, her rifle still at the ready. She held
her lips pressed tightly together and might have looked
pale, in better light, as she studied the body. Then she
turned and started back toward Chavez, muttering angrily
in Pushti as she pocketed the wireless microphone/receiver
from the sled.

"Dumb," she said, slinging her rifle and straining to hoist
Chavez to his feet. "That was dumb, running off like that.
How did you expect me to keep up with you? Dumb."

"I know," Chavez said, his voice a little slurred from the
impact of the stunner blast, "but I think I love you anyway."

"And bloody well you should," she said without even
breaking the rhythm of her tirade. "Come on, you're going
to have to help me here, I'm no weightlifter, stand up."

She came clattering back into their little redoubt,
carrying two jerry-cans of water, the headhunters' rifles
slung over her shoulders. The recess in the ridgeface was
too shallow to be honestly called a cave, but it provided
cover from above and somewhat to the sides. Shasti had
drudgingly hauled the bundled hides up from their hiding
place and stacked them in the niche's entrance, walling it
off. Then she had gone back to their camp for the supplies
they had hidden, and made a second trip for more, all while
Chavez had lain in the hole helpless and worrying, as the
numbness in his side slowly faded. It was coming up on
dawn, now; and he'd feared she would get caught out in the
open.

"How are you feeling?" Shasti asked.

"Better," Chavez said, and wiggled the fingers of his left
hand at her. He'd been trying to lift his arm.

"Perfect timing," she said.

"Well, I didn't want you to have it easy, now, did I?"

She said something short and pungent in Pushti and sat
down by the barricade to keep watch. Chavez stiffly worked
his way back down under cover again. He already knew
what there was to be seen out there: the sleds had come

rushing back toward their campsite at the headhunter's truncated announcement. Not ten minutes ago they had begun circling in and landing, even as Shasti was making her way back to their strongpoint for the last time.

"They'll wait for the light, I think," she said.

"If they're smart."

"Still think we can pull this off?"

"We haven't got a whole lot of choices."

"No, I guess not."

The headhunters spread out in a ring at the base of the hill. Trebig hadn't bothered to call for reinforcements; he had everything he would need right there.

They moved up slowly, making good use of the available cover, toward the little cavelet. Then a burst of sliver-fire spattered the rock ahead of him, and Trebig hit the dirt, followed by his men.

"That'll do for now, Anders," Chavez's voice came down thinly.

"What the hell do you think you're playing at, Blackstone?" he shouted back. "You aren't going anywhere!"

"You and me both."

"Why don't you just knock this crap off and come out of there?"

"No, thanks. I've seen how you play that game."

"Then we'll just have to shoot you out of there, won't we?"

"Go ahead. It'll come out of your salary."

"What?"

"You want to shoot up fifty thousand standards' worth of skins, you go right ahead."

Trebig cursed. He could see now how the two renegade skinners had barricaded themselves behind the stolen hides.

Then he grinned, nastily.

"Don't go away, Blackstone. We'll think of something."

"Take your time," Blackstone muttered, as he lowered himself down behind the skins again. "Standoff," he told Shasti.

Then the cavelet was full of fragmenting splinters as fire

came pouring over the top of the hides. The slivers
themselves passed hopelessly high because of the angle of
fire, but then they struck the roof of the niche. Some
ricocheted down into the sand floor, but others shattered
and filled the air with tiny fragments. Chavez and Shasti
ducked down reflexively, then she popped back up and
snapped a burst down the hill. Slivers clawed at the air
around her with renewed savagery and she dropped down
beside Chavez, arms wrapped around her head as the firing
went on and on and on—

—Trebig grinned as the headhunter with the long-
barreled sniper's weapon canted his rifle forward on its
bipod and popped free the spent magazine. This was going
to be easier than he'd thought.

18

"Mister Santer, *Irish Missed* is braking for reentry."

"Damn. What's happening with Trebig?"

"He says they have Blackstone and Keane penned up and expect to finish them soon."

"Tell him to finish it *now*. And get me Security again."

Several security men entered the sleds' maintenance hangar, carrying bulky cases between them. The cases bore Wolkenheimen ordnance markings. The mechanics began readying their contents for fastening at the prows of two sleds.

It was an hour later, and Chavez and Shasti were still alive. There had been two attempts to rush them, both beaten off; but both of them were bleeding in several places from stray sliver fragments. Chavez had perhaps a quarter-drum of ammunition left, Shasti's rifle was empty.

Trebig was angry. He had sent four men back by sled already, two of them dead, one of the others questionable. His last five men were concealed not ten meters from the mouth of the niche; and if he could just get them to charge a final time, he could finish it. They weren't terribly willing, though; they were unused to such stiff opposition. Stiffly, sore because he had gotten no sleep that long night, he set off to prime them to attack.

All pretense of accident behind them, the *Missed* dropped swiftly through the sky, aimed directly at a single unimpressive ridge on the edge of the great sand flats.

Two sleds rose away from Santer's depot, oddly balanced

under the weight of the new additions at their bows and
their heavy warheads.

Chavez stuck his head up and quickly pulled it down as
fresh sliver-fire spilled over their barricade.

"There's a lot of moving around down there. I think
they're going to try again."

"And I think they'll pull it off, this time."

"Yeah, I think so, too."

"Ah, well—as I said, it's been a disappointment."

"So it has." Chavez rubbed at the back of his neck. The
air seemed oddly thick, and his scalp itched.

Trebig leaped to his feet and lunged forward with a cry—
and was spun and thrown from his feet as a great invisible
hand snatched at his rifle and tore it away. He looked up
and saw a solid wall of metal as three hundred feet of
intrasystem freighter bore down on him, broadside on.
Beyond and beneath the ship he could see the tangled ruins
of the grounded sleds it had passed over. The rest of his
men, similarly disarmed as the fringes of the *Missed*'s drive
field passed over them, were scrambling desperately down
the hillside, certain that the great ship meant to come down
right on top of them. Hastily, he joined them.

The *Irish Missed* drifted to a halt just outside Chavez and
Shasti's impromptu fort. A hatch slid open and Moses
Callahan was there, throwing them a winch-line and hook.
Chavez caught it and ran the line through the cording
binding the hides, then slipped the hook back around its
own line. Then he and Shasti hung on for dear life as the
winch tugged their spoils clear of the ground and hoisted
them toward the hatch. Several headhunters, weaponless
but angry, came running around the bow of the *Missed* just
in time to see them scrambling aboard.

"Nice of you to drop in," Chavez said.

"It was good of you to rise to the occasion." There was a
muffled, booming impact deep in the ship, shaking the deck
under their feet.

"What the hell was that?" Moses demanded of the air,
and slapped at an intercom switch. "Maureen. What the
hell's going on?"

"Sleds, Cap'n," O'Shaunessy's reply came. "They're

shooting at us. Looks like some kind of tactical ground missile."

"Can they hurt us?"

"That last one went off in Number Three Hold. Blew up nothing but empty. I'd hate to be taking one in the drive room, though."

"Well, damn it. We don't have to put up with this nonsense, do we?"

"If you don't get up here and drive, certainly we do."

Moses broke all records for the corridor dash. He threw himself into his couch and stabbed and punched at his keyboard. The status board in front of him was flecked here and there with scarlet, where shrapnel had plucked at 'tween-decks circuitry.

Even as he poured more power into the magnetics, several of the red motes winked out under Maureen O'Shaunessy's ministrations.

The *Irish Missed* carried no weapons save a few stunners and light sidearms in her armory. She'd never had need of more. But she was three hundred feet of steel and alloy, with a fine mass-to-thrust ratio. That was more than enough.

Santer's sleds had separated for their attack, one diving in while the second held back to observe the results. Now the second sled canted over and began its run. The driver held his fire, closing, aligning his sights on the ship's bow—and it was gone.

The *Missed* canted upwards and leaped away from the little sled, clawing for altitude. The sled brushed the fringe of its drive field and flipped wildly away, the driver fighting desperately for control.

The first sled wasn't as lucky. Coming out of a high, banking turn, it struck the *Irish Missed's* drive field dead-center. It whipped around wildly, trapped at the interface between the drive field and the planet's magnetic field, and was cast spinning away below. A tiny blossom of fire stood out briefly against the sand behind the climbing freighter, then was obscured in its own smoke. The remaining sled leveled off and climbed half-heartedly after her, hopelessly outdistanced.

Chavez and Shasti crowded into the *Missed's* control room.

"Are we clear?" Moses asked.

"Of the sleds, yes."

"Any other ships on the planet?"

"Just the *Abilene*," Shasti said.

"That antique; we're clear."

The *Missed* rose above the curvature of the planet. The fusion drive flamed into pale life and Trollshulm dropped away behind her.

Two hours later, Moses and Chavez found Shasti down in the hold, staring at the bundled hides. Fifty thousand Confederate standards, at least, more than enough to bond the *Missed* at their next destination, more than enough to pay all of their passages to just about any world in colonized space, with quite enough to live on for a good while besides.

And she was frowning.

"Eli Santer has three hundred hides in storage in Trollshulm," she said.

"Well, he hasn't got these."

"So what? You think this is going to hurt Eli Santer? Stealing ten hides he never even saw? What did we hurt, Chavez?"

"His pride. . . ."

"You can't eat pride. You can sure as hell live without it."

"So what do you want?" Moses asked.

"I want to do what we wanted to do in the first place. I want to hit back at Eli Santer. I want to take something from him."

"What have you got in mind?"

"Ten hides are worth fifty thousand. What are a hundred worth, or two hundred, or even three hundred?"

Moses Callahan said, "I don't know. I've got no quarrel with Eli Santer—"

Shasti looked at him, started to say something.

"—except that he took advantage of a friend. I'll have to check our position, see if we can pull it off and still make rendezvous. Excuse me." He turned and left them there. In a little while, back in their cabins, they heard the sound of the engines increase in pitch and a gentle hand tried to push them down into their couches.

Santer's desk tried to kill him.

It ripped itself off its brackets on the floor, spinning wildly. One corner caught Eli Santer on the shoulder and threw him against the wall. The desk smashed into the far wall of his office and hung pinned there.

He picked himself up and stumbled to the door, which flung itself open violently when he turned the knob.

Outside, he was too late to see most of the damage. Everything ferrous that had been in the street was already gone—tracs, sleds, equipment, everything scattered about by the magnetic drive of the massive ship that hung low overhead. A trac had been hurled through the front wall of the accounting office. The wall of the sled hangar was a mass of dents and buckles that hinted at the havoc contained within. Men were running in every direction to get out from under the vast metal shape descending out of the sky above the warehouse—the warehouse. Santer didn't need to see any more. He ran from the depot, toward the lonely shape of the *Abilene* docked a mile away.

Markov was already there, staring out of the personnel lock at the spectacle of the *Irish Missed* descending on the depot.

"What the hell is going on?" he demanded.

Santer ran up the ramp to the lock.

"I'll tell you what's going on!" he shouted. "If you want to keep this damned ship, you get it powered up and you get it airborne and you get over there! *Now!*"

And he shoved past Markov and disappeared into the ship, running for the bridge.

The street was clear as the hatch opened in the flank of the *Irish Missed*, and Chavez and Shasti were lowered by cable to the ground, along with the collapsible pallet of strong aluminum tubing. Chavez set quickly to work assembling the pallet as Shasti ran into the warehouse. As they'd hoped, it was deserted. She was already dragging the first of the hides outside as Chavez finished the pallet. They worked quickly, but the pallet would only hold twenty hides at a pinch. Several trips would be necessary. The hides were heavy, but Chavez was strong, and Shasti worked with the fervor of the truly screwed-over. The pallets were filled rapidly.

When they saw that the ship was not about to crash, men began to filter back into the depot. Many of them saw the activity at the warehouse and ran forward to protect their livelihood. They were unarmed, but there were many of them.

A streak of scarlet light scored a building to the left of the mob, and seared across the street before them. Maureen O'Shaunessy stood in the hatchway of the *Missed* with a welding laser tuned for its tightest collimation. Actually, it probably wouldn't have done the men much hurt, but the scarred building and the scorched track across the street were ominous suggestions to the contrary.

Chavez and Shasti were on their fourth trip up when the *Missed* lurched violently, nearly throwing them from the pallet. They held on desperately as the ship rocked. Their faces were pale as they finally reached the hatch.

The IF *Abilene* hovered over the *Irish Missed*, their fields locked, trying to force her away from the depot and down. Moses Callahan came into his own.

Santer hung over Markov's shoulder in the crowded bridge, staring down at his master screen, fists clenched in the thick padding of Markov's acceleration couch.

"Bring them *down*, Thomas! Push them off that warehouse and ground them!"

"I'm trying, damn it!" Markov answered, almost inaudible over the howl of the straining generators. "But that's a damned big ship!"

"And this is *your* ship, damn it!" Santer shouted. "If they get those hides, you'll lose her! That's a goddamned promise, Markov! I won't give up those hides!"

Markov bent to his board again, tapping in commands. The howling of the generators rose to a new, even fiercer pitch, like icepicks driven through the two men's eardrums. The deck below them began to shudder, as Eli Santer fought with all the power at his command to crush the *Irish Missed*—and Moses Callahan came into his own.

Normally, piloting was a fairly dull affair; there were no

currents in space, no storms. A planet's magnetic field was a predictable thing and easily coped with. Moses was almost grateful for the challenge. His hands flew over his board, matching the *Missed*'s upward thrust to the downward pressure of Santer's ship. The *Missed* lurched, wavered, steadied. Stalemate. Not good enough. It was time to be creative. Moses's hands flew.

The *Missed* spun end for end, seeming to pivot almost on her own stern. Then she climbed up and out at a sharp angle, and almost before the movement was perceived, she was out from under *Abilene* and reversing her course. *Abilene* barely had time to check her own descent; she had no time to respond to this new attack. The *Irish Missed* forced her attacker down with a great, thundering impact, directly atop the warehouse. *Abilene* lay grounded, her back broken, her structure irreparably sprung out of line, among the ruins.

The *Missed* halted, hovered for an instant, and then vanished upwards into the cobalt Trollshulm sky.

Santer didn't know how long he'd been unconscious.

He came to sprawled in the angle of the corner between skewed bulkhead and deck. Panels and wiring and beams dangled from broken fittings on all sides. The only illumination was the thin red glow of the emergency lamps.

He sat up and saw the bulk of Thomas Markov sprawled in his couch. Santer struggled to his feet and lurched over. Markov lay back in his couch, face peaceful, eyes open and calm and unseeing, lifeless. Santer couldn't see any obvious injuries in the weak scarlet light. It was as if the man had simply decided not to outlive his ship. Santer turned and made for the lock, leaving the dead ship to its dead master, to survey the wreckage of his own dream.

Eli Santer stood, drained of rage, of ideas, of everything, staring at the wreckage. Nothing had been moved, no attempt made to clean up after the disaster. There was nothing the dozen or so men left in the depot could have done, even had they been so inclined; the only reason that even they were still there was that there really wasn't any place else they could go.

It was finished, and he knew it. It didn't matter how many hides, if any, they could ultimately salvage from beneath the dead *Abilene*. Between the loss of the ship, and the buildings, and the equipment, he was as good as bankrupt. He might have tried to hold on, through strength of will and with the backing of his guns; but his headhunters were scattered all over the desert after the rout at Blackstone's camp; and their biggest advantage, supply and organization, was lost. He had no hold over the skinners now, none. They had taken his world from him, broken it and handed him back the scraps.

A trac rumbled into the ravaged depot, an unsuspecting skinner delivering his take. Santer saw the realization strike the man as he noticed the devastation. He couldn't even work up the energy to resent him as he grabbed for his microphone and began to speak. He could only stand and stare into the hard eyes of Adrienne Santer, facing him in the wreckage of the depot as though waiting to loot his grave.

Four days later they passed the radio beacons that marked the limits of Hansen System Space. Ahead the gigantic starliner *Natchez* loomed like an immense stiletto hanging in the darkness. They were clear, now. There was a saying out between the stars: "System law stops at the starliner hatch"—which, considering the wild variations in colonial law, was only sensible.

They would sell the hides directly to the ship herself, in exchange for a draft on her accounts. *Natchez* would have no trouble selling the hides; all starliners were *de facto* extraterritorial and beyond prosecution or liability.

"All squared, Cap'n," Natchez announced. "We're offering barnacle rate. Just lock on aft of hatch four."

On their screens a tiny blister detached itself from the *Natchez* and moved toward them, slowly growing into a blocky, efficient, dull-looking agrav freighter, hitching a ride on the starship to greener pastures.

"*Irish Missed, Irish Missed*, this is agrav freighter *Cumulus*, outbound from Caledonia Nova. Any agrav traffic in this system yet?"

"Irish Missed to *Cumulus;* one other ship, have at 'em. The merchants will love you."

"Thanks."

"Oh, hey, and *Cumulus,*" Moses added, "when you've grounded, would you do us a favor and convey our deepest thanks to a Mister Eli Santer? You won't have any trouble finding him."

"We'll do that thing."

"Thank you." Moses switched off. "Just because they're the future, doesn't mean I have to make it easy for 'em."

"What are you going to do with your share, Cap'n?" Chavez asked.

"Oh, forty-six hides should buy me a pretty fair cushion, I should think. I imagine I'll just take my time and find someplace where the *Missed* won't be ready for the museum for a long time yet. What about you?"

"I think I've had enough of the rugged frontier life. I think I'll head somewhere peaceful for a change, like Earth."

"Back to His Excellency and his niece?"

"I doubt that he'll still be around by the time I get back there."

"Pity."

"Why? He was no prize, Cap'n."

"No, I mean about your going back to Earth and all. Means I'll have to hire someone else."

"For what?"

"Groundside man, general crew, that sort of thing. Handling the shore end of the ship's affairs. It doesn't matter, though; I'll find someone."

"I'm not exactly a heavyweight businessman, Cap'n."

"No, but you do have a certain flexibility of outlook. . . ."

"As of four days ago, I'm a straight-out criminal."

"Precisely what I meant. Just the sort to deal with these infernal colonial types."

"Well—you talked me into it. But I'll want someone to handle the managerial aspects."

"I rather thought as much. Miss Keane, would you be looking for employment, by any chance?"

"Well, actually, I did find myself at liberty the other day. And I do have some administrative experience. . . ."

"Done. Welcome aboard, the both of you."

The *Natchez* gleamed in the starlight like a pile of silver coins waiting to be pocketed, as the *Missed* settled into her berth.

THE WILD SHORE

Kim Stanley Robinson

'Simply one of our best writers' Gene Wolfe

'A powerful new talent' Damon Knight

2047: for 60 years America has been quarantined after a devastating nuclear attack. For the small community of San Onofre on the West Coast, life is a matter of survival: living simply on what the sea and land can provide, preserving what knowledge and skills they can in a society without mass communications. Until the men from San Diego arrive, riding the rails on flatbed trucks and bringing news of the new American Resistance. And Hank Fletcher and his friends are drawn into an adventure that marks the end of childhood . . .

A stunning debut by a powerful new talent.

'There's a fresh wind blowing in THE WILD SHORE . . . welcome, Kim Stanley Robinson' Ursula K Le Guin

'Beautifully written . . . with a vivid depth rarely encountered in science fiction' *Washington Post Book World*

FUTURA PUBLICATIONS/AN ORBIT BOOK
SCIENCE FICTION

ISBN 0 7088 8147 5

WORLDS APART

Joe Haldeman

For the inhabitants of the Worlds – the artificial colonies orbiting silently through space – Earth was finished. Devastated by nuclear war and now ravaged by the after effects of horrific biological weapons, the mother planet was torn apart. Humanity's home would soon be gone forever.

But Earth would not loose its ties so easily. And for Marianna O'Hara there was work to be done in the ghastly ruins of the stricken planet before she could, at last, look outwards to the stars.

WORLDS APART, the second volume of the brilliant trilogy of mankind's future by the award-winning author of THE FOREVER WAR.

FUTURA PUBLICATIONS/AN ORBIT BOOK
SCIENCE FICTION

ISBN 0 7088 8121 1

HOSPITAL STATION

James White

A vast hospital complex floating in space, built to cater for the medical emergencies of the galaxy. There are patients with eight legs — and none; stricken aliens that breathe methane or feed on radiation; an abandoned baby that weighs half a ton. And there are doctors and nurses to match, with a bewildering array of tentacles, and mental powers stretching all the way to telepathy.

Faced by the illnesses and accidents of the universe, fired by the challenge of galactic medicine, O'Mara, the hospital chief, and his crack team, including the altogether human Conway, with his insatiable curiosity, and Prilicla, the brilliant and fragile insect telepath, battle to preserve life in all its myriad forms.

HOSPITAL STATION — the astonishingly inventive saga of a vast hi-tech community, a cross between an emergency clinic and a zoo.

FUTURA PUBLICATIONS/AN ORBIT BOOK
SCIENCE FICTION

ISBN 0 7088 8181 5

All Futura Books are available at your bookshop or newsagent, or can be ordered from the following address:
Futura Books, Cash Sales Department,
P.O. Box 11, Falmouth, Cornwall.

Please send cheque or postal order (no currency), and allow 55p for postage and packing for the first book plus 22p for the second book and 14p for each additional book ordered up to a maximum charge of £1.75 in U.K.

Customers in Eire and B.F.P.O. please allow 55p for the first book, 22p for the second book plus 14p per copy for the next 7 books, thereafter 8p per book.

Overseas customers please allow £1 for postage and packing for the first book and 25p per copy for each additional book.